THE HOLY FATHER'S NAVY

Philip Purser

SAPERE
BOOKS

THE HOLY FATHER'S NAVY

Published by Sapere Books.

24 Trafalgar Road, Ilkley, LS29 8HH

saperebooks.com

ISBN: 978-0-85495-551-0

PART ONE: *ACT OF NODDY*

CHAPTER ONE

The plane must have flown in low from the west, the pilot trying to get below the cloud and not realising that it reached right down and wrapped the islands. Maybe he just saw the high bird cliffs solidifying ahead and the gap in them where this strange circular lake spilled over into the sea. Anyway he came through it and was obviously climbing as steeply as he could as he swept across the lake and up the valley. Another ten feet, even, and he might have made it. The point of first impact was at a kind of grassy lip where the ground started to level off. There was a great score in the soft shallow earth. Next came an empty old barn or something, half its roof sliced off. Then a quarter-mile-long fan of debris as the plane started to break up, finally the burnt out house which it had showered with blazing fuel before burying itself in the hillside beyond. There was a heavy drizzle and the smell of the wet charred timbers was sharper and somehow more upsetting than the paraffin smell that had been in our noses for the past quarter of an hour.

That was as close as we got. A Danish sailor with a rifle slung upside-down over his pea-jacket emerged suddenly from the house. He looked disconcerted as if he should have noticed us sooner. I saw him glance anxiously up the hill to the terminal wreckage, where there were other figures moving, some military, some civilian, and a tractor and trailer, and one of those little forward-control Chrysler utilities. Some of the men were pacing the ground with heads bent, as if looking for bits and pieces.

An officer in a shiny waterproof looked up and saw us and shouted. The sailor became very officious, scowling and waving us away. I said okay and took Irby's hand and we walked back the way we'd come.

It would have been two days — two and a half — since the crash. The first we'd heard of it was in the little dining room at Midvag with old Niclasen shaking his head and grunting as he listened to the news on the radio. The news, plus what was evidently a painstakingly detailed weather forecast, seemed pretty well all there was on the Faeroese radio apart from some mournful chanting and, on Sunday, interminable readings from the Bible. Old Niclasen lived from bulletin to bulletin and would translate bits and pieces for us about the momentous events then going on — prophetically, I now see — in the Middle East. If there was anything from home he always gave us that too, though how accurately it was hard to say. He informed us once that the Queen had dismissed the Foreign Secretary. I expect we misunderstood him, because he had skippered a trawler from Hull for five years and knew Britain quite well. The trouble was the impenetrability of his English.

This time it was obvious the news was of something nearer to hand. The reader's voice had taken on a special urgency and Niclasen hung over the set, twisting the tuner to try and improve reception. When his daughter came in with the coffee pot he shushed her and she, starting to listen, creased her round smooth face into an expression of concern. Niclasen flattened a big red hand and zoomed it at the table-top to show us what had happened. It was a jet, we gathered, somewhere on the main island, a place that sounded like 'Saxon'. A woman on the ground had been killed, as well as the pilot.

We looked suitably distressed and an hour later had forgotten all about it. For once no rain or mist was threatened in the weather forecasts which old Niclasen followed even more closely than the news and qualified with his own head-shaking, eye-cocking lore. We could go wandering on the fells behind the village without fear of getting lost when the thick white fog rolled in from nowhere.

CHAPTER TWO

Irby and I had been married the previous summer. There were seventeen years between us, which was a biggish gap. I'd worked out that when she was my age I'd be nearly sixty. There were all the readjustments and little rows that I'd expected, plus a bigger one that I hadn't. I suppose I'd had some awful patronising idea that I might mould this slim, serious girl to my own design, like Pygmalion. Instead, her own particularity flowered. She revealed obstinacies I hadn't foreseen, determinations I'd never even suspected. She changed the furniture in my living room, took a shine against several old friends of mine, including Rosie and Gerald Mann, got at me to close drawers and clean the bath after I'd used it and launched a long-term campaign for us to move to the country if we had children. That little plot had turned sour for the moment — Christ, I'd have settled in Potter's Bar if that's what she wanted and if it would have put the clock back five weeks...

But when I was feeling optimistic it seemed that something nicer was happening to me than had ever happened before. It really was an enormous act of flattery, an act of faith, even, for her to commit her life and youth and all the things she might become to tatty old me, who had failed to achieve anything very much, even to exploit the two or three rather odd adventures in which I had been involved, and was now once more safely doing time in the B.B.C.

She had northern leanings and loved to make me talk of my Spitsbergen trip fifteen years before. She'd suggested Iceland or the Faeroes for the honeymoon and I'd gone to the length of getting the literature from the Iceland Tourist Office in Piccadilly. But idiot prejudice had made me insist on somewhere more languorous, with the result that we both had gastroenteritis in the south of rotten Spain. Next time, I'd promised we'd go north. The opportunity came sooner that I'd planned, and in sadder circumstances. I'd arrived home latish, having forgotten we were supposed to be going out to dinner. Irby, who was five months on the way with our first child and had given up her job already, was a bit scratchy. She said, 'Why is it we can never go anywhere on time?' The worst of it was that she was actually ready herself, and looking very disturbing in a maternity dress that might have been designed to accomplish pregnancy rather than accommodate it. 'I asked you especially to get home early tonight because we were so bloody late last time we went to John and Sue's.'

I was trying to clean my teeth. 'I'm sorry, love, I just couldn't get away.' At least that's what I meant to say. It came out the usual mumble you produce with a mouth full of toothbrush.

'I can't hear a word you say. And you've sprayed all over the looking-glass. Honestly!'

'Mirror,' I said. 'Bathroom mirror. Why use three syllables when two will do? I was having a diplomatic drink with C. Exec. Tel.'

'Drink, drink, drink! That's all you ever do there.' She waved her hands vigorously in the air, fingers splayed out to dry her nail varnish. 'I suppose after you've been drinking all day you say to each other, "How about a spot of work before we go home, old boy?" and the other man says, "Well all right, but only one memo. I promised the wife I wouldn't be late."'

I ignored that.

'And hurry up, I want to do a wee.'

'I'm not stopping you.'

She hovered for a moment. 'No, leave me.' Her voice had suddenly changed, though I didn't remark it then. I sighed extravagantly and took the shaver into the bedroom. She cried out, just two words that skewered the air.

'*There's blood!*'

It shone in the seam of her tights, thick and red and enough to cover a half-crown.

I got hold of her and said, 'It's all right, it's nothing, I bet it often happens.' But after she'd lain in bed and bled for two days they took her into All Saints and the third day she lost it. She was still under anaesthetic when I arrived that evening, waxy and bruised around the eyes. There was a blood drip above the iron bed.

The doctor said, 'We were rather blowing on our fingers but she's all right now. It's a bit unusual to abort so late on, she lost rather a lot.'

A nurse told Irby later that it would have been a little girl. I thought a break would be a good idea, so a couple of weeks later we were among the only five passengers on the Saturday evening Icelandair flight from Glasgow.

Out in the Atlantic Mykines reared up like a sea monster, its bowed head capped, even on this perfect day, with a wisp of cloud. Below us Midvag and its neighbour, Sandavagur, were hidden by the brow of the hill, but we could see the long curling inlet from which old Niclasen had hooked last night's supper of pink-fleshed trout, and beyond that the great tilted slab of cliff that marked the southern extremity of the island. We sat by a rivulet splashing its way down to the sea and ate chocolate biscuits and drank sweet orangeade from cartons. Scruffy brown sheep grazed. An oystercatcher circled around making loud remarks and occasionally a whimbrel went *wheeeeee*, very thinly and plaintively. But in the midst of the stillness there was one small centre of activity.

At the head of the long curling water was the airstrip where we'd arrived so spectacularly at the end of the flight from Glasgow, the little F.27 sinking steadily into a bloodshot dusk, rocks and islets starting to appear in the sea below, the arms of a fjord into which we flew converging and steepening until they seemed to tower above us, then suddenly falling away again, gone, and ground directly below, indeed coming up fast — approach lights, a glimpse of runway and next instant a wreath of smoke blowing briefly off the tyres. The brakes went on hard and as the pilot turned to taxi back you could see why: there wasn't much airstrip left.

In fact there wasn't much of anything: one low, modern terminal building, a few odd huts, the skeleton of a hangar. But the Faeroese had tried to make it look welcoming and cosmopolitan, with a line of flags fluttering in the breeze, even if there were only six or seven flights in a week and those all by the same Icelandair plane. From where we now sat it looked like a toy aerodrome, not quite to scale. Only on this particular day it was abnormally busy. One after the other an assortment of propeller-driven aircraft flew in — it was obviously much too restricted for jets. I identified an HS 748, what was either another F.27 or a Herald, a DC-4, and finally, with a blast of reverse-pitch revving that must have carried right across the island, a big Hercules transport. The white stars of the United States Air Force stood out on its flank.

Back in the village the Niclasens were still shaking their heads over the news. Nothing like this had happened since the war. The dead woman had been distantly related to the wife of the boat-builder, who said that she had been married only last July. Old Niclasen said there would be many questions asked in the parliament, especially by those head-men who were opposed to the Faeroes' involvement with NATO. Meanwhile more aircraft had arrived and some earlier ones had left again, a little helicopter shuttled to and fro and the taxis bounced by on their way to the Vestmanna ferry filled with important-looking passengers.

We moved on ourselves next afternoon, as planned. Old Niclasen insisted on carrying Irby's case down to the harbour. The departure of the twice-weekly boat evidently counted as a minor occasion, with much seeing off and shouted gossip. The subject today wasn't hard to guess. Niclasen stood on the quayside, solid and stocky in his blue trawlerman's jersey, and watched us go. Midvag's straggly line of bright-painted wooden houses and Sandavagur's more formal grouping, dominated by the shining black and white church, dwindled in turn behind us. Then there were only beetling cliffs, and one strange spire of rock, and looming ahead an island whose steep face was scalloped into the shape of a monster jelly mould. Loose formations of puffins sped across the waves on madly beating wings. It was the slow way to Thorshavn, but on another rare day incomparably the best way.

The following morning brought more typical Faeroese weather. Waking, I heard the rain pattering down. In the street people were going to work under umbrellas or waterproof hats, the cars crawled by carefully. Our window looked across to a stone house and a tall dripping tree, both rarities in the islands. With the clean, varnished, neutral modernity of the hotel room we might for the moment have been in any rainy European town.

At breakfast I tried reading the local daily, without much success. Faeroese preserves the digraph *ae* and the broken-backed *d*, which gave the headlines a bizarre quality but hardly assisted understanding. The aeroplane incident seemed to have been given curiously low prominence. The main story was of the events in the Middle East. Yet it could have been only the second opportunity for the paper to worry about what was surely a very big local issue.

Irby said, 'Where shall we go today?'

I looked out. The rain had eased, but everything still looked damp. 'You wouldn't like a day in the swinging capital?'

She shook her head decisively. 'There's plenty of time for that in the evenings.' Irby was an industrious tourist. Besides, it was true — we had already explored most of the interesting parts of Thorshavn, the harbour, the Tinganes, the old houses of tarred timber and turf roofs. There were no pubs, no restaurants. Shopping we could leave until the last day.

I thumbed through the duplicated island timetable, trying to make sense of the bus and boat and taxi schedules. We'd missed most of the more promising possibilities; they seemed to like early starts in the Faeroes. But a name caught my eye. Perhaps I'd been looking for it all the time. It was the name that figured in the newspaper story, the name that had sounded like 'Saxon'. I said, 'There's a bus going north at ten-thirty, if you like.'

It turned out to be a kind of overgrown station-wagon, by Mercedes, with seats for up to about twenty. We ground out of Thorshavn through untidy areas of new housing, past a rubbish dump, the engine whining in low gear as the road zig-zagged upwards.

The surface was reasonably well metalled at first, then road-making gear and piles of material marked the resumption of the lurching, bumping, pot-holed progress that was more familiarly Faeroese. Sometimes low cloud blotted out the view, at other times we would look down into wide fjords. In each village of red and green and ochre houses someone left the bus, until only Irby and I were left. At the next village the driver pulled into the side of the road and switched off the engine. Pointing to a taxi parked across the street he conveyed the idea that it would take us the last stage, which — after we'd waited ten minutes, until the taxi-man emerged picking his teeth — duly came to pass.

It took perhaps a quarter of an hour. The road ran alongside a reedy marsh, then forked at the head of the valley. To the left it led to a cluster of houses and a church half a mile off. To the right the way was barred by a hurdle and a portable No Entry sign. Indistinctly in the drizzle I saw a roofless building, some vehicles half-hidden by it, rawly exposed earth.

The taxi driver looked inquiringly over his shoulder. To the left? I shook my head. He pointed to the red and white sign. So we compromised and got out there and watched the taxi splash away back to civilization (or comparatively so) before setting off on foot past the barrier.

'How do we get back?' said Irby.

'Something will turn up,' I said cosily.

Christ, it would be hard to imagine a more desolate setting for a haphazard little tragedy of the times. The strange circular lake was the focus, the navel of the landscape. It lay away and below defeating scale so you couldn't be sure if it was vast and distant or small and close — perhaps it had deceived the luckless pilot in the same way, in the fleeting moments between sighting it and extinction.

From its far shore a silvery thread of water led to the gap in the cliffs and a glimpse of the Atlantic blurring into the sky. The silence was so complete it was unnatural. What was missing? It took me a minute or so to work out that for once in the Faeroes there wasn't the din of seabirds.

The wet clouds pressed down, and as we retreated from the aggrieved Danish sentry the rain started in earnest again.

CHAPTER THREE

'With the whole north Atlantic to fall into,' I said, 'it just had to be this little patch of islands instead. And from however many hundred square miles of empty moors it had to be the one house in sight. And instead of a sheep, of which there are plenty, a human being — someone's wife. Isn't that what your lot would call an Act of God?'

We were hiking back the way the taxi had brought us — well, one of the ideas had been to do lots of healthy walking. Only now the rain was driving hard. I could feel it running steadily off the hem of the oilskin coat I'd bought especially from the healthy walking department at Gamages, and soaking into the eighteen inches of trouser leg left foolishly exposed. The man had said I should get the over trousers to match but they'd looked much too square and waddly.

I said, 'Well, isn't it?'

With the hood press-studded into place I could only see forwards. I had to swivel awkwardly from the hips to look at Irby. She only had an anorak, and was turning dark with wetness from the waist down.

'Oh shut up. I don't know. I'm getting soaked.'

'I told you to bring that nylon mac. How would *you* explain it away, then? If there is Someone Up There either he's malevolent or he's inefficient. God is nodding. Goddy is Noddy.'

It was the miscarriage of course, which had stirred up the religious thing between us. There'd been a trying time before we were married, when I'd had to take instruction from Father Freeloader, so called because he always managed to organise things so that only his lunch hours were free. I got the virgin birth over oysters and sole at Bentley's, the infallibility of the Pope between the pâté maison and roast duckling at Shirreff's and the hard line on family planning with the délices de fromage and cassoulet at the Ecu de France. With wine (and Father Freeloader was never shy of making a suggestion as to growth and vintage) it cost me twenty-five quid. But one was in love, wasn't one? And he was a likeable rogue: in his time he'd taught at Lancing, been R.C. chaplain at Oxford and landed in Normandy with the Guard Armoured. Now he was on all sorts of committees and boards of governors. He had the plump chops of the priest and a dry, deferential manner.

He made no attempt to convert me. All that was asked was that I should try to understand Irby's faith and give some voluntary undertaking — it was no longer a condition — that our children should be brought up in it, though he liked to tease me into little admissions which he then claimed as proof that I was at heart a religious being. Once he wanted to know the last time I'd prayed for anything.

'In the war, I suppose.'

'Never since?'

I thought. 'At a party once there was a girl I suddenly wanted desperately and she seemed quite keen, but there were others after her and I wasn't very competitive. I remember closing my eyes for an instant and thinking, "Please God, let me have that girl".'

'And did this come about?'

'Actually, yes.'

'There you are.'

On the honeymoon Irby had slipped away early one Sunday, to mass. When we were home again, for the time being in my old flat in Pimlico, she'd sometimes trot along to the Byzantine folly of Westminster Cathedral. But between coming out of hospital and our departure for the Faeroes she'd been five or six times. From certain silences and bitten-off remarks and sudden weepings I knew she was trying to elevate losing the baby into some kind of punishment for neglecting her observances and hardening her heart and marrying a worldly unbeliever and sleeping with him beforehand and continuing to do so after she was pregnant ... it was a self-indulgence, of course, which is why I had to keep getting at her, I really did. The kid had been lost through some set of physiological circumstances, just as the jet had crashed where it did because of some set of aeronautical and meteorological circumstances. Unless it were that less predictable thing called pilot error. What was he doing in these parts, anyway?

Irby said, 'Who?' I must have voiced the question.

'The pilot. He'd never have got a jet down on the Vagar airstrip. Where was he making for, where'd he come from?'

'Does it make any difference?'

'I suppose not. Probably it was a ferry trip. He'd staged at Iceland and was on his way to Norway or Scotland. I wonder who he was. We haven't heard anything of him, poor bugger!'

We'd brought a picnic lunch of sorts — rye wafers, Danish salami, tomatoes. We ate it in a sort of bothy by the side of the road, a low hut of stone and wood under a turf roof. It might originally have been someone's primitive home, such as we had seen preserved as a little museum at Midvag. Now it was being used to store hay and stuff. Inside it was dim and draughty but quite dry; the timbers had kept a bleached, pale colour. I spread the oilskin.

Irby said, 'I'm sorry, I can't sit in these wet things.' She peeled off cotton trousers and then cotton pants. It was a long time since I'd sat in the hay with a girl bare from the waist downwards. I remembered suddenly the one work of fiction which had driven me into a sleepless fever of lust.

I said, 'When I was about eleven I was much stirred by some clean-limbed children's story. There were these boys and girls camping in tents, all very innocent of course. In the middle of the night one of the boys and one of the girls woke up and it was pouring with rain — like it is now. The guy ropes! The guy ropes would have to be slackened or tightened or whatever it is. How could they do it without their pyjamas getting soaked. Answer: they wriggled out in their nothings. I can't tell you how it inflamed me. The first — and last — time pornography ever really worked for me.'

She smiled — ah, that fond, chiding smile as when in former days I'd confided bits of seedy autobiography. The aftermath of the miscarriage had taken a long time to dry up. Besides, there were other barriers: a vague feeling on my part that to be too eager would show a lack of respect to the late occupant; for Irby, renewed perplexities as to the means of birth control — they'd put her on to an oestrogen drug that our doctor hinted was a form of birth-control pill, without actually saying it was; for both of us the symbolism of initiating the risk of another messy disappointment. But affection needs love as much as love needs affection. And, if I can put this without being indelicate, there was perceptible in the musty air of the hut a distinct, disturbing, girly aroma. I put my hand on her cool damp thigh and kissed her.

She said, 'What are you thinking of?'

'Guess.'

'You must be joking.'

'I'm deadly earnest. And Deadly Earnest wants it.' Every couple has its private, awful jokes. 'It's seeing a scene of disaster. Well-known syndrome. After earthquakes etcetera the fields are full of survivors, screwing.'

'Well, thanks very much.'

'I didn't mean it like that.'

'They said to wait at least three months.'

'That was before starting another baby.'

'But — well, you know.'

'I think that pill makes you safe.'

'Did John say it did?' Even though she had her arms round my neck now, her voice had an interrogatory edge.

'He implied it would help in all sorts of ways.'

She relaxed. 'The things I do for you.'

Afterwards she had to resume clammy clothes, wincing at the unpleasantness of it. Full of protective love I said, 'We'll buy you something in the next village.'

The rain had eased but there were plenty of puddles. I goofed through a version of Gene Kelly's *Singing in the Rain* routine which made her giggle. In the middle of it the Chrysler utility overtook us. The officer in the shiny coat nodded stiffly without offering us a lift, the sod.

There was a general store in every Faeroes village, sometimes more than one, but all selling everything from chewing-gum to seaboot stockings. Language was a difficulty, not to mention the translation of sizes. A kindly fellow-customer who had a few words of English came to the rescue. We bought blue jeans, white knicks and as a bonus while I was in the giving vein, one of the enormously thick Faeroese sweaters. When she pulled it on once after a bath instead of a dressing-gown it was very sexy but a bit like cuddling up with a sheep.

Our benefactress took us to her house where Irby changed in a bedroom and I waited in the living room and we were both pressed to stay for coffee and cheese and bread. The place was furnished in the style that I was beginning to realise was general throughout the islands: thirtyish furniture in pale, shabby wood; house plants; few signs of such precautions against the grim winters as double glazing, but always central heating or a big stove or both.

Inevitably the subject of the crashed jet came up. What couldn't have been foreseen, unless I'd missed earlier references by retreating into the glassy-eyed, fixed-smile, head-wagging act I usually donned in the face of alien tongues or boredom, was the kind lady's reaction. As if assuming that's what we'd come for she vanished from the room and we heard her calling. When she returned she said, 'She comes now.'

'Who comes?'

'The mother of the dead girl. She was from the next house here.'

I shot a look of dismay to Irby and when she didn't acknowledge it, made an elaborate show of looking at my watch and exclaiming about the bus. If we'd gone there and then we'd have escaped. But one of the things that I'd had to discover about Irby was this perverse capacity she had for interesting herself in other people's troubles. When she'd given up her job to have the baby she'd actually taken up good works.

While we waited the kind lady filled in the background. Apparently the young couple had married only the previous year. The girl had gone to live with her in-laws on the remote farmstead and help with the sheep and the two cows and the knitting while the husband went out with one of the deep-sea fishing fleets from Klaksvik. He'd been at sea when it happened and still wasn't back.

The bereaved mum came in then, red around the eyes but very voluble. There was much womanly talk with our lady acting as interpreter and Irby sometimes seeming not to need her mediation. Snapshots were produced, plus a wedding group in a plastic frame which the poor mother had in her handbag. I studied these with unfeigned interest. The girl had been pretty in a fair, round-faced way. The husband was big and beefy with the prominent cheekbones and slight cast of eye I'd observed several times among the islanders. The extra awful thing we learned was that they'd been expecting a baby too. Had we children? Irby shook her head. I looked at the likeness of the husband again. We didn't have much in common; for a start he couldn't have been much more than half my age. But he'd lost both — wife as well as unborn child. I looked at the curve of Irby's cheek and her narrow shoulders and how she was totally in communion with these two middle-aged women she'd never met before, and wondered what I would have done if I'd lost her.

On the bus later she said, by the way, had I taken that in, we'd been asked to the funeral on Friday and she'd said we'd go. I said, 'I thought we were supposed to be on *holiday*.' But I didn't really mind. Outside the next house as we left, the bereaved mother's house, the Chrysler utility was waiting. The officer, standing by it, had stared.

CHAPTER FOUR

That evening we found the hotel dining room almost crowded. The night before we'd returned late from our exploration of the town to dine alone amid the tasteful murals of fjord and cliff. Now there were one or two families having what passed for a night out in Thorshavn, a pale young man and his girl, one or two lone souls and a group I couldn't quite place but instinctively knew were something to do with the crashed jet. They wore what amounted to a uniform of soft tweed jacket, dark grey trousers, button-down shirt. They were keeping both heads and voices down but the low exchange of monotones was unmistakably North American. When they spotted Irby I was gratified to note their self-absorption wavered. She *was* rather beautiful. The soft Faeroes air and soft Faeroes rain did for her complexion what a Mediterranean sun would do for my old girlfriend Rosie Mann. She bloomed.

The food matched the décor of the place, which was impersonal and vaguely Scandinavian. We were filled with nostalgia for the meals at Niclasen's little guest-house in Midvag, the pink trout and salt lamb and casseroled sea-birds and buttery potatoes from the peaty soil of the fells. Worst of all, the Faroes were 'dry'. Old Niclasen had turned a blind eye if I'd carried a tooth glass of Scotch to the table. Here you could have only a feeble, fizzy lager. I forced down two bottles and couldn't feel anything except wind. One of the button-down brigade caught my grimace and smiled in rueful sympathy.

When after the others had gone he lingered over a last cup of coffee it seemed only courteous to beckon him over.

'Dennis,' he said. 'Paul V. Dennis.'

'My name's Colin Panton. This is my wife Irby.'

He looked at her with renewed appreciation. 'It's too bad about the liquor situation.'

'It's uncivilised.'

'Of course, we Americans have some experience of it.' I blinked at him sceptically. He wasn't old enough to have been born during Prohibition, let alone have known it; not more than thirty-five, with a studious, nut-brown face and bright brown eyes.

He said, 'I mean aboard our warships.'

'Oh yes, I remember. We have a little Scotch in our room if you'd care for one…'

'I was about to suggest the same thing.'

'We asked first. Yours another time, maybe.' Actually we were already on the second of the two bottles we'd bought at the duty-free shop at Abbotsinch. But the Atlantic Alliance came first. Besides, it was reassuring to know that further supplies of the old revivifier were being hoarded elsewhere in the hotel.

In the little lift I said, 'You're in the Navy, then?'

'No, sir. I can't claim that distinction. My work brings me into contact with the Armed Forces a good part of the time.' But he didn't elaborate at this stage.

In our bedroom, amid such evidences of intimacy as Irby's wet things drying over the radiator he seemed slightly ill at ease. To tide over the pause while I hunted up glasses and rinsed them and filled them and took them back into the bathroom for water Irby launched into the story of the emergency shopping. She did it well, improving it a bit in a rather disreputable manner she must have caught from me.

Dennis thawed visibly. Inevitably it led on to the bereaved mother and the whole subject of the crash.

Dennis's good spirits were stowed away. He shook his head. 'You might say it's my business, dealing with this kind of incident. I still find it saddens me.'

I said, 'Out of all those millions of miles of nothing, to hit that one house.'

'Not even hit the *house*, Colin. The people in the house were unharmed — the father-in-law, the mother-in-law, the young boy. The house was only damaged by fire from the J.P. fuel. There was time enough to escape. The dead young woman was actually some little way from the house. It was five a.m., she was going to the, er, outside privy.'

'We didn't know that. What about the pilot?'

'The pilot?' He shrugged. 'Yeah, well he was killed.'

'But who was he?'

'Is it important?'

It was my turn to shrug. 'It's just that we haven't been able to make out much from the paper here. I knew I should have read Old Icelandic at university.'

He was still wary. He looked as if he were coming to a decision. 'Colin, I have to ask you…'

'Go ahead.'

'I mean, you're not a newspaper man yourself?'

'Good God, no.' I saw Irby glance guiltily at me and added, 'We're strictly on holiday — or in Irby's case, recuperation.' The rest of *that* story followed.

Dennis frowned in sympathy. 'I'm sorry, I would never have asked but … well, we have to be careful. There are aspects of this incident which are classified.' He fished out a card and handed it to me. I read his name, Paul V. Dennis, Ph.D., and underneath, Office of International Logistic Negotiations, the designation of a U.S. government arms agency.

I said, 'It was an American plane.'

'Well, I guess the official news release has already confirmed that it was of American manufacture. It was in fact a Firestorm. But we are nearly one hundred per cent satisfied that there was no contributory failure of airframe or power plant. Some instrument malfunction is a possibility, we may know more certainly in due course. But all the indications are of some unfortunate, er, tragic accident on the pilot's part.'

We were back with the pilot. I said, 'He must have been in radio contact with someone, somewhere…'

'That I cannot answer for.'

'Was he American, too?'

Dennis didn't reply at first. I thought, I've been too curious. Then he said, 'To tell the truth I couldn't tell you if I wanted to. I don't even know. That shows what a callous bastard you get to be in this job.'

The language had rather departed from the courtliness he'd first displayed towards a member of the, er, fair sex. Nor did the callousness quite accord with the sentiments he'd expressed a little earlier. I said, 'I suppose he was ferrying it somewhere.'

'The ship was carrying ferry tanks, that is true.' He set his glass down and looked at his watch. If it hadn't been for the laws of reciprocal hospitality the dialogue might have terminated there and then. He held up his hand against a second drink and said, 'You must let me return the honour. There's a choice of Scotch or Rye, as far as I remember.'

In other circumstances I wouldn't have bothered. I'd have made excuses, enjoyed a more reflective drink from my own bottle while Irby fiddled around washing out things, and returned with pleasure to whichever paperback I was then reading from the hand-picked bundle of paperbacks we had brought. But the scent was strong of something not quite what it seemed. Besides, there's nothing like a dry environment for sharpening the appreciation of the offer of a drink.

We followed him up to the next floor and along the corridor, clutching our glasses. There was a buzz of voices from behind one particular door.

Dennis said, 'We pooled our resources, if you don't mind the crowd.' He looked at Irby.

Irby said, 'As long as they don't mind me.'

'Are you kidding?'

Inside it was hazy with tobacco smoke. Several bottles stood on a table. The button-down brigade were in shirt-sleeves and from the animation with which they greeted us, had been getting in some hard drinking.

The conversation was loud and cheerful and bitty. Irby was the centre of attention. I tried to pay attention to what individual button-downers said to me, with varying degrees of prolixity, while keeping an ear cocked for anyone else mentioning the jet business. For a long time they kept off it, unless by references so cryptic that I didn't catch them. They had a jargon all of their own, much of it composed of initial letters and numbers. They were mostly full of the dreariness of the Faeroe Islands, comparing them with other desolate spots such as Newfoundland, the Aleutians, Alaska and Guam. I left it to Irby to take them on, which she did with spirit.

'You mean to say you *chose* to come here,' a red-haired one kept saying. His red hair was curly and covered his head tightly. He had also been drinking the most determinedly of all.

It was he who raised the spectre of the jet crash, literally. There was one of those lulls in the chatter. He'd just refilled his glass. He held it up and said, 'Gen'lmen — and excuse me, lady — I give you a toast.'

In the hush that fell he couldn't think of anyone at first. He frowned and then it struck him. He said, 'A toast to a brave man. To what's his name again — Kuchinski.'

No one spoke.

'C'mon,' said Red-head obstinately. 'To Kuchinski, who died for his country whatever that may be.'

'Shut up,' said Dennis.

'Why should I? So we have to be the heavies, eh? We have to be the friendly power that bats down outa the sky and kills off some girl — and her baby —.'

'I said shut *up*,' said Dennis again.

'It's all right for you, just the ship is yours. We have to have the human element.'

'Listen, I'm warning you.' The others joined in, telling Red-head to leave it alone.

'Well, I'm drinking to him.' He glugged back half a tumbler of whisky. 'I trust he's in Heaven. If he isn't there ain't no justice…'

Suddenly there was a fight in progress. One moment everyone was standing there, the next moment there was confusion, shouting, and the red-head knocked against the table with a crash, his face white except for a bright red mark on his cheekbone. It was ugly and demeaning. Irby grabbed my arm. She hated anything like that. It seemed best to go.

In the corridor Dennis said, 'I should apologise for Mac and the other.' He added, as if in explanation: 'He's a Canadian.'

I said, 'Who's Kuchinski?'

'Forget him.'

'Was he a Canadian, too?'

He was definitely twitchy now. He said, 'There's a NATO public affairs officer assigned to the investigation. Maybe you should talk to him.'

'Thanks, but its only idle curiosity.'

There was one more awkward moment. In the morning I put a call through to London. It was easiest to write the number on a slip of paper and take it to the reception desk. I was waiting for it to come through when the button-down brigade arrived to settle their bills. Dennis gave me a courteous good morning, the Canadian red-head looked subdued. I was afraid the call would come through while they were still there, and rehearsed throwaway explanations — an S.O.S. for a case of Scotch, perhaps? — but in fact it was another ten minutes before I was speaking to Ken Iles, who was editing *Panorama* these days. I'd asked for him because I knew him as well as anyone and the programme had to keep tabs on all the news while not needing to cover it all from day to day.

He said, 'Where did you say you were?'

'The Faeroes.'

'Where are they, for Chrissake?'

'That's a good start. Didn't you ever listen to the weather forecasts for trawlermen?'

'All right, I know. Is this instead of a postcard...'

'Listen. What's appeared about a plane crash here?'

'Don't remember anything. When was it?'

'Three days ago. Early Tuesday a.m. should have made the evenings. A Firestorm jet hit a house, killed a woman. Also the pilot.'

'Hardly world-shattering. Just a minute ... Jennie says it was just an agency paragraph, likewise in the dailies next morning. Nothing on television, nothing else very much ... slight hoo-hah in Denmark ... usual anti-NATO stuff.'

'Did they name the pilot?'

'Um… no.'

'Or give his nationality, or the nationality of the plane?'

There was a pause. Then: 'No, apparently, it just said NATO — a NATO jet. What's the mystery?'

'That's the mystery. There isn't anywhere called NATO. It's an organisation.'

'It sounds a bit like splitting hairs, honestly.'

'I tell you, the whole thing is slightly odd. Even the local paper is keeping mum, and they haven't had a plane crash here for twenty-five years.'

'The trouble is Dad, it's all a bit off the map up there, isn't it. And everyone's in Beirut except me.'

'I'm glad I reversed the charges,' I said.

'Give my love to the Penguins.'

'They don't have them. Just sheep.'

CHAPTER FIVE

The funeral took place in the church across the valley from the destroyed farmhouse. Irby and I were late, mainly through inconclusiveness on my part in getting a taxi for the last part of the journey. The thing was that if it was running to a scheduled service it only cost a few kroner. If you engaged it privately it could cost the earth. How to tell which hat the taxi-man was wearing? A few heads turned as we entered and Irby did her little bob but we obviously weren't the only strangers.

Inside it was all pale, smooth unvarnished pine, beneath one simple brass chandelier. The coffin of the same wood, with handles of the same metal, might have been a matching fixture. The back-rest of the pew was unyielding in the middle of my back, forcing me to sit as upright as an elder. There was a harangue from the pastor and much unaccompanied singing. In the churchyard afterwards we hung back while the immediate mourners stood around the grave. The poor raw boy of a husband looked bewildered, his red hands clenched, his wiry fair hair plastered down. There was the mother we'd met, leaning on the arm of her man and weeping; the other parents, our kindly lady and her husband. The older men wore high-collared coats and woollen knee breeches with silver buttons.

Many of the headstones were surmounted by a carved seagull, its head tucked under its wing in sleep — a curiously touching symbol. The ocean seemed close, you could hear it faintly booming under the cliffs. And down in the valley the circular lake reflected the sky like the disc of water at the bottom of a deep old lavatory pan.

As the coffin was lowered there came an incongruous flash from a photographer who didn't trust the murky light. If the pastor was aggrieved he didn't show it. There was quite an official turn-out: the Danish High Commissioner would attend, they'd said at the hotel, as well as members of the Faeroese parliament. Among the official black overcoats were several uniforms including the blue of the U.S.A.F. I became aware of the stare of a tall man in a long navy raincoat. He had thick iron-grey hair brushed back off his forehead, and when I caught his eye, gave me a gesture as if of recognition. I guessed who he might be.

As we left after shaking hands and nodding our heads and stepping aside, he caught us up. He was wearing a rakish naval cap by now and gave an airy little salute.

'You would be the English couple from the Hafnia?' and without waiting for a reply, 'Paul Dennis said I should look out for you.' His accent was strongly American. 'I'm Hank Jansen, NATO public affairs officer.'

I was a bit thrown by the name, and perhaps showed it.

'Lieutenant-Commander, Royal Danish Navy,' he added. 'Maybe I could offer you a lift back to Thorshavn.'

'That would be very nice if you're sure it's no trouble.'

'My pleasure. I surprised you a little, eh?'

'Only the name, really. Hank Jansen was the name they used to put on a series of piggy-book thrillers in England —'

'Sure, I heard that.' He laughed rather unconvincingly. 'It's an easier name, international-wise, than Hjalmar, that's all.'

We climbed into a black Volkswagen and set off.

'Rather a moving little ceremony,' said Jansen.

'I thought it was just *sad*,' said Irby with sudden vehemence. 'Sad and inadequate and — oh, I don't know.' I glanced back at her. She was dry-eyed but her lips were pressed together. 'Did you see the husband? He looked as if he'd been stunned.'

'The question of compensation is being considered. Of course, nothing can make up for the...' He lifted a hand from the steering-wheel to reach for the unsaid words.

'And the pilot?'

I caught his eye in the rearview mirror. He said, 'The body was flown out. He was a Canadian citizen, as maybe you heard.'

Nothing much more was said for a while. I couldn't be sure what Jansen's motives were. We drove alongside a long fjord and he pointed out the last whaling station in the islands, a corrugated iron place down by the water's edge. Steam drifted from a tall chimney and the VW's ventilation system gave us a brief oily taste.

Then at last he came to the point. 'Mr Panton, Mrs Panton, if I am quite frank with you, will you be quite frank with me?'

We blinked at each other. I said, 'I don't altogether understand.'

'Well, let me be frank first, then. The situation here as regards the NATO presence is a little delicate. The Faeroese have a considerable degree of independence from Denmark, and some of them would like to have even more. You will be familiar with that situation in your own country.'

'Yes.'

'Unfortunately, it is only through Denmark that NATO is here — you follow? So our little presence, which is not much — little more than a meteorological and communications centre — becomes for the students and agitators, you know, a symbol of foreign domination. Secondly, this is a part of the world where we prefer not to show the flag, not to advertise our armed forces. There are close ties with Iceland, which is outside the Alliance. The Russians are watchful. There is a tradition of neutrality. Normally we keep only one small cruiser in these waters, and she is primarily for fishery protection. So you see what bad luck it was that plane should have come down where it did.'

He paused to negotiate an even bumpier and more broken stretch of road than usual. 'We have some good luck too. They flew me in to deal with the public affairs side, but in fact the Press boys have left us alone. I guess they've been too busy elsewhere.'

'I still don't see how this concerns us.'

'You had some drinks last night with the Americans in your hotel?'

'Of course we did. Dennis would have told you.'

'But what you didn't tell *him*, Mr Panton, was that you work in the communications field, namely the British Broadcasting Corporation —'

'I make historical documentaries,' I said, which was in fact exactly how I had been misemployed for the past five months. 'I'm not interested in anything that happened later than Queen Victoria.'

'He specifically asked you if you were in communications.'

'He asked if I were on a paper.'

'Your answer was — shall we say less than completely frank?' I let that pass.

'Anyway,' he said. 'The point is that one of Dennis's colleagues was apparently not so discreet as Dennis himself. You know who I mean.'

I said with an impatience that wasn't altogether feigned, 'All I heard him say was something about the nationality of the plane and pilot. Is that such a vital secret?'

'Put that way, of course not, Mr Panton.' I caught the reflection of his eyes in the driving mirror. They gazed at me speculatively. 'But look at it another way. You will admit there are certain member countries of the Alliance — Germany, should we say? Or the United States — whose names carry more emotional associations than the others.'

I began to see what he was driving at.

Irby said, 'What difference does it make? It's not going to bring the girl back to life.'

He inclined his head. 'That also is true. Let's just say that for reasons that may become apparent shortly it is … convenient, uh? … that people should think it was a Canadian plane. Canada is a country no one minds. Right?' When neither of us answered, he added, 'After all the pilot was a Canadian. That is established, is it not?'

'Kuchinski?'

'Kuchinski,' he agreed.

We came to a building I'd noticed before, and wondered about. It was long and low, buried into the hillside high above the head of an enormous fjord, so that from the road only the grass-thatched roof showed.

Jansen was slowing down to turn off. He said, 'This is what all the trouble is about.'

Irby said, 'How do you mean?'

I'd already guessed. It was the NATO headquarters.

Jansen said, 'If you wouldn't mind waiting a moment while I see if there are any messages for me.'

The turning led down to a gravelled terrace cut into the slope. There were half a dozen other cars there. The red and white Danish standard drooped from a tall flagstaff. Otherwise it could have been an egg packing station.

Jansen was back within five minutes. I thought he looked put out but he said equably enough, 'Nothing to detain me, thank goodness. They say a few kids demonstrated outside at the time of the funeral, but in the Faeroes that is not so impressive.'

He was right. We overtook them on the outskirts of Thorshavn. There were less than twenty of them, straggling a bit now. They had a banner and a couple of handwritten placards on poles which I couldn't read except for the word which I think meant 'murder'. They hardly looked the touchy political force that Jansen had been invoking earlier.

At the hotel Irby got out first.

'Mr Panton?'

'Yes.'

'One last word if you don't mind.' He shut the door again and spoke in a low voice. 'The deal was that you should be frank with me as well as I with you.'

'I don't know what you mean.'

'You made a call to London this morning.'

Christ, surely they didn't tap the lines in this backwater! How much did he know? He'd certainly have checked on the number. I said, 'It was only to my secretary. Routine check.'

He revolved that for a moment. 'I see.' He opened the door again and said more affably, 'I'm sure you'll agree it would be better all round it we can keep this out of the hands of the hairier kind of security guys.'

I tried hard to be non-committal. 'I imagine so.'

He reached back through his repertoire of movie slang for the acknowledgement which had the hint of caution he sought. 'That's dandy,' he said. 'Goodbye, Mr Panton.'

CHAPTER SIX

'That's what I've been trying to tell you,' I said. 'Either they're not saying whose plane it was — or they don't bloody well know! It's all very sinister.' Back in London I saw no reason why the story shouldn't be reopened from there. The trouble was that I'd moved into documentary and was no longer directly concerned with current affairs. The *24 Hours* crowd seemed the likeliest to be interested, which is why I was now drinking with them in their scruffy club down the road from the Television Centre in the old Lime Grove studios.

'We'll certainly have a look at it,' they said. And that afternoon I had a long phone call from a researcher who didn't seem very bright. But when I bumped into the duty editor a couple of days later he said, 'I'm afraid we're not having much luck with that story of yours in — where was it?'

'The Faeroes.'

'Oh yes. Well, no one seems to be able to help.'

'Are you sending up there?'

'Not until there's something to go on.'

'How about the aircraft company?'

'We had Keith in Washington try them. They referred him to that agency you gave us. And they back to NATO. So we tried NATO again and they say, off the record you know, there's nothing in it, it was simply a mix-up at the time, there's no mystery.'

'The plane *was* Canadian, then?'

'So it seems.'

'Did they actually confirm that?'

'Not in as many words. But the chap was apparently quite open about it.'

The brave days at the B.B.C. were past, I thought sourly. The memorable victory over government interference which I had once witnessed had been in vain. The next administration had simply set out to achieve the same end by subtler means. From a new chairman, new governors, a reorganised directorate, a philosophy of caution and conformity seeped steadily down through the ranks.

Of course, the initial incident was unimportant and remote seen from this distance. I had to admit that. The Faeroes were as far from London as Naples and the whole population was less than that of many a rural district. But surely the implications were momentous. If I'd been with the opposition, it was the sort of thing that might have attracted the attention of *World in Action*, which loved exposés, no matter how obscure. Or of Alan Whicker, who would have tramped cheerfully through official denials and evasions to elevate the deaths of an unknown ferry pilot and an unknown young woman into a parable of the cold war or the armed peace, or something.

Couldn't I do that myself, though? Not as a performer like Whicker, but as a documentary film maker. *Act of God* — the title suggested itself at once. The theme would be the impact, literally, of technology and strategy and everything on a remote, peaceful community. There was a Scottish film unit which was begging to be worked, and Glasgow was a third of the way there already. There was a marvellous Orkney poet who I'd wanted to use for a long time. He would be perfect for the commentary. For the research I could ask Malcolm Freundlich, whose overdeveloped sense of conspiracy would be useful. I'd first employed him on a feature about refugees who'd come to Britain, mainly from Nazi Germany, and how they'd been treated and what contribution they'd subsequently made to the country. He was of refugee stock himself, a German-Jewish family that had settled in Glasgow. On top of being young and Jewish and Scottish — indeed a Zionist and Scottish Nationalist — he was an atheist, a Marxist and possibly a homosexual. It was difficult to think of a subject which one way or the other didn't arouse his deepest suspicions. But he was efficient and not easily fobbed off.

It wasn't difficult to get approval to go ahead, at least on the research. I summoned Malcolm. He listened carefully, his dark eyes unblinking.

At the end he said, 'Why confuse the issue by bringing superstition into it?'

'How do you mean.'

'Calling it *Act of God*. It's a political consequence, like anything else. It was the system that killed that girl.'

'Okay, but "God" is six letters shorter. Are you interested?' He hesitated.

I said, 'It ought to be right up your street. Your friends in Young Napalm — is it? would approve.'

'Young *Mapam*' he said patiently. 'But I no longer belong to it. I have severed all connections with the Communists in view of the Soviet attitude to Israel.' He thought again for a moment, then said, 'Very well. I'll do it.'

'Good. For a start you might look into the life and times of the other victim, the pilot. His name was Kuchinski.'

We started work. I wrote personally to the dead girl's family and to the kindly lady who had introduced them, discreetly outlining the idea and looking forward to their co-operation. Malcolm pursued his inimitable methods of inquiry. I should have known it couldn't last.

The department head was at this time deeply involved in a special project of his own. On the phone he said, 'I'm not sure what this is all about but there's hell to pay over your Faeroes idea. Did you give some sort of undertaking when you were up there?'

'Certainly not.'

'Well, Fulton Goodman's handling it. Would you mind seeing him?'

Fulton was my old boss from current affairs days. He had now been shunted into a post concerned with the Corporation's relations with the government, the unions, the civil service and other august bodies. Well, at least he had some old-fashioned integrity. If there had to be such a functionary, better Fulton than some of the smoothies who were rising to power. He kept up his Canadian bear-with-a-sore-head act.

'Jeez, Colin,' he said by way of greeting, 'you've really stirred things up again.'

'Who with?'

'With just about everybody. We've had the Danish embassy on, we've had the Foreign Office, we've had the Ministry of Defence, the 'D' notice people, we've had NATO, we've even had the Canadian High Commissioner, which was a little galling for me personally, to put it mildly.'

'Over what?'

'No bullshit, Colin. You know what. And in particular all these questions about some pilot —'

'Kuchinski.'

'Kuchinski, that's right. Good old Canadian name. Listen, Colin, did you give some kind of undertaking to a Commander Jansen up in Thorshavn, or however you say it?'

'None. He gave me a modest gipsy's warning, that's all.'

'Well he says you did. He says that he only got you off a hook with the security people by vouching for you personally, and you've now let him down.'

'It's simply not true. Or anyway, not more than fifteen per cent true. They are playing this one altogether too craftily. They really must have something to hide.'

'Well, they don't have to worry hiding it from us any more.'

'There's a stop on it, you mean?'

'As far as the Corporation is concerned, an absolute stop.'

'But, Fulton, you're a Canadian. It's the Canadians who are taking the rap for something that's nothing to do with them...'

'We have our problems. Cutting back on our NATO commitments, withdrawing a little. Maybe we don't want to rock the boat.'

'Don't rock the boat! — it could be the B.B.C. call-sign these days.'

'I'm sorry. But that's C. Exec. Tel's decision.'

'I'd like to see C. Exec. Tel.'

Fulton grinned his old grin. 'He's expecting you. And Colin —'

'Yes?'

'I should tell you I'm going back.'

'To Canada?'

'Yeah. If I have to be a no-man, it might as well be there as here. Seriously, it's a nice offer: a director of the Radio and Television Commission. The Corporation are kindly releasing me soonest.'

I said, 'I'm sorry, Fulton.'

'Well, I'm sorry too. But this job' — he indicated the papers on his desk — 'shit.'

I said, 'When you get settled in, could you do me a small favour?'

'Sure. What is it?'

'Find out what you can about this Kuchinski.'

'Get out!' said Fulton irritably.

The new Chief Executive, Television, was a smooth young man with bags under his eyes. He was busy on the telephone but waved a limp hand in greeting. I looked through his ceiling-to-floor window to the untidy urban landscape beyond: houses, trees, cranes, churches, office blocks, the Post Office Tower and the distant nipple of St Paul's.

'All right,' C. Exec. Tel. was saying. 'Cinquente-sei livri Omo, uno mezzo-gallon Teepol. Si.' I flopped into the black leather armchair designed to put his clients into a posture of inferiority and tried to work out what it could possibly be about.

'Guiseppi,' C. Exec. Tel. explained a moment later, ringing off. 'I'm trying to teach him to bulk-buy. So much cheaper.'

'Manservant?' I said incredulously.

'We don't think of him as that, but I suppose so, yes. We got so tired of au pair girls, you know.'

'What's this nonsense about my programme?'

'What programme?' He seemed genuinely uncertain.

'*Act of God* was the working title. You know perfectly well —'

'Oh, that. Hasn't Fulton put you in the picture. There was some trouble —'

'So he said. The first time I've heard of us being intimidated by mighty Denmark. We'll be paying Danegeld again next.'

'Now Colin, you know there was more to it than that. I don't remember the details. NATO came into it. But this isn't a great climb-down. It was an editorial decision as much as anything.'

'*What?*'

'Now don't get excited. It wasn't a bad idea, though I think if Nick had been less occupied with his own special at the moment he might have been a little more critical. My own view was that it was — shall we say a little unambitious for a Colin Panton special?' This was the flashing candour bit.

'Well, thank you very much.'

'But that's not really why I asked to see you.'

I thought I'd stormed in to see him, but let it pass.

He turned on the look of keen concern. 'What else have you been doing lately, Colin?'

A good question. I said, 'There were a couple of *It Happened Heres*'. This was a B.B.C.2 series of reconstructions of historical events on the actual site.

'Exactly.'

'There have been worse ideas.'

'Indeed — though it was a pity about those electricity pylons getting into shot at Bosworth.'

'What else do you expect from the nationalised industries? Anyway, Bosworth wasn't mine.'

'I know, I know. Unkind of me. But Colin, can you honestly say you've been — fully *stretched* lately?' The full extension of persons had been a favourite Corporation image ever since Lord Reith had used it of himself on a T.V. interview.

I said, '*Act of God* might have given me a slight tug.'

'Which leads rather aptly to what I have to say. Are you by any chance a Roman Catholic?'

'No. My wife is.'

'Mmm.' He paused fractionally as if before finally committing himself. 'Have you heard of an organisation called Nova Candia?'

'I've heard of it, that's about all.'

Nova Candia was a lay Catholic order, somewhere between the Knights of Malta and Opus Dei and until quite recently much less well known. It had started to become better known because of its efforts to enlist young Catholics into an aid organisation rather like the American Peace Corps, or our V.S.O., which was obviously of news value in a youth-conscious world. Then it had really fizzed into prominence — and out again when nothing seemed to be happening — with a proposal to convert an old aircraft carrier as a relief ship equipped to sail to any scene of disaster.

'It's strongest in the traditional Catholic countries of course,' C. Exec. Tel. was saying. 'France, Italy, the Rhineland. Hardly established at all in this country. Which makes the invitation all the more singular.'

I wasn't going to act as his feed. I waited.

He said, 'The B.B.C. has been offered full facilities by the Order to make a documentary account of its work, particularly the relief ship, of course.'

'But do we want to?'

He managed a look of mild professional surprise. 'I should have thought it was a subject of fairly immediate potential. The relief ship story alone is full of dramatic possibilities.'

'There was a lot about it a year or two ago, and then it never came to anything.'

'It's going to now,' he said confidently. 'And very soon. But I think you fail to see the point. The real point here is that we end up with a film which is going to have tremendous international appeal. Indeed it will be an international project from the outset. Every Catholic country and many others, America, Latin America — they'll all be in the market. We could earn thousands in foreign currency, which I don't need to remind you is an important factor these days.'

I was silent for a moment. 'Why us?'

'We should consider it a great compliment. Because we've done so well with — well, the Royals film, things like that.

Because we have a reputation for independence and integrity. Because they evidently don't want just a public relations job—'

'But won't it be exactly that? Should the British Broadcasting Corporation be in the public relations business?'

'If we were in the public relations business, as you rather insultingly put it, would I be offering the job to someone who is not a Catholic, nor even, I suspect — though it's not my concern, and I shan't make it so — a believer? This is a bona fide approach, without any conditions attached. Likewise my offer to you has no strings to it.' He softened again. 'It's simply that I think you're the right man for it and so does Nick. If he weren't tied up he'd be here now to say so.'

'Can I think about it?'

'Of course. Let me know as soon as you've decided. But Colin —'

'Yes?'

'Isn't it time you took on something worth your energy and your talents again?'

CHAPTER SEVEN

'I think you should do it,' said Irby. Her voice was strained because she was concentrating on the bend looming ahead.

'Change down!' I screamed. 'Always drive round corners, never coast.' It wasn't a good idea, trying to teach her to drive. I said, 'Well, I don't want to do it. I want to get back to *Act of God*.'

'But you said they killed it.'

'I could have beavered away on the side.'

'Can't you still?'

'In Rome or somewhere? Hardly very handy for the Faeroes.'

'But handy for God.'

I gave her a suspicious look. On top of everything else she was starting to develop a nasty turn of wit.

She said, 'Anyway, it's time you did something big and —'

'Worthwhile?'

'If you like.'

'C. Exec. Tel. used the same expression.'

Irby herself had found much that was worthwhile, not to say worthy. She hadn't returned to journalism for the time being and was pursuing her Good Works instead. A young unmarried mum and a girl who'd had three abortions in fifteen months she'd acquired in hospital. Then there was Mary, who came to clean the flat and suffered from nameless guilts. And the Mooneys across the road. The Mooneys numbered eleven with a twelfth in the offing, occupied the basement and ground floor of the last dilapidated house in the street and were preserved — I sometimes thought — solely as a picturesque reminder of the old feckless London poor, a little bit of living history to provide fuel for dinner party anecdotes. Over the leeks vinaigrette the latest Mooneyisms were swopped nightly.

There was the blast of a horn and a taxi driver who'd been coming up on the inside lane was mouthing something nasty.

I said, 'Stop just past that bus stop there and we'll change over. My nerves can't take any more just now.'

She pressed her lips together. Her face still hadn't plumped out fully after the miscarriage. Perhaps it wouldn't. She'd grown up.

I said, 'You're not doing so badly, actually. But I think you should go to a driving school after all. Have someone who's not involved emotionally with you. At least, I hope he wouldn't be.'

Later we picked up the other argument. She said, 'You could go and talk to them about it.'

'I'll see.'

'I mean, you wouldn't be concerned with faith or dogma, would you. This is to be about practical things, isn't it? Feeding the famine-stricken, ploughing the desert, saving the children. You're always complaining the Church doesn't *do* anything.'

'That's exactly what I don't complain. It does too much. Look at Mrs Mooney — a great mascot for the street, practically a status symbol. But she's having her tenth kid soon because the Pope says she mustn't go on the pill.'

'She likes children.'

'Ten of them? And with Mooney himself off work for two years now with his leg or whatever it is. Doesn't seem to hinder his sex life.'

'With the family allowance and sickness benefits and everything they do well enough.'

'Yeah. And that's why I had to pay thirteen hundred quid income tax last year.'

'You're being inconsistent now.'

Actually it was rather a hollow display on my part. I had a growing inclination to take on the job, even felt a preliminary tingle of excitement at the prospect. An extra nudge came from Malcolm's attitude. It seemed only logical to continue with him on this project. When I explained it to him, his antennae quivered audibly. This was something aimed at everything he held dear.

He said, 'You won't accept, will you?'

'Why not?'

'It's an irrelevancy. It has nothing to do with the realities of the world today. It's — it's a sentimental, reactionary, out-of-date gesture.'

'That's for me to decide.'

He looked at me with that blank, sceptical look of the young these days. They don't know about the little pretences that make life easier.

I said, 'I shan't know for sure for a day or two, but the job's yours if you want it.'

He said, 'I don't want to be a researcher always. I'm twenty-two.'

I sensed some kind of proposition. 'What do you have in mind?'

'I want to direct.' Of course: that was another thing about the young, their veneration for the image. The word was dead. They all wanted to direct. I found the mechanics of film-making acutely boring — the endless re-takes, the interminable delays. Having someone to take on the drudgery would be nice.

I said, 'I can't make any promises, but something might be arranged.'

He said, 'I will make some preliminary inquiries.'

That night I had an off-putting if silly little dream. I'd been transferred to the religious department and instead of the reasonable comforts of life in the B.B.C. heretofore, it was all grimly austere — a dusty, dark room just like an old schoolroom; an old B.B.C. hen with a stern face making cocoa and saying, 'Oh no, you can't have a drink *here.*' I was still trying to do something about that aeroplane in the Faeroes but I didn't know how to begin, there wasn't even a telephone. I woke to a feeling of being trapped and desperate and inadequate.

CHAPTER EIGHT

It transpired that it was in fact the Head of Religious Output, or H.R.O. in B.B.C.speak, from whom I should learn more about the project. Nova Candia's original approach had been to his department. An invitation to H.R.O. to discuss the matter over a spot of lunch confirmed all my worst misgivings. 'I hate cocoa,' I sobbed to Fulton in the club. It was his last day, and I would have dearly loved to stay and get maudlin with him, but the Religious Department wasn't even in the Centre, the address was somewhere in North Kensington.

'They'll probably be able to find a bottle of Communion wine,' he said consolingly.

I said, 'Don't forget to look up my old friend Kuchinski.'

The place turned out to be a rather swanky new office block and after the customary wrangle with the commissionaire as to whether or not I was entitled to park in the private car park, I made a reconnaissance in a more hopeful frame of mind. There was certainly a little dub room, with one or two people already sipping drinks. On the other hand the restaurant was a clinical self-service establishment without a bottle of plonk in view. One might get the business over and plead an urgent need to go and edit something in Ealing.

Locating H.R.O.s office turned out to be tricky. I found doors marked with the names of various underlings but not his. Finally there was one that said 'MGR' followed by a vaguely familiar name. I poked my head in.

'My God,' I said. 'Father Freeloader.'

He was sitting behind a desk, plump and sleek as ever. He looked at me over his half-spectacles and said, 'I wondered if it might be you when Gerald mentioned your name.'

'How long have you been here?'

'A matter of weeks, dear chap. Quite the new boy.'

'And manager already?'

'You always liked teasing me, didn't you?'

'It's on the door.'

'Monsignor, actually.'

'Of course, how silly of me. Congratulations. When was this?'

'Likewise quite recently.'

I saw what I should have spotted earlier, the little purple flash just below his dog collar. I said, 'You'll always be Father to me.'

'I'm touched. Shall I take you to meet Gerald?' He slipped from behind the desk. He moved lightly on little feet that always seemed to be shod in dancing pumps. His clerical suit was black and nicely cut from a fine silky material.

H.R.O.'s dress was opulent in another way. Though according to the note he'd sent me he was the Rev. Gerald, there was nothing clerical about his off-white jacket, flared trousers and floppy Mr Fish shirt. The face above didn't quite match the ensemble, being insecure and anxious: the usual Anglican sheep in Tom Wolfe's clothing, I thought, which was a poor joke, but no doubt I would be able to polish it up. He had thinning fair hair and a diffident approach.

'Shall we have a drink here while we're waiting or try the club perhaps…?' he suggested helplessly.

'It's all arranged, Gerald,' said Father Freeloader firmly. Ushering me back into the corridor he murmured, 'They had rather Low Church, not to say Noncomformist, ideas of hospitality when I arrived. I've managed to persuade dear Gerald to exercise a few of his privileges as head of a department.'

He certainly had. It was a little private dining room with the table laid for five. Two jolly ladies in shiny black dresses and white aprons, quite unlike the dragon of my dream, hovered over a side table bearing an assortment of bottles, glasses and other cheering items. I chose dry sherry which I thought had the right ecclesiastical associations. Father Freeloader bent to scrutinise the labels on the wine bottles and I heard him question one of the ladies rather tetchily. H.R.O. said, 'We're all rather excited by the invitation. It's the first time the Department's had a chance to venture into what one might call the, er, big time. It's all due to the Monsignor, of course. He brought us the business, so to speak.'

Father Freeloader warded off the tribute with a very small motion of a soft pink hand. 'Old friend,' he said modestly. 'Geoffrey Moodleigh, rather senior in the public relations field. Know him?'

'Just by name,' I said tactfully.

'He does tend to function at the level where the object is to maintain anonymity rather than obtain notoriety. He's acting for Candia purely for an honorarium — old Catholic family, has actual ties with the order.'

'And *he's* bringing along a very senior official from the embassy,' said H.R.O. eagerly, 'but we're not supposed to remember that — about the embassy — because of course we're dealing with him only in his *unofficial* capacity as a Member of the Order. I say, you don't think they've forgotten, do you?' He was consumed with sudden anxiety.

'They're on their way,' said Father Freeloader. 'I telephoned.'

'Oh, good. Of course, the Order isn't very active in this country, though I gather they've been quietly recruiting a few of these, er, young volunteers from some of the stauncher Catholic families. Isn't that so, Monsignor?'

'I believe so.'

'But *il Conte* is very highly placed in its councils. It's still rather amusing — not to say flattering — that they should come to us. Apparently they're most particular that it should not be a propaganda exercise. They didn't want a Roman producer, nor necessarily a Christian. I said, 'Well, you've come to the right place, we're all Humanists here'.' He added hastily, 'Except the Monsignor, of course.'

Father Freeloader grunted.

The others arrived. Moodleigh was an immensely well-preserved English gent of the old school: healthy pink cheeks, figure so trim it might have been corseted, but probably wasn't, silvery hair and voice to match. He wore a carnation in his buttonhole and bent over Father Freeloader's outstretched hand with a little bob that seemed to speak of the old complicity of priest and recusant. The Count was a man perhaps in his early fifties, dark-complexioned with thick black hairs on the back of his hands. He had the practised bearing of the professional diplomat but also a disconcerting habit of suddenly directing the stare of hard dark eyes at you while at the same time producing an unexpected piece of information. The first time it happened to me was when H.R.O. had trotted out another feeble witticism about my being peculiarly qualified to bring an agnostic detachment to the film.

The hard eyes bored into mine. 'You have no religion, Mr Panton?'

'None that I admit to.'

'But you wanted to make a programme called *Act of God*, something like that?'

How had he known? I said, 'It was using the phrase merely as a figure of speech,' and old Moodleigh chimed in with some long-winded explanation of what it meant at Lloyd's. Another time he said out of the blue, 'I saw *Britons from Europe*. It was extremely interesting, though possibly you were a fraction too complacent over the internment camps in 1940.'

This was the documentary about refugees. Though it had done quite well and won some awards it was odd that he should have remembered the exact title after — what? Nearly two years. He must have been doing some research on me.

The meal was indifferent but Father Freeloader's choice of wines impeccable, even if they had brought him the '64 Pomerol and not the '62. I was thinking that I may not have known much about claret but I knew what I liked when the eyes came my way again.

'The *Columba*, as we've called her: an old warship now declaring herself to be a ship of peace, her crew composed largely of young idealists, her first voyage no longer far off — what would your attitude be to such a madcap scheme, Mr Panton?' His English was betrayed only by such usages as 'madcap' which look all right in print but sound all wrong.

I said, 'If it worked, all in favour.'

'Why?'

I hesitated. The usual pieties wouldn't impress this character. He offered a lead. 'You wouldn't find it — incongruous?'

'It's the incongruity that interests me.' Before I could expand on this, old Moodleigh dredged up the fable that was bound to be dredged up sooner or later. He said, 'There was the famous story during the war, you know, when Churchill and Roosevelt sought to impress on Stalin the importance of having the

Church on their side. Stalin replied, "And how many divisions has the Pope?"'

'At least you now propose to give him a navy,' said H.R.O., going quite pink with glee.

The Count wasn't much amused. That is, he didn't disapprove. He simply didn't bother to pretend he hadn't heard it many times before. He made it plain he was waiting for me to go on.

I said, 'What I mean is that I'm always attracted by active things that express abstractions — you have to be if you're in this business. Like the way an army expresses the nature of the people whose army it is. Compare the Israeli army, say, and the Swiss. Or the way a bullfight expresses a whole lot of things about the human race, mostly nasty. The very idea of an aircraft carrier spells ... what? War and imperialism and aggression —'

'As we have been made only too aware,' he murmured.

'— but more than anything it spells Power. It's the symbol of Power. If you can take a carrier and make it spell something else, then you have expressed, better than in a million words of propaganda, what Christianity is supposed to be about.'

'And what is that, Mr Panton?'

'Why ask me?' But he was asking me. I riffled through all the poor old words that had been devalued by abuse and over-use, Charity and Compassion and Concern, and finally chose the one that had been abused most of all but could still sound like new. I said, 'Love.'

The Rev. Gerald looked embarrassed again, Father Freeloader faintly surprised.

I added hurriedly, 'Of course, it might equally well turn out to express what Christianity is in fact about, more often than not.'

'Which is?'

'Intolerance. Superstition. Regimentation.'

That could have ended the proposition without more ado. But the Count only said quietly, 'And which would you expect to emerge if you made our film? The love or the intolerance and regimentation and what was it — superstition?'

'I wouldn't know until I started on it — perhaps not until I finished it.'

'I see.' He thought for a moment. 'You say that when you began *Britons from Europe* you had no idea whether it would turn out an enthusiastic or a cynical report?'

'It could have gone either way, yes.'

'Then this *Act of God* — it was to have been about a disaster of some sort, was it?'

'A very minor one; a plane came down.'

'And again you had an open mind?'

'I think so.' But I saw where he was heading.

He said, 'Yet you started with a title that clearly indicated an attitude. *Act of God* — from what Geoffrey has explained about the common understanding of the phrase you meant that here was a random, a meaningless accident.'

'Not necessarily. I might well have concluded it was very much an Act on *someone's* part, if not God's. As a matter of fact, that was precisely the angle that interested me. Who was to blame? They weren't even saying whose plane it was.'

No man to leave a joke while there was still breath in it, H.R.O. came in with, 'I hope you're not suggesting His Holiness also has an air force.'

The Count said sharply, 'If he had, I doubt that he would employ it to kill one young woman.'

I gaped at him. 'You knew — how did you know?'

He didn't even blink. 'I have represented my country at the Councils of the Treaty Organisation. I like to keep in touch. Mr Panton, I think we would be pleased if you undertook this film.'

But did I want to do it? In search of spiritual guidance I sought out Father Freeloader next day with the suggestion that we might investigate the bourgeois cooking at a little bistro lately opened off Kensington Square.

'I noticed you didn't have much to say at the lunch.'

'Did you, dear boy? Perhaps it became me not to say much. I am, after all, but a novice in the world of television.'

'But you are the Roman Catholic adviser. Your duty is to advise.'

'If all the advice in history were withdrawn, would the world be a worse or better place?'

'I know perfectly well you don't approve of the film, just as you don't really approve of lay orders.'

'Why shouldn't I approve of a film which will depict, with great skill and honesty I am sure, work which is being done in God's name?'

'Ah, but is it according to His will?'

'You don't make a very good Jesuit, Colin. Leave that kind of speculation to those of us who have nothing better to do.'

'All right, so you have no reservations at all?"

He ruminated for a moment. 'I suppose that for me God is about being, not doing.'

I said, 'The trouble is, for me He's not anything. I wish I knew more about your stuff, dear Father.'

'There is always time.'

'The subject's too big, I've left it too late. It's like *War and Peace* or Beethoven or —' my eye caught the label of the

Margaux which Father Freeloader had gently proposed after scanning the wine list — 'or claret. If I was going to master any of them I should have started years ago. So I stick to the lesser things I do know, like reliable Rhônes and Berlioz and Hardy.'

'Unbelievers both,' he sighed. 'As for the Rhône, it is all right with some coarsely-flavoured dish in winter, when one has a cold. I will give you a letter to someone you may find both helpful and amusing, or anyway surprising. Every society within — or around — the Church has its protector at Rome. Nova Candia's is one Cardinal Stefani. I knew him many years ago.'

'Thanks, but look — it's still not too late for me to pull out. Do you think I ought to?'

'Since it was I who urged your candidature, hardly.'

The devious old rogue, with his affectation of having wondered if I were the same Colin Panton he'd once instructed!

CHAPTER NINE

Until I actually saw the *Columba* I never quite believed she existed. Even as the Trident climbed away from Heathrow, and I watched the gravel-pits wheel and recede, and pressed the button for a little drink to mark the fact that from now on the New Order of the Knights Protector of St Mark of Candia was paying my way, and hunted in my case for Malcolm's notes on the subject — well, it remained curiously unreal.

The ship was being fitted out in Venice, or so the illusion maintained. I would scout out the ground. The film unit would follow as soon as they'd finished another job, in ten days' time. Malcolm was supposed to accompany them as assistant producer, part of the job being to dogsbody the gear through Customs. He'd said, 'But shouldn't I be with you, planning what we're going to shoot?'

'You can't have it both ways. You said you wanted to branch out.'

His attitude to the project had changed with the change of function he'd gained. He was no longer dismissive. Instead, his habitual suspicions had re-formed around the carrier. 'There must be some ulterior motive,' he'd say. 'What could it be?'

'You're mixing it up with the last job,' I'd reply. 'That was the great conspiracy, wasn't it? This is what it says it is — if it ever puts to sea, which I doubt.'

But once when I bowled into the office unexpectedly he looked up from the telephone with what was almost — in someone normally so tightly-controlled — a guilty start. He said into the mouthpiece, 'Thank you very much, that's very kind of you,' and rang off.

'Who was that?'

'Oh, the Imperial War Museum with some answers.'

The only thing was that it had sounded, as I opened the door, as if Malcolm was imparting rather than gathering information. I turned to his notes.

It seemed that the original Knights of St Mark, drawn mainly from France, the Venetian Republic and Southern Germany, had constituted one of the smallest and least effectual of the crusading orders. After the fall of Acre of 1291 they'd settled on the island of Candia, or Crete, from where — shielded by the more powerful Knights Hospitallers of St John in Cyprus and Rhodes — they'd indulged in some minor expeditions against the Infidel. But the Venetians who owned the island were more interested in trading with the East than raiding it, and for the knights who stayed in Candia chivalry gradually gave way to commerce. Only the Frenchmen, who withdrew to their *commanderie* in the Dauphine, tried to preserve the old traditions. Here they fell under the cloud of envy and suspicion directed at their rich comrades the Templars, and were suppressed by Philip Le Bel after their Master, Jehan de l'Arbois, confessed under torture to heresy. Their name was subsequently cleared by a Papal commission but their property had long been dispersed.

Nova Candia, one of two hundred and fifty lay orders registered with Rome, dated from 1932. It had no links other than sentimental with the old chivalric order. At first an ultra-conservative secret society dabbling in right-wing politics — and still likely to be, Malcolm implied — it had started to become more publicly known in the 1950s, and almost famous in the 1960s with the formation of the *Auxilia Candiae* or youth corps. It was non-apostolic, seeking to further the cause of Christ by example rather than preaching. Thanks to an investment policy said by *Newsweek* to be even more astute than the Vatican's own, its finances were extremely sound. Within its ranks the emphasis was now on service rather than on giving money. It had won much respect, Malcolm was forced to concede, for its rescue and relief operations in the Italian floods.

The dossier on the *Columba* herself included photocopies of old *Jane's Fighting Ships* entries, one or two news clippings and Malcolm's neatly-typed summary. It seemed she was originally H.M.S. *Talus*, a Colossus-class Light Fleet Carrier of the Royal Navy, 13,190 tons, launched at Birkenhead in 1944, commissioned the following year and with the British Pacific Fleet in time for the last few weeks of the war. She'd taken part in some early experiments with catapult launching before being transferred to the Australians as H.M.A.S. *Bligh*, 1947. She saw service in Korean waters in 1951-52 and was sold to the Argentinean Navy in 1954 as the *Fernando Colombo*, but apparently spent most of her years with this navy laid up. In 1962 she was sold to a firm called Expo British-America S.A. who had a plan to convert her to a mobile exhibition vessel. But after some extensive refitting the scheme was abandoned and she was put up for sale again, being finally bought by agents for the Order at little more than scrap valuation. Restoring the ship would add a great deal to the cost but as Malcolm sourly added, the owner of the shipyard was known to be a member of Nova Candia and presumably wouldn't screw his own Order too harshly, at least by Venetian standards.

Some vital statistics followed, then a section about the manning of the *Columba*. Part of the Expo conversion had been with a view to ease of handling: they'd claimed she would need a crew no larger than that of a conventional cargo vessel of the same tonnage. According to Italian Press reports the Order proposed to employ a minimal professional crew; they would depend otherwise on the youth volunteers, some of whom had been sent for sail training under French, German or Italian auspices. The master was to be one Giovanni Belli, formerly master of a cruise ship, but a Captain Durand, late of the French Navy, was named as director of operations.

Next came a historical note on the civilian application of aircraft carriers. It had been first suggested in the 1950s that they might be used as relief ships, after naval carriers had proved their usefulness at scenes of disaster, notably the Greek earthquake. Carriers had large storage space, workshops, hospital facilities, etc., plus the obvious capability of air-lifting supplies and aid teams where needed, presumably by helicopter. A United Nations committee reported favourably but nothing came of the idea at the time.

Finally Malcolm itemised some of the misgivings about the *Columba*. In Italy there were doubts about both the physical and the moral safety of the volunteers. The whole idea of a former warship sailing under the Church's colours was under attack from the Communists. There were the jokes that the Count had instanced, about the Pope's Warship or the Holy Father's Navy. And outside Italy, it was rumoured that several governments had expressed diplomatic anxiety about the presence of such a warlike silhouette upon the seas and the confusion it might cause. There were assurances that the ship had been entirely disarmed and would be clearly painted as a bringer of peace, not war, but Malcolm had saved to last the sardonic caption from a left-wing journal which read, *God's Armour is 5 cm. Thick.*

CHAPTER TEN

They were supposed to be meeting me at the airport. After twenty years in films and television and journalism, not to mention a stint as a travel agent, I still disliked making myself known to strangers. I wished I could follow the other passengers to the water-bus and the old city basking in its vaporous haze across the lagoon. But the *Columba* was being fitted out in Mestre, the industrial dump on the mainland. I rested my bag and waited gloomily to be accosted.

Eliminating the usual touts and motorboat operators, there only seemed to be one likely candidate. I felt more cheerful. She was a big fair girl wearing a blue linen suit and sunglasses. A deep leather bag of the kind photographers use was hung over her shoulder, along with an expensive-looking camera in a case. She was making it as obvious as possible that she was searching for someone.

I caught her eye and we converged. Nearer to, she had shiny yellow hair held back with a band and a deep suntan and would have been handsome — rather than pretty — had it not been for the scar of a badly-rectified harelip.

She said, 'For the *Columba*?' in an American accent.

'That's right.'

'It's awful of me. I forgot what name I was supposed to be asking for.' Her smile made the scar much less forbidding.

'Panton. Colin Panton.'

'I'm Lisa Thompson. Hi.'

I said, 'You're American,' not very brightly.

'So my passport says. I've been living in Europe a few years now.'

Outside the sun was burning down. There was a little Fiat in the car park, the inside like an oven.

'Wow!' she said. 'Sorry about this. I wanted the one with a roll-back roof but I guess it would have been another ten lire a week or something. The Order rents it for me while we're here. Did you eat?'

'On the plane, if you can call it that.'

'So we should go straight and see the ship, or do you want to go to your hotel first?'

Since we were already on the mainland and since there was no point in getting freshened up and then all hot and bothered again, I opted for the ship. On the road out of the airport she put her foot down and with all the windows open it got more bearable. She said, 'You could call me a kinda Press agent on the project. I'm a photographer, really — freelance. I came down to do a portfolio on the ship and they asked me to stay on. There were other factors involved but I won't bore you with them.' Again the grin softened the accusing expression the lip built into her face.

'Tell me about it.'

'Like what?'

'Is it ever going to work?'

'Surprisingly, yes.'

'When?'

'We're scheduled to sail in two weeks' time.'

'And will we?'

'There's an even chance.'

'Where to?'

'You didn't hear?'

'No.'

'The buzz is that it'll be straight to Africa.' She named the beleaguered rebel province whose starving children were at this time the most notorious cause in the world. Well, even Malcolm wouldn't want to quarrel with that.

'But no shake-down cruise first?' I asked.

'That's what it is, officially. But Durand figured why shouldn't we take some food and stuff out while we were about it. At least, that's what Leo says. It would also be good for the image.'

'Tell me about these people.'

'Captain Belli's around. He's sweet but kind of distant. Durand will be the real boss, they figure. Have you met him?'

'Not yet. He's director of operations, isn't he?'

'Yeah. He's not here yet but his reputation came ahead.'

'As what?'

'As a toughie. The word is, Captain Bligh had nothing on Durand. Then there's Leo, that's all. He's nice. It should be Padre Leo really, he's the priest — chaplain, I guess you'd say — and also a doctor. You know, trained as a missionary. But everyone calls him Leo. One way or the other he's in charge of the kids' welfare.'

'The kids being the volunteers — what do you call them, the *Auxilia*?'

'Right. We have sixty already and more to come.'

As Lisa threaded her way through the mess of crossings and railway tracks and sheds that surrounds any dockyard I still didn't quite believe it. It was a great scheme on paper, and on paper it would stay. Then suddenly the superstructure of the old carrier was towering above the roofs. Round the next corner she came into full view, a flat-topped ark shimmering in the heat, a slab of iron against the sky.

We drove right on to the dockside. Here, out of the glare, I could see the hull was in the process of being painted. Half was still a rusty red, half a gleaming white. Painters were at work in cradles slung from the decks. I pitied them, perched against the hot iron and, if they turned their heads, seeing the acres of dingy, dented red that stretched ahead. They looked young, in paint-stained shorts. One of them had a transistor with him, from which came the voice of Rita Pavone belting out some urgent lyric.

I said, 'They're not —?'

Lisa said, 'Sure they are. These kids have come to *work*.'

The gangway took us to what must have been the gun deck. We climbed to the hangar deck. The hangar ran nearly the whole length of the ship. Cables snaked everywhere, there was a confusion of hammering and sawing. Lisa said, 'It's some fantastic number of cubic metres of storage space which I've forgotten. Like two hundred trucks or something.'

We climbed again to the flight deck. Big and bare as it was it didn't seem to stretch the 690 feet Malcolm's notes had specified. The deck plates were irregular and far from flush fitting, criss-crossed with slots and conduits, studded with covers and cowlings and other junk. Near us gaped the square hole of one of the aircraft lifts. Workmen were everywhere, also more of the volunteers, wearing what was almost a uniform of jeans or shorts and denim shirts.

'Come and meet the captain,' said Lisa.

Belli was tall and thin and on the old side for this job, I thought. He was wearing drill trousers and sandals and a cotton pullover that hung loosely from his bony shoulders. He was also deep in conversation with a dockyard engineer or someone, and gave me a polite but abstracted welcome. Perhaps we could talk a little later, when he had more time…

In the next hour we tramped about three miles of white-painted passageways, ascended and descended a thousand iron steps, ducked through a hundred bulkheads. Sometimes a ventilator blew a cool draught of air, more often a hot blast, mostly it was just still and stifling. I was shown messes, dormitories, a club-room, the sick bay complete with operating theatre, in varying stages of readiness. The one place that seemed completely finished was the chapel, which was large and simple and — Lisa said — had been converted by the volunteers themselves.

They'd somehow made it cool and tranquil with flat white paint and rush matting on the iron deck and a single decoration, a Madonna fashioned from tiny mosaic tiles, blue and yellow and palest pink. Lisa had looped a chiffon scarf over her head before we went in, and as we left I noticed she gave a little bob in the direction of the altar. She was one of them, then. Father Leo, she said, was visiting one of the kids who'd had to go into hospital in Venice, but ought to be back soon.

Finally we were back on the flight deck. Belli hailed us. He was relaxed now, and smoking a large cigar. We paced slowly aft. The deck seemed to have stored all the day's heat and here there wasn't a hint of the wind off the lagoon which sometimes made the Venetian summer bearable. I could think only of a shower and an enormous drink, an ice-cold lager perhaps or a litre carafe of chilled white wine, the outside beaded with condensation —

The next thing I knew, as they used to say in boys' stories, the deck had come up to meet me. It was hard and hot and it hurt, and for a moment I was too winded to move.

'Are you all right?' Lisa was saying. She and Belli helped me up. There was dust and paint all over the front of my second-best lightweight suit. One knee throbbed and blood oozed from a black graze on the heel of my left hand. I managed a rueful smile and looked to see what had tripped me. A steel cable as thick as a modest drainpipe lay across the full width of the deck. My hand had encountered a second one. Beyond that was a third.

Belli was full of Latin protestations of regret and alarm. Lisa inspected my hand and said more practically, 'We'd better get that cleaned up.'

As I hobbled back between them I asked with the jokey curiosity of someone bravely concealing his pain, 'Did they *have* to keep the old arrester gear?'

Lisa took the question as meant and passed it on. Belli shrugged. She said, 'They decided it was simpler to leave it than get rid of it. But he will have the cables covered over with matting or something.' Belli was pointing at something further forward. Lisa added, 'The catapult is still there, too.'

I screwed up my eyes against the glare. There wouldn't be much to see, though; just a long furrow in the deck. I said, 'Does it work?'

'*Si, si.*' But it was meant to be a joke. Belli showed many gold teeth as he laughed.

I said huffily, 'It was one of the first hydraulic catapults. Rather historic.'

Lisa translated. 'Yeah, he knows that actually. There are some plaques that tell the history of the ship he's going to have cleaned up.' She listened to him for a moment. 'He says there is something else they are keeping you should see.'

'What's that?'

'He'll show you.'

Amidships, to the side of the deck rose the island superstructure of the carrier. As Belli led the way towards it I said, 'How serious is this suggestion that they will actually fly stuff off or on?'

'It's quite serious. Only with helicopters, of course. Not aeroplanes.'

'And they can get helicopters?'

She checked with Belli. 'Sure. They already have one. Just now it is in Torino. Others could be hired or borrowed or something.'

A man stepped out of the companion way to meet us. He was young and immensely handsome with thick dark hair and lean features. He was buttoning on the garment in which I was nearly always to see him: one of those high-necked, short-sleeved white overalls worn by the more fashionable housemen and dentists.

'This is Leo,' said Lisa with, I thought, a touch of college-girl awe.

'You have had an accident?' he said in smooth English.

'I made an arrested landing.'

White teeth flashed in polite appreciation. He said, 'Come down to the sick bay. We'll soon fix you.'

It didn't take long. He cleaned the place with spirit and put on a dressing. His hands were expert. 'Anything else?'

'I don't think so.' Afterwards I found my knee was grazed but not nearly so deeply. I attended to it myself with after-shave and a Band-Aid.

He said, 'I suspect you might find a drink helpful.'

'I wouldn't say no.'

He opened a cupboard and produced a bottle of grappa.

'With a lot of water or soda,' I said. 'I'm thirsty.'

He produced soda from a refrigerator. 'All of it?'

'Please.'

It was still a stiffish drink. I gulped it back in one beautiful draught, declined another and returned to the others. On top of the heat and the fall the instant alcohol made me feel nicely light-headed.

'This way,' said Lisa.

We ascended steep iron steps. The backs of Lisa's knees were perceptibly paler than the rest of her visible surface. Her camera bag bounced lightly on the seat of her well-filled linen skirt. We peered into what had been the aviation bridge, into some other bridge, and then *the* bridge. It had been newly perspexed in, rather smartly, and there were some obviously new instruments. What Belli wanted me to see, though, was the fitting familiar from the several documentaries I'd seen on the last of the Navy's carriers. Raised high on a pedestal was a tubby leather throne, the seat the captain would have occupied — sometimes for many hours on end — when the carrier was at work.

I said, 'Can I try it?'

'Why not?'

I swivelled around and lolled back and then sat forward again and surveyed the long rectangle of the flight deck and tried to imagine what it would have been like steaming fast into the wind, the whine of the jet engines running up — no: in those days the roar of piston engines, the clatter of propellers — perhaps a hostile shore on the horizon, and thought with drunken wonder, God, what an image for the Seat of Power.

CHAPTER ELEVEN

A week dragged by unsatisfyingly. Until the film crew came out there wasn't much I could do. On the other hand I wasn't anxious to yell for it too soon. The painting and scraping and other preparations would have to be covered but a little of that would go a long way. With Father Leo's help I chatted up some of the volunteers with a view to picking out one or two on whom we might focus in the film. They were nice young people, very much like the kids you would expect to find in community service, only with a dutifulness, an acceptance of discipline which was more reminiscent of cadets at a military academy. A few of them had tried to organise the others in a pale imitation of boring student solidarity but without much success at this stage. Leo was clearly the dominant influence among them, as priest and doctor, as person in authority closest to them in age and outlook. This outfit he wore of high-buttoned white tunic over black trousers seemed to express his role exactly: dedicated, aseptic and by derivation from all those Hollywood doctors, glamorous. He was already on very good terms with Lisa and showed friendliness towards me. I put him down as an ally.

Durand arrived. I happened to be aboard when a taxi deposited him on the quayside. He was wearing a grey suit and a summer hat pulled squarely down on his head and he strode up the gangway as if expecting the screech of bosun's whistles to greet him. When I was introduced he turned bleak grey eyes on me and did not bother to feign either interest or pleasure. He clearly was not an ally.

Away from the job it wasn't much better. I'd resisted all suggestions about staying in Mestre and was lodged in an hotel near San Marco, not one of the famous ones but comfortable enough in any season except high summer. Unfortunately this was high summer. The sun beat down by day, the nights were close and airless, the canals ponged. The Lido would have been better, but that would have meant extra journeyings and anyway, just going to the beach one day for a swim cost me eight quid.

I missed Irby, of course. It would have been fun showing her the city. She'd have loved the little squares and alleys, the absence of the motor car, the unique background sound which you eventually identify as the thunder of conversation. But she would have suffered in the heat. This was Rosie Mann weather, and I couldn't help remembering that it was with Rosie Mann that I had last been in Venice, in a sticky orgy of sex, wine, fritto misto and Ambre Solaire. I had to suppress an ignoble impulse to telephone her and see if she wouldn't come winging out…

On top of loneliness and randiness there were odd, unclassifiable uneasinesses. Once I thought I was being followed. Another time a figure crossing San Marco seemed familiar, but the context was all wrong and I couldn't place him.

Inevitably I saw quite a lot of Lisa Thompson. The first time I took her out I decided she was heavy going, the second time she was quite amusing and certainly better than dining in the company of a paperback. Likewise her looks seemed to vary widely; sometimes everything about her was dull; other times her hair shone, her complexion softened, her eyes held deep hints of green. Even the scar on her lip came and went. In some lights, some moods it all but vanished. The next time you looked up it transfixed her face.

She only mentioned it once, in the course of another confession. We'd lingered late over a meal — it was our third and probably our last little tête-à-tête, as next day the unit would be arriving. Midway through the second bottle of Valpolicella she assumed that particular solemnity that signals a girl is going to reveal some dread secret. More than once in my experience it had turned out to be no more than that she was an adopted child, which I couldn't find very important. Lisa's was a variant on this revelation.

She said 'You should know something. I'm not really an American. That is, I'm an American citizen but not American born. I was born in Bingen, which is in West Germany, and taken to the States when I was two. Maybe if this had been done sooner, or better —' she pointed to the lip, which obediently glowered — 'it wouldn't have been such a lousy job.'

She must have been talking about 1945 or 1946, when I was a soldier in Germany and the civilian population didn't get enough to eat and the hospitals were all to hell. I said, 'I don't even notice it any more.'

'These people, these good people that brought me up — Thompson is *their* name. Mine's really Reussher, for Christ's sake.'

'So who cares?'

She said, 'I'm a Kraut. Deep down they don't come any Krauter than me.'

I jollied her off that plane and she told me how she'd come to Europe and worked for some crummy picture agency in Paris, then gone freelance. She'd been doing quite well, then she'd lost the apartment she'd been loaned free, and the rent of her studio went up and laboratory charges in Paris were just crazy, so when she came to Italy to shoot a portfolio on the *Columba* and the Order offered her a niche as official photographer she decided to give it a whirl. It didn't pay much more than bed and board and film stock but she would still be free to sell her own stuff…

By the end she was animated again. She was wearing a dress cut low enough to display the incipient swell of her breasts. A little gold cross hung at the confluence where her tan paled. It would have been logical to have ended the evening in bed somewhere. But where? She was in a hostel, I in this stuffy hotel. Besides, traditional seduction routines had always bored me. With her it should be on the impulse, perhaps out of doors.

I said, 'Let's take a day off tomorrow and go somewhere. Have you been to Malomocco? There's a steamer in the morning. It's nice there.' It was, too, with a decent little restaurant and a stony shore that was often deserted. I could leave the unit to find its own way to the hotel.

Infuriatingly, she shook her head.

'Why not?'

'I should be around every day, just in case.'

'Why?'

'In case of someone coming or something.'

'One day's not going to matter.'

'Besides, there's an assignment I have to get finished.'

'What assignment?'

'Some Swede who wants a total deck-by-deck, bulkhead-by-bulkhead breakdown of the whole ship. That's about a hundred, a hundred-fifty pictures.'

'What's he want that for?'

'Oh, some picture magazine that wants to do a cutaway drawing of the ship, something like that. He offered two hundred bucks, so who am I to worry?'

It crossed my mind even then that it was an unlikely story. Mainly, though, I was miffed by her refusal.

She said, 'Maybe another day, if we can fix it ahead.'

But once we began filming it would be work all the way.

Walking back to the hotel I had the feeling again that I was being followed. Only this time it was more positive and also rather more alarming. I was somewhere around the Arsenal, which at the best of times is one of the lesser frequented parts of Venice, and at one a.m. was deserted. The obvious thing was to get among people. The Riva degli Schiavoni would still be thronged, and was only a few minutes away if I could find the right combination of alleyways and bridges. I branched off left, hurrying while trying not to appear to be hurrying.

Too late I realised this was a mistake. If his knowledge of the city were at all better than mine he would have the advantage. I twisted and turned in approved story-book fashion but without losing him. In the maze of little passages his footsteps echoed and re-echoed, now seeming to come from one direction, now from another. All that was clear was that he, too, had speeded up.

The incident resolved itself messily. Suddenly I realised I could no longer hear him. I stopped. He must have manoeuvred himself to cut me off and was lurking in wait. When I didn't move he evidently lost confidence. There was a pounding of footsteps as he came towards me. I saw an opening off the alley and plunged into some little courtyard, knocking over a dustbin with an almighty clatter. I thought I heard my name called but this was no time for stopping to find out. There was a low wall and what could have been another alley beyond. As it happened it wasn't; it was one of the tributaries of the tributaries of the canals of Venice, one of those tiny, silted-up backyard canals not much bigger than a ditch. I landed in two feet of stinking mud and water.

I swore loudly and in English. A long-legged Venetian cat stared at me for a moment and then skipped away. All around lights started to come on. Windows were being opened, people calling. Nearer at hand the voice said again, 'Mr Panton? Colin?'

'*Malcolm*?' I screamed. 'What the hell's the idea?'

'I'm sorry if I gave you a start —'

'Why were you following me? What a bloody silly trick —'

'Following you? I wasn't.'

I waded towards a gap in the wall. 'Come off it, Malcolm Freundlich. What's the game?'

'I *wasn't* — at least not until you came running round that corner and I thought I recognised you.'

I stared at him suspiciously. 'And anyway, what are you doing here? You're not supposed to arrive until tomorrow.'

'I came on ahead.'

'What about the gear?'

'The others said they could manage it.'

The lights of the Riva were just ahead. I squelched towards them. Malcolm kept his distance, perhaps because he didn't want to be associated too closely with such a dripping scarecrow.

I said, 'Why did you come on ahead, and who said you could? The whole point of having an assistant is that he should look after the admin.'

He said, 'I'm sorry. I had to come via Paris, you see.'

'Oh you did, did you? May I know why?'

'There was someone I wanted to see.'

Bloody Malcolm, somehow he could get away with anything. It was his sheer, unsmiling belief in his own rightness.

Back at the hotel I shovelled my suit into a laundry bag to send to the cleaners, but it would never be much good again. The trousers, after all, had already taken a beating when I tripped over the arrester cables on the *Columba's* flight deck.

CHAPTER TWELVE

Came the day of — should one speak of the consecration or the commissioning of a holy battleship? Anyway, it was one of those elaborate Catholic ceremonies that disarm non-Catholic prejudice by also being so casual and cheerful. In the sunlight the vessel now shone a dazzling white. The island superstructure was dressed with yellow bunting. On the scrubbed flight deck were assembled a comic-opera band, a children's choir all in white, and the volunteers combed and brushed and clad in what was now accepted as their uniform of blue denim. On a white and gold dais set up by the after aircraft lift sat an impressive array of dignitaries.

There was an ancient admiral in full dress, several other uniforms, three priests in lacy vestments in addition to Father Leo, a bishop and — in vivid crimson — a cardinal. There were prayers both spoken and chanted, much brassy music, some singing, several speeches. But people laughed sometimes or gossiped among themselves or scratched their bottoms. It all added up to some highly colourful footage for my film unit, especially as the cameraman, who was called Reg Hayho and had a ginger beard and a lot of South London truculence, had out-shouted and out-manoeuvred the local television people and Press photographers for the best positions.

I wondered if there was anyone we ought to make sure of zooming in on. The cardinal was an obvious target, as a prince of the Church and a striking symbol, particularly in Eastman Colour, of the institution in whose name, if not with whose unreserved blessing, the whole venture was being mounted. My attention was also caught by a figure in the most unexceptional of dark suits but who seemed to be accorded much deference by the others. As I watched he turned to speak to Durand, who nodded in enthusiastic agreement. He had a large bald head and rubbery features, solid during the prayers, mobile and expressive when he chatted.

'Who's that?' I whispered to Lisa.

'I guess it's the French guy — the Grand Master he calls himself. He's a Professor Somebody.'

I remembered the name from a reference in Malcolm's notes. 'Levegh,' I said. 'He's professor of canon law at Lyons. And the cardinal?'

'Stefani.'

'Of *course*.' I'd completely forgotten Father Freeloader's letter of introduction — not that I'd been to Rome to be able to use it. 'He's the Order's protector?'

'They figure so. Unofficially, that is. Strictly speaking he shouldn't get mixed up with us, being in the Secretariat of State. This is the first time he's actually appeared in public at anything to do with Nova Candia. We'll probably get requested to play him down.'

I looked again. Here was your real Vatican prelate, statesman as much as priest. Father Freeloader had said I might find him — what was it? Both amusing and surprising? How could he be so wrong? The man I gazed upon was gross, old and unlovely. Even at a distance of sixty yards I could distinguish the slab chops of his face, the little piggy eyes, the eunuch arrogance. Everything I hated about organised religion was concentrated there.

Lisa whispered, 'He's not much liked. People don't know much about him. He's been in the Curia since anyone can remember, but elevated to cardinal only last year. The Romans promptly nicknamed him the Ice-cream Cardinal.'

'Why?'

'I can't say. He just is. Leo will know.'

'Get the cardinal,' I instructed Hayho. 'Get him looking as porky as you can.'

A reception followed, down in the hangar. Two long tables had been set up and barmen imported. There was bubbly wine, Campari-soda, gin and tonic and little mouthfuls to eat. The air-conditioning wasn't working properly, as it never did in my acquaintance with the *Columba*, and the lights the Italian T.V. crew had insisted on installing made matters worse. The professor was mopping his domed head with a handkerchief when I caught his eye. He twisted his rubbery features into an exaggerated mask of suffering.

'Name of a dog, it makes one hot,' I said idiomatically.

'It is unforgivable. What will it be like when the vessel has to go to the tropics? — as of course it must. Is that not the first object?'

'Africa, you mean?' Rumour had hardened into an assumption that the shakedown cruise of the *Columba* would — if all went well — develop into a practical exercise in bringing aid to the rebel province.

The professor said, 'You must ask Durand about that,' and looked as if he were going to button up.

I said hastily, 'They say it's the shore electricity while we're here — the ventilation, I mean. Once the ship's on to its own generators it will be all right.'

'I sincerely hope so, for all the people's sake. You are an English journalist?'

'Television.'

'Not the one who makes the film?'

'The same.'

'Aaah.' An extravagant *aaah*, but whether of distaste or pleasure it was hard to say. He mopped his head again. It was partly his own fault: his suit was of thick winterweight stuff, with the tiny red bud of the *Legion d'Honneur* in the lapel.

I said, 'You don't altogether approve of it in France?'

The disclaimer was almost as vehement as the *aaah*, expressed with a frown, a shaking of the head and a sequence of *nons*. 'We have nothing against a film at the proper time, if others want it. But let us achieve something first. Always in publicity, it is the gesture which counts, not what is actually achieved.'

'I'm not in the publicity business,' I said edgily, because in French *publicité* means advertising. 'I shall decide what counts.'

'Of course. We have a great respect for the B.B.C. in France. But let me explain. The Order, as you perhaps know, was traditionally secretive, almost a secret society like the Freemasons. This was especially so in France' — he invested "France" with a Gaullist sonority — 'where during the Occupation we were a part of the Resistance. We understand that in the West today, at all events, it is no longer practical to strive in secret. It is necessary to do one's work in public. But we shall never believe in the need to sell the work of the Order, as one might sell a new aperitif — or a new politician!' There was no love in the last word.

Durand had drawn close as the professor spoke. He stood in silence, radiating approval of what he'd heard and disapproval of me. If he was conscious of the heat he showed no sign of it. It was the first time I'd seen him hatless. His hair was iron-grey, cut *en brosse*. There were those cold eyes. When he bared his teeth in a brief smile at the professor's last sally, they were wide spaced, like pegs.

'We are not interested in coaxing or persuading people to help, any more than we hold out to these young volunteers the promise of an adventure which will be gay or — what is the word? Glamorous! We tell them it will be hard work, digging latrines or building huts or unloading heavy supplies in the heat. It will be tending the sick or caring for filthy refugees. From the world at large who will see your film, Mr Panton, we want more than sympathy or sentiment or a quick cheque which costs the donor nothing. We are interested only in service, duty, dedication — all the qualities which are now out of fashion, no?'

'Not if someone could still manage to inspire them.'

He looked at me keenly. 'Have you met the cardinal?'

I wasn't sure if I wanted to, at this stage. Doing so might impair my warm prejudice against him. Besides, I didn't have Father Freeloader's letter with me. But Levegh swept me along. As we approached I could smell the faint, musky smell of his robes.

'Eminence,' hissed the professor. 'Eminence.'

His use of English, on top of Father Freeloader's hint, might have prepared me for what followed.

The cardinal turned. The old porky face under the crimson skull-cap was bedewed with sweat. He extended his hand to Levegh, who bowed and kissed his ring.

Levegh said, 'This is Mr Panton from England, who is to record our venture for the screen.'

The hand came my way. Uncertain what was expected of me, I tentatively put out mine. The cardinal took it, turned mild brown eyes on me and enveloped it in both his hands. He said in purest downtown Glasgow, 'How are you, then?'

I said, 'Christ.' It slipped out.

He didn't seem offended. 'On the contrary, but one of the lesser servants of the servant of His servants.' His hands squeezed mine and then let me withdraw it. He said, 'It has been forgotten, I suppose, after nearly fifty years.' On hearing more, it was no longer the purest downtown Glasgow. It was like a very good imitation of downtown Glasgow by a foreign mimic, with the 'fifty' authentically nearer to 'fufty'.

'That you're Scottish, you mean?' I mumbled.

'Ah, no. For I am not really. Merely that I spent my boyhood there. My father went to manage a restaurant in Glasgow. I lived in the city until I came to Rome as a student, and it was my intention — my hope — to return there as a young priest. The Lord willed otherwise.' He smiled without rue and asked, 'You know Glasgow, Mr Panton?'

'No, not very well. But my assistant, Malcolm Freundlich, comes from there.' I called him over.

'Govan, Shieldhall, Parkhead, Shettleston, Glasgow Green,' said the cardinal. 'I knew them all. And in the summer "doon the water" to Rothesay.'

Malcolm listened to him, for once dumbfounded.

'Is it the green cars that go west, Mr Freundlich? You see, professor, in Glasgow the tramway cars are painted different colours according to the quarters of the city they serve. It is most ingenious. I had a brother who remained in Scotland until he died — oh, twenty-five years ago now. I have grand-nephews and grand-nieces I have never seen.' The thought seemed to still the flow of reminiscence. He said more briskly, 'Well, we are in your hands as regards the film you shall make. Your actors to dispose as you incline.'

He touched the massive cross that hung on his breast, as if perhaps to signal the pleasantries were over. He said, 'Of course, I don't need to tell you that the result could do much to help the venture that has brought us together today.'

'It's a bold venture.'

He looked at me reflectively. 'It is perhaps something to fire the imagination of men. If it can prove itself also to be of real service to the world...' He paused unhurriedly. 'Let me put it this way: my duties in the Curia include the administration of those services we conveniently assemble under the heading of Relief. I assure you that such Relief could be multiplied a hundred fold without abolishing the need for it.'

I said, 'I had a letter of introduction to you but I'm afraid it's at my hotel,' and gave Father — or rather, Monsignor — Freeloader's name.

The cardinal nodded. 'I remember him. A good man.' He indicated he had to turn his attention to the young volunteers who waited expectantly for an audience but said in parting, 'I hope we may meet again.' He added with a slight smile, 'After all, you still have your letter.'

I watched him with the kids. He put his arms round two of them — a boy and a girl — drawing them close to him. Others crowded round. They seemed to be talking and laughing without much awe. The big ballooning figure in his musky robes was someone they accepted as naturally as I might have accepted a favourite uncle. I turned to Malcolm, who had recovered his composure.

He said, 'There haven't been trams in Glasgow since I was in Infants. They're all buses.'

Later I learned more about the Glasgow background. The cardinal had been born in Nervi, near Genoa, where his father was a maître d'hôtel. They'd gone to Scotland around the turn of the century. Eugenio, second son in a family small by Italian Catholic standards, did brilliantly at St Aloysius' and the

University before going to the Scots College in Rome on the eve of the First World War. He interrupted his studies to serve with the Italian army and was wounded at Caporetto. After ordination he returned briefly to Scotland as secretary to the archbishop but was already earmarked for Vatican service, to which he was called in 1920. His elevation to the Sacred College came only in his seventy-fifth year, when he was within a few months of the age at which the Pope was now urging his prelates to retire.

At the time all I knew was that while I wasn't prepared to admit I liked him any more, he had certainly made a large impression. There are people who, when first you meet them, gate-crash all your private broodings for the next day or two. Eugenio Cardinal Stefani was one of these — or would have been if there hadn't been so much to organise, if the sailing of the *Columba* hadn't been so imminent and if there hadn't been one further encounter, or near encounter, to distract me.

On the last evening the crew proposed a farewell binge, on the reasonable expectation of lousy cooking when we were at sea. They were inclined to be boisterous on occasions like this, but they considerately asked Lisa along as well, so I accepted. We were to assemble in Harry's Bar. I met Lisa first. She was clutching a bulky packet bound with much Sellotape.

I said, 'What is it?'

'The great portfolio for the client who wanted the deck by deck breakdown.'

'Oh, that?'

'Yeah, that. The point is, he's been yelling for it. Can we drop it in at the Danieli first?'

'That's the opposite direction.'

'But only a little way. It won't take ten minutes.'

I might have thought that the Danieli was high living for any journalist and especially for the kind of journalist that deals in cutaway plans in magazines. I might have reflected that the whole commission was slightly implausible. I might even have asked the client's name. But I was too busy being aggrieved.

Lisa went into the hotel. I hung back and looked into the B.E.A. window and allowed myself a little homesickness — how much longer before I could be on my way back to Irby? — so that when I did follow her, he was just disappearing. I only saw a three-quarter rear view, at fifty yards' distance. And he was in civilian clothing instead of uniform. But this time there was no mistaking the gait, the brushed-back grey hair. Two removed worlds crashed together. It was Commander Jansen.

PART TWO: *THE EARTHLY AIR FORCE*

CHAPTER THIRTEEN

I'm not going to chronicle the maiden voyage of the *Columba* in any detail. For one thing it's all in the film we made, or as much of it as a film can obtain. For another, as is demonstrated by those who look back fondly on old wars, the mind sunnily erases the tedium and discomfort while keeping gayer moments shiny bright. If I try I can still see that horrid little cabin with weeping iron walls and dribbles of rust. I can still feel the vibration of the engines. I can hear the clanking of pipes and the whirr of the puny fan that just stirred the sticky air. I can smell the particular smell which every ship acquires; the *Columba's* was of oil and baking bread and incense mixed with a whiff of garlic. I can taste the soggy pastas and sour wine of the mess — but how much sharper is the memory of the piercing pleasure of an ice-cold Coke from a dispenser I found hidden away in an obscure corner and whose refrigeration unit had somehow escaped the almost continual breakdowns in the electrical system. It remained a beautiful secret for two days.

Captain Belli had been dissuaded from making another ceremony of the departure, and had ordered an early morning sailing to avoid a fuss. The local Catholics had still contrived to have a band playing, a crowd cheering and a flotilla of small boats to escort the carrier on her way. We'd hired a launch from which to cover her progress to the sea gates before boarding her. Gleaming white and firm in outline against the milky iridescence of the lagoon, dressed in bunting, her yellow and white standard beginning to stir in the breeze, she looked — she really did — a marvellous sight. In the film we amplified on the sound track what in reality could only be heard faintly — the bells of San Marco and San Gorgio and San Sulspice and all the other churches of Venice bonging out in salute.

In the Adriatic we did nothing but a few linking shots, bow waves, other vessels dipping flags as they passed. Durand had specifically asked for a grace period in which to launch a training programme without distraction. But the size of the ship made careful advance planning necessary if we weren't to be forever lugging equipment from one location to another. The voltage of the ship's electric system was all wrong for the lighting Hayho had brought and the socket adaptors didn't fit. There was lots of improvisation to be tried out. I was busy enough to be able to stow the strange encounter of the last night into a corner of my mind.

At Bari, spilling over with light and life, we had a meal ashore while the *Columba* took on the rest of her supplies. Off Catania the helicopter came aboard. It was a little Agusta-Bell piloted by an equally little Italian and clearly incapable of any serious load-carrying, but we filmed it in case nothing better turned up to dramatise the purpose of the voyage. It was still not absolutely certain that anything was going to be attempted. Father Leo flashed his film star smile and said, 'I think it is mostly politics, this time.'

Pantelleria rose theatrically from the sea and subsided again. Gibraltar's gaunt profile prompted secret feelings of patriotism. Then we were in the Atlantic and stiff breezes and rolling seas were taking toll of the volunteers, not to mention my crew. We started to film some training sequences and lined up our selected volunteers to talk about themselves and their ideals and what had led them to enrol, but Durand's attitude could hardly have been less helpful, and Durand seemed more and more in charge. There was endless trouble when we tried to organise the helicopter for some aerial shots. Even a request to film from the top of the stubby lattice mast met with objections. Silliest of all was the swimming pool incident.

The pool was rigged up from canvas and stanchions on the flight deck abaft the superstructure. Though it was draughty the kids loved it. Naturally we wanted to include it and equally naturally Reg Hayho wanted to populate it with the shapeliest and most briefly-bikini'd girls. It's one of the common lies that the camera tells but it didn't seem worth arguing with him. He was organising a merry splash-in when Durand stormed down in person and ordered the models to some mythical duty elsewhere. Probably he disapproved of the pool in itself. All his life at sea, whether in the Navy or in the training ship, would have been in an all-male environment. The presence of the girls perplexed him. He even tried to enforce segregated bathing until he was calmed by Father Leo, who after all was in charge of the volunteers' spiritual welfare and would often come and sit by the pool in his Dr Kildare overall and smoke a little cigar.

Durand had brought with him the dozen youths who had previously been on training ships. They wore a lanyard with their denim shirts and acted as petty officers. They stayed noticeably apart from the rest of the *Auxilia*: more disciplined, more reserved and all being French, not altogether popular with the others. One of them precipitated another row.

We were working in the hangar, where some of the kids slung their hammocks — they were certainly living spartanly — and where, in the space not taken up by stores, they all liked to congregate in the evening and sing and make music and sometimes debate among themselves. It was the only high-ceilinged, airy place available to them. Hayho and Malcolm were clambering up a stack of crates when one of these seniors started shouting at them to get down. I wasn't going to stand for that and we had a loud wrangle. He went off very mottled about the face and later Durand sent for me. He was sitting in his seat of power and this once was unexpectedly polite. He explained that the crates in question contained fragile hospital equipment.

'Yeah, well, the union should know about it,' said Hayho when I returned. '*We're* not in his rotten navy.' He'd already wanted to cable the union with complaints about the food, the seawater showers and the crowded accommodation — 'Yet they waste all that space on a bloody great chapel.'

There were tensions within our own group, too. Malcolm had irritated the film crew by trying to organise them in things they'd been doing for themselves when he was still in short pants. When I drew him aside and gently pointed this out he withdrew into himself for the next three days — his human relations were as fraught as his political sensibilities. At the best of times he would spend hours by himself reading or covering blue airletters with dense, minute script. Somehow the sun and air emphasised his Jewishness to a degree I'd never noticed before. He took a dislike to Lisa and did not conceal it. Whether this was because she was American or German or a woman I wasn't sure; perhaps a mixture of all three. She in turn drew away from us. She spent long hours by the pool talking to Father Leo. In a swimsuit she looked rather splendid, her stalwart legs slimmed by sheer longitude.

But as the *Columba* sailed round the great bulge of Africa and into the tropics, and the air-conditioning proved ever less adequate, all differences were forgotten. Federal MiGs flew over and once came down for a closer look. It was the first, and least alarming, of the buzzings the carrier was to suffer in the next few months but unnerving if you'd never before seen a jet fighter skimming at you with the condensation wrapping it in visible pressure waves, the sound only hitting you as it passed. Durand had an enormous cross, red edged with white, painted on the flight deck. The upright bar ran the full length, the cross-piece was forward of the superstructure, so that from above it looked like a crucifix. A sense of imminent action gripped everyone. At last the carrier pitched in the Atlantic swell off a distant coastline. From the flight deck we thought we heard the faint roar of the surf. Beyond that blue smear on the horizon was civil war, and beyond that a beleaguered people whose children were swollen with hunger.

CHAPTER FOURTEEN

The swimming pool was emptied and dismantled, the flight deck cleared. There was much high-level poring over maps on the captain's bridge, which we were graciously permitted to film. I noticed that both Belli and Durand were in their best whites and that Durand, rather than Belli, sat himself in the swivelled throne.

What followed was in one sense an anti-climax, in another heroic and rather moving. In my case it was further confused by the onset of some kind of sickness. I'd been dosing some preliminary symptoms with Entero-vioform and aspirin. Then this morning I'd woken up with a throbbing head and sore glands. When I climbed out of my bunk I was so dizzy I had to hold on to it. Anyway, Durand's élite volunteers ranged themselves on the flight deck. The chopper hoisted itself and took up a waiting station. We heard the brittle sound of piston engines and saw a stiff high-wing outline in the sky. I was suddenly certain as to who and what it would be.

There was an aeroplane that had been famous six months or more earlier, when a few brave lunatics had first begun to fly supplies into the beleaguered people. It was a venerable Scottish Aviation Twin Pioneer, admirably suited — by virtue of its sturdy construction and short take off performance — for making use of improvised air-strips, even if its useful load wasn't very big. The papers had been briefly full of old Baker Charlie, as it was nicknamed from its registration letters. Its pilot, a former British naval aviator and general chancer, had been snapped in all the T.V. newsreels. He sounded like a bit of a golf-club fascist, but what he was doing was undeniably commendable.

Now, as the carrier steamed into the wind he lined the old crate up for a deck landing and what's more, an unarrested deck landing. There was no sign of a hook on the plane, even if the *Columba's* old gear still worked. It had tripped me, but I weighed a lot less and moved a lot more slowly than a Twin Pioneer. I remember wondering how many of us watching knew enough — or had enough imagination — to hold our breath as the wings wavered jerkily and the engine note hardened for the final approach...

Two hundred and thirty heaving yards of iron: no catch-net, no arrester, no mirror landing sight, not even a batsman, just that raw bleeding cross.

He made it. He made it, in the event, without much trouble: a beautiful piece of piloting which would become an exciting shot in the film. He slewed no more than fifteen feet off the centre line and braked to a halt with ninety feet to spare ahead. The élite volunteers who, to give them their due, had chased recklessly after him to grab at tailplane and landing-gear struts, wheeled him back amidships.

Hayho went in with the little silent Bolex to get a close-up as he clambered out. I studied him with a burning interest that wasn't wholly the result of the fever. He couldn't have been more fittingly turned out if he'd been dressed by the B.B.C. wardrobe department. He was wearing the uniform of his kind — linen trousers, blue blazer, silk square at his neck, yellow sun-glasses which he clawed off to shake hands. He had a lean Navy face, receding dark hair, a great corrugated scar on his forehead as if he'd once been smashed with a hot iron, and this mad light in his eye.

While the volunteers started to load the plane with bags of meal and cartons of milk powder, and Malcolm supervised the filming of it, I took him for a drink in the cubby-hole just off the flight deck which Belli had let us have to keep the gear. He looked as if he could do with a Scotch, and one might help me, too.

He drank his standing to attention, elbow lifted high.

I said, 'Sorry I can't offer you pink gin.'

'That would have made me altogether too homesick.' He looked around, twitching slightly. 'Wasn't this the old *Talus*?'

'Yeah. They cleaned up the old crest down on the gun deck if you want to see it.'

'No thanks, cock. Never sailed aboard her myself, but did a tour on a sister ship, *Theseus*. *Talus* was always thought a bit of a — well, not exactly a jinx ship but a joke ship. They used her for a lot of experiments with catapult take off, you know. She had one of the first hydraulic ones their lordships installed. Remember seeing trials off Devonport once. Three Barracudas went plop into the sea one after the other, exactly the same trajectory, very moving. Another time she was supposed to be on a goodwill visit to Hong Kong when she only just missed the Kowloon ferry, which wasn't quite the best way of winning the hearts and minds of the locals.'

I said, 'Another drink?'

He looked at his glass and twitched again. 'Better not, old boy. I've a slightly hairy moment ahead.'

'I don't know how you do it.'

'Oh, it's been done plenty of times before. Off Malaya in the early fifties the Pongos used to set down Pioneers on *Bulwark* without any arrester nonsense. They were the single-engine sort but the principle was the same.'

We were back on the flight deck. He donned the big yellow shades again and surveyed it critically. 'Mind you, if they want to start moving any worthwhile loads one will have to use some sort of helping hand.'

'I gather the worldly powers thought that idea a bit suspect.'

'They would, old boy. But even old Baker Charlie isn't going to lift much without. Mind you, one would need to glue on a few extra bits and pieces if one were going to attempt the amazing catapult trick — that's if the catapult still works.' He smiled at something he'd just thought of. 'Or one might try the old RATO lark. That's rocket-assisted take-off. Used to play at that with the Barracudas again. Bags of smoke and flame and one was, so to speak, farted aloft.'

At the plane the loading had stopped. The kids stood around. In the foreground a small dramatic tableau was being presented. Hayho stood belligerently behind the camera, arms folded.

Malcolm was looking defiant and Lisa was flushed and unhappy. They all turned accusingly to me.

Malcolm said, 'No one gives us orders.'

Lisa said, 'Will you explain to this young man that he is not taking evidence, he is making a film.'

I said, 'What's the matter?' but could already guess. As soon as the plane was full the volunteers had started to unload the stuff again. When Hayho had stooped behind the camera as if to continue filming the argument had broken out.

The fever chose that moment to stage a little show of force. The iron deck seemed to yield beneath my feet. I shut my eyes and tried a deep breath.

Lisa was saying, 'The plane has to be lightened before it can take off — that was how we fixed it all along. But there's no need to advertise the fact.' The scar on her lip was like a weal.

I looked at the pilot. He made a face and pushed the glasses further back on his nose with the tip of his middle finger. He said, 'Sorry, but that's how it is. I'd hardly get the tail up with that lot. I did warn you.'

'How much can you take?'

'Less than half of it. Four hundred kilos at the most.' He must have been watching Malcolm's face, which was dark with the disfavour of the young. He clapped him affectionately on the back. 'For you, my friend, I'll make it five hundred.'

I said, 'Four hundred will do.'

He turned on me. He said, 'I'm the one that no one gives orders to — no one.' To soften it he added, 'The original free spirit.' He looked at Malcolm again. 'He shall have his pound of flesh.'

I said faintly, 'He didn't mean it like that.'

The pilot watched the unloading carefully, and directed exactly when it should stop and supervised the securing of what remained. Then he dusted his hands and sniffed the wind and said, 'Might as well be on my way.' He lowered his voice to make one last point.

Since we'd tagged along so far we might as well go all the way. I said to Hayho, 'Can you stop down to make it look like dusk?'

None of the pilots on the supply operation risked the Federal MiGs in daylight. Our token cargo of meal and milk powder would be put down on the offshore island and when darkness fell the pilot would make his usual run. To complete the falsehood we had now to make it look dark. Hayho said nothing but I knew he would do what I asked and do it well.

The *Columba* built up speed and headed into the wind. The volunteers rolled the Twin Pioneer back to the very lip of the deck. The pilot kicked the arrester cables as we passed them.

'Look as if they'd pull up a Hercules, never mind old Baker Charlie.'

We shook hands and he climbed aboard.

As he revved up the twin Leonides radials to screaming pitch I thought, 'Bloody Malcolm.' An extra hundred kilos was the weight of two small people. It could make all the difference. I was filled with a sudden feeling of disaster. Then he was rolling. He was rolling terribly slowly. He was past the superstructure before he got his tail up. I started to lumber along the deck, with what idea in mind I can't imagine. Then slowly, sluggishly the plane rose into the air. From where I stood, it looked as if there'd been zero feet to spare. From the flying bridge, they said, you could see he had about three metres of deck in hand. He made one circuit, giving a thumbs-up signal in cheerful parody of nonchalant movie aviators and flew off to the south-west. Five weeks later he overshot the airstrip on a routine run, hit a petrol bowser and was burned to ashes along with the half a ton of stockfish he was carrying.

Aboard the carrier we were all silent for the moment.

'It is a demonstration,' said Father Leo. 'A demonstration of what can be done, of what more could be done if only we were allowed to use the proper equipment. The powers that have obstructed us will perhaps now be persuaded to change their minds.'

That night the *Columba* anchored off the island air base, a hundred miles farther away from the beleaguered territory. In the morning the kids began the laborious task of unloading her supplies on to lighters for ferrying ashore and onward transmission by the regular airlift. Someone said there were hundreds of tons already waiting. It might be months before they reached their destination. But I was too sick to care.

CHAPTER FIFTEEN

The worst of it was that there was a chance of a lift home on a Swedish DC-7, anyway as far as Paris. I was determined to catch it. Nothing should stop me. But each time I woke during that long night, shivering or sweating or needing to stagger to the iron heads, the prospect grew more remote. By morning it was all mixed up with bits of delirium. I had a confused dream in which the DC-7 was somehow going to take off from the flight deck. The next thing I knew with any clarity was that I was in the sick bay and Father Leo was smiling a reassuring smile and getting me to swallow a couple of pills. Later, when it was nearly dark Malcolm and Hayho were looming by my bed. The unit would catch the plane if I didn't object. They had shot 5,800 feet of film, Hayho was urgently wanted on another job, they might otherwise be stuck here for another week…

The drug I was on must have been a great sanctifier. I gave them a wan blessing. Of course they were to go. I was only sorry poor Malcolm would have to cope with all the paperwork again. I even remembered to suggest that they leave the Bolex behind. It had its own documents and if anything sensational were to happen Lisa Thompson or I could point it in the right direction and press the button. They promised to let Irby know I was all right.

After that it was a pleasant recovery. The sick bay was comparatively cool, even airy. At first I wasn't allowed to eat anything, just drink boiled water. Father Leo said it was some kind of acute enteritis that I might have been hatching since Bari, or even Venice. He would sometimes perch on my bed for an hour or more, flashing his film star teeth and chatting. His conversation was informed and intelligent if always directed, with the relentless consideration of the professional, at what he thought would interest me. Because I was in television he told me about television programmes he'd seen. Because I was British he dredged up pointless stories of Britons or Americans he had met. I used to switch off and wonder if any pain, any doubt, any real symptoms of life ever throbbed behind the bland, handsome exterior — what sexual urges, for that matter. Celibacy was still the rule for the priesthood, though weakening everywhere. Had Leo ever had it? I asked Lisa, which perhaps wasn't very kind as I suspected she had a crush on him. She said, 'Oh, I don't know. He talks about it freely enough — whether the kids have been behaving, all that. And he touches you. That is, he pats your derrière or puts his arm round you, but that's all. At least, so far.'

The one topic on which I found him genuinely enthusiastic, and therefore genuinely interesting — admittedly I was already curious — was Cardinal Stefani.

'He was brought up in your country, you know,' he would never fail to say, 'In Scotland.'

'Really?' I would reply, and try to elicit something new. 'Why do they call him the Ice-cream Cardinal?'

'It is said to come from that very thing. His father was a hotel manager, but at that time many Italians went to other countries to make and sell ice-cream. Everywhere in Europe the Italians sold ice-cream. It was a joke. Maybe at the college in Rome his fellow-students who came from greater homes made a joke about him.'

'Probably,' I said. 'They were like that in those days. But he *isn't* popular?'

'How can anyone be popular who has been in the Curia for fifty years, who has never been an archbishop, never a bishop, never even a parish priest? There is also his appearance. He is very large, he is not handsome. Though we may know this is an illness, for the Communists he is the perfect symbol of wealth and greed while the poor people starve. Yet if he were to be elected Pope tomorrow — of course he will not be, but if he were — the people would take him to their hearts as warmly as they take to any Pope. Colin, I believe he is a great and good man.'

Between times I dozed and felt nicely detached from the world. The perplexities of the past weeks seemed unimportant. Only as I recovered did I resume worrying about the fraud we'd compounded. The film would already be on its way to the labs. Soon the raw footage would be running through the machines for a first check on content and quality. At every stage thereafter the fake would become more and more authoritative, until eventually it would annul the truth altogether.

The near-encounter of the last night in Venice also bothered me. For the third or fourth time I cross-examined Lisa about the man. She repeated that the request to do the deck-by-deck portfolio had originally come by phone to the Nova Candia office at the shipyard. He'd said he was speaking from the Nordic Agency bureau in Rome but he also worked for magazines and this was for a magazine, he didn't say which. They wanted to do this great cut-away job. They would pay for the service.

Then there'd been a second call, saying he'd be in Venice for the sailing. Could she deliver the pictures to the Danieli? The rest I knew. He'd seemed preoccupied, thanked her, given her the envelope with the money, and excused himself.

'You're quite sure Olsen was the name?' I said. 'It couldn't have been Jansen?'

'Olsen.'

Of course for a Scandinavian that was like Smith or Jones.

When I was on my feet again we ambled round the decks together. Sometimes we'd join the volunteers in their hangar meeting place, which was even roomier now, though one great stack of crates hadn't been unloaded — the ones which Durand had said contained hospital equipment.

The kids had changed. They were still well behaved and polite compared with the revolting students seen on television, but they were now questioning the aims and means of the *Columba* much more openly. They held interminable inquests on what had been accomplished so far. They rejected the token airlift and were critical of the landing of the stuff at the island. An ordinary freighter could have done that, and more cheaply. A few innocents still believed that love would conquer all. They said that if only the *Columba* could cleanse herself of lingering associations with war and hatred she would be accepted everywhere. She ought to be known as the Peaceship *Columba*. The flight deck must become the Fellowship deck, the gun deck the Love deck.

But others argued that the Order should be more militant. It should have insisted on sailing into the Federal seaport capital and driving the supplies through to the rebel enclave itself. If the convoy had been attacked that would have been a far more productive demonstration than the airlift. Some urged that the rich nations of the world should be shamed into providing cargo helicopters or other suitable aircraft which would enable the *Columba* to function as planned. One or two radicals maintained the Order should dissociate itself altogether from

Capitalism and the unjust society and work only with the Communist world.

I piped up in French, 'Who do you think was flying those damned MiGs, then?' which produced a few laughs and also some scowls and — as things turned out — was oddly prescient.

Father Leo would often sit in, and smoke a little cigar and try to draw the sting of what had been said in that mellifluous, bland, liberal way of his. He would have made a natural television commentator. Durand or the other officers never came. But always there would be one or more of the élite volunteers. They would sit slightly apart, attentive, silent, disciplined, as if from another world.

CHAPTER SIXTEEN

We must have been about midway between Madeira and the African coast — I tried to get the exact position from Durand afterwards but we'd had a dispute and he refused all information. It was about eleven in the morning of the fourth day of the homeward voyage. The pool had been set up again and I was lying in its lee, feeling the sun soak into my still tremulous flesh. Lisa had been in for a splash and was towelling herself and trying to get the water out of her ears — that unromantic little action that nevertheless puts any girl into a provocative pose, head to one side, weight on one haunch, feet planted a little apart and arms raised just enough to ripple the muscles of the back. With eyes narrowed against the glare I was vaguely admiring Lisa's version of it when this shadow flicked across the deck. It was like negative lightning, a blink of darkness, a god whirling his sword across the sun. Next instant the compression wave hit. It hammered against my eardrums, made me catch breath, cry out wordlessly. I felt as much as heard the bang — then everything was engulfed by the onslaught of jet noise. I found myself on my feet, hands over my ears, looking for the receding dot of the plane, catching it as it banked and the wings flashed in the sun. Lisa was frozen in her pose, her mouth open in dismay. From some of the girls by the pool came thin cries of pain.

I heard myself, faint and muffled, shouting, 'Watch out, there may be another.'

There was. As I turned to look back I spotted it low in the sky to the south, so low that I lost it in the blur of the horizon. I picked it up again, for the moment seemingly motionless, a stone suspended above the sea. I shouted again and made a grab at Lisa to get her down on the deck — there was no rational reason to, it was a pure reflex. Suddenly the stone was a boulder, hurled at us. I saw the cocoon of vapour, ducked and pressed my hands heard over my ears and swallowed. Perhaps because I was ready for it this time, the boom was more tolerable, but I heard the cries from the pool rise to shrieks. Lisa turned a blank, aghast face to me. I shouted, 'Your camera — have you got your camera with you?'

She shook her head.

'Calm those kids if you can, then.' I ran towards the island superstructure, not feeling until half-way there the hot iron deck scorching my bare feet. So far no fresh stone was poised to strike. The Bolex was still in the cubby-hole the unit had been allotted, because that could be locked while my cabin couldn't — Jesus, I didn't have the key! I had to skedaddle back to where I'd left my jacket. Out of the corner of my eye I saw Lisa already consoling a thin girl in a one-piece bathing costume.

The third pass hit as I was inside the cubby-hole, wrenching the thing from its box. Behind a lot of thick steel the shockwave hurt less again, though for some reason it sounded louder. The fourth pass followed hard on the third — it seemed there were two planes, the longer interval had been as they wheeled round for a fresh run-in. I gained the deck in time to squirt off a few feet at the dwindling arrowhead shape but it wouldn't show up as anything more than a speck on the screen.

A strange silence fell on the carrier. Even the crying of the group by the pool had ceased. Bruised eardrums no longer heard the sounds of motion and machinery. It lasted for perhaps a minute. Then whistles began to blow. One of the élite cadets came running, herding the people by the pool below decks. I started towards a better vantage point aft, ignoring his shouts, though feeling increasingly certain that the planes had gone; two passes each was the ration.

So it proved. Father Leo treated nearly twenty of the young volunteers, mostly girls, mostly for shock. Three of them plus one member of the regular crew had suffered real damage to their eardrums. Another kid had tumbled down an iron ladder in the first impact of sound and broken his wrist. The casualties might have been worse if a large number of the volunteers had not been at a class in the hangar.

The strange quiet persisted for the rest of the day; those who weren't physically deafened were emotionally stunned. I exposed some more film, without any great confidence in the result — my knowledge of cinematography was academic rather than practical. Lisa, who in her tough Kraut way had recovered quickly helped me a bit, besides shooting off a couple of cassettes of her own.

Durand must have seen one or both of us from his bridge. He sent for us. He had his head braced back and his mouth shut in a little hard line, as if he'd had to take a blow in the face while his hands were tied behind his back, which for a former naval commander was exactly what the buzz-up must have felt like.

I said affably, 'What did *they* think they were playing at?' but he ignored it, as he was to ignore all my questions about the incident.

He said, 'I wish nothing of what took place this morning to be communicated to the Press.' He looked at me. 'Or to the radio and television.'

The thought hadn't actually occurred to me. It was hardly world-shattering news. But I wasn't going to take orders from him.

He said to Lisa, 'You will give me your film, please.'

She wound back the Yashica, flipped open the back and handed him the cassette. I knew for a fact it was one she'd only just loaded. A little hesitation would have been more convincing.

Durand said, 'And the one you have in your pocket.'

She gave him that, too.

He turned to me.

I stowed the Bolex symbolically behind my back. I said, 'It's in the agreement: no one vetoes what I choose to shoot, no one says what or what not I include.'

He wasn't used to being resisted. He glared and said, 'You are nevertheless subject to customary maritime law, Mr Panton. Which means that at sea you come under the captain's orders.'

'Very well, I will see the captain.'

For a moment I thought he was going to lose his temper. But instead he forced his head even further back on his shoulders.

The little peg teeth bit out the words. 'Captain Belli is indisposed. For the present I am in command.'

It seemed that he had been in command all along. But I said nothing, just held his gaze as equably as I could.

He said, 'May I also remind you that your task, as I understand it, ended with the relief operation this ship conducted some days ago. Your colleagues left us then. You would have gone with them had it not been that you needed Father Leo's care. In a sense you are now only a guest aboard the *Columba*.'

He had a point of sorts there, and saw that it had struck home.

He said, 'I have a heavy training programme to carry out. I would have preferred no distractions. But while you are our guest I trust we shall do our best to make you comfortable and see your health restored.'

I nodded.

'In return, is it too much to ask that you do not abuse our hospitality?'

'Of course not.'

He held out his hand. 'So you will hand over the film?'

I shook my head. 'I can't. And anyway it's not necessary. I will give you my word that the film won't leave my possession. It won't be given to anyone else, not even anyone else in the B.B.C. It will be used only — if it's used at all — in the film we have contracted to make.'

He stared at me. I could imagine the options available to him being weighed up, one by one, behind those bleak grey eyes. Finally he nodded stiffly in agreement.

I said, 'Anyway, I doubt if anything will come out.' But he wasn't in the mood for Anglo-Saxon diffidence.

He said, 'Can I have your word you will film nothing else.'

'Of course.'

Gradually the ship came back to life. The chapel was crowded for a service Father Leo held, ostensibly of thanksgiving that the harm done had not been greater, in reality — I guessed — as a reassurance. Captain Belli attended, looking pale and strained. It was rumoured that the incident had upset him deeply. Later, the attack was the subject of a particularly long, earnest and inconclusive hangar conference on the part of the volunteers; inconclusive because they had no means of telling — as none of us did — whose planes were responsible.

No one had caught a good look who also knew anything of aircraft recognition; at least, no one who was going to offer any information. One or two of Durand's former cadets may have had an idea, but they preserved their usual taciturnity. All I could say with any confidence was that the planes didn't have one of the more distinctive outlines, such as that of the Phantom or Lightning. I couldn't even be sure whether I'd seen conventional swept-back wings or a delta configuration. The only persistent detail was of a snouty look about the fuselage. I'd have to initiate some tactful research back in London.

Where they'd come from was equally open. Drawing a circle on the map gave at least three countries within comfortable range: Portugal, Spain and Morocco, not to mention Gibraltar — as indeed some of the kids did mention it, with evil looks in my direction — or the possibility of another, real, aircraft carrier. If they carried any markings, no one had seen any.

I said, as another lousy joke, 'If we're the Holy Father's Navy they must be the profane air force.'

They looked at me woodenly.

'The air force of the world, then — of secular power.'

'Ah, yes.'

In their unpredictable way they adopted the conceit immediately. I never heard them talk about the jets in any other terms. In English I made it the Earthly Air Force, which had a nice contradictory ring. But whose planes were they in reality?

Father Leo relayed a mystifying piece of news. He said, 'Captain Durand has complained in the strongest terms. But it seems no one will take responsibility for the attack. They all deny having any warplanes in that area at the time.'

CHAPTER SEVENTEEN

The old Jeep had stood on blocks in a corner of the hangar since anyone could remember. It had come with the carrier when the Order acquired her. It may have dated from the exhibition scheme, even from her days as a warship. It was painted a faded orange and innocent of any registration markings. There'd been some idea that a Jeep would be a useful thing to have aboard, and to be able to put ashore, in certain emergency operations. Two of the volunteers with an interest in mechanics had worked on trying to restore it during the voyage, but without success. They finally gave up, but not before they'd got the wheels to turn and managed to inflate the tyres. One day the kids took it on the lift up to the flight deck and pushed it around to burn off excess energy, with a lot of whooping and cheering. Durand didn't interfere but said later that as long as it could roll on its wheels it was a bad weather hazard and it would either have to be immobilised again or jettisoned.

It was decided to give it a ceremonial burial at sea. Durand again raised no objections. I could see that he appreciated the need for some sort of end-of-voyage screech. What was surprising was that he should have approved the means of consigning the old Jeep to its last resting place. It was proposed that it should be dispatched in style from the *Columba's* — or rather, the *Talus's* — historic hydraulic catapult.

'If the Jeep doesn't work I'm damn sure *that* doesn't,' I protested. 'Not after all these years.'

'Captain Belli said it did,' said Lisa. 'When you asked him that time.'

'That was a joke.'

We were sitting in a sheltered spot on the gun deck, watching the sun set astern. To the north the mountains of Sardinia were just visible in the dusk. It was the last evening of the voyage. Father Leo drew on his little cigar. He said, 'It was Captain Durand, I understand, who had the artificers look over the former machinery.'

Was that a loaded remark? But it was difficult enough in broad daylight to tell from those melting brown eyes what — if anything — Father Leo was trying to imply. In this light it was impossible.

He continued smoothly. 'He is not the man to tolerate any equipment in his care being less than fully efficient.'

That was true enough. And such apparently redundant devices as the aircraft lifts had already proved their usefulness in all sorts of ways. Had not the mad pilot of the Twin Pioneer said that with a catapult he could have lifted a much greater load?

I said craftily, 'Did Durand ever serve on an aircraft carrier?'

'Oh yes, I am sure he did. He seems conversant with all their properties. And our French Navy still has two in service, you know.'

Now there certainly was an inflection in his voice — an inflection of pride. I'd forgotten, as it was easy to forget, that despite his Italian name and Italianate looks the young priest was a Frenchman.

Next morning the old Jeep was brought up on deck again. The kids had painted it with strange and beautiful designs and decorated it with streamers. I fancied a resemblance to a bull being led to some ritual slaughter. People assembled in a big hollow square around it. Obviously it was going to be a colourful, light-hearted occasion. I still had fifty feet of film in the Bolex. Surely Durand wouldn't mind my filming it. But instead of asking him I wondered if I couldn't contrive something without his knowing. Besides, I needed a good vantage point.

Durand would be on the captain's bridge, I felt sure. There was the old aviation bridge below his, and therefore invisible to him, Hayho had used it once or twice and I knew it was usually unmanned. I fetched the camera and Lisa and I stealthily ascended the steep iron steps. I opened the door and entered.

Captain Belli turned and stared at us.

I said, 'I'm sorry,' and started to back out.

'Please, please.' He waved us in. He was wearing the cotton pullover he'd worn when I first met him, only now it hung even more loosely on his shoulders. He looked frail. He turned away and studied the scene below again. I eased a sliding window open and poked the lens out.

Down on the deck one of the volunteers was delivering a mock oration over the Jeep. It was in Latin, which was a nice idea even if it meant that I couldn't understand what it was all about. Otherwise they'd avoided all resemblances to a religious ceremony; the tone was nearer that of a heroic Roman occasion, which wasn't entirely inappropriate. What adventures had the old anonymous Jeep seen in its day? Had it been an admiral's perk? The scarred veteran of a forgotten Pacific war? Or the everyday transport of some early export hero?

From the bowels of the *Columba* came preparatory groanings and thumpings. Two of the élite cadets fixed a wire loop from the Jeep's bumper to the cocked thumb of the catapult shuttle. There was a blowing of whistles, a pushing of people back from the immediate area. The eyes of those in charge were turned interrogatively to the bridge above our viewpoint.

I peered into the eyepiece of the camera. Now all the chattering and laughing had ceased. There was a long moment of silence. I pressed the button. The Bolex's clockwork motor whirred. Then suddenly the Jeep was hurling forward. I heard the deep iron clang of the catapult mechanism.

The Jeep seemed to hang in the air, far ahead of the lip of the flight deck. The streamers fluttered. The nose dipped gracefully and then it exploded into the ancient depths of the Tyrrhenian Sea, to join the galleys and wooden walls and ironclad battleships and twisted aluminium aircraft and all the other deposits of five thousand years of belligerent man.

From the deck came, first, nothing; then a sigh; then laughter and cheering. But on the aviation bridge old Belli was shaking his head slowly from side to side.

I left until later the same day, when everyone aboard would be occupied with preparations for landfall, a close look at the cause of one last little perplexity. Even the hangar, which had become the market place of the ship, seemed for the moment deserted. But I strolled with elaborate casualness towards the stack of crates from which Hayho had been shouted off, which Durand said contained fragile medical equipment, which had remained aboard when most of the *Columba's* other stores had been off-loaded.

Of course it was perfectly reasonable that contingency stores should be kept until some specific need for them arose. That was the whole point of the carrier, to be permanently ready to rush aid to any disaster. There was already a lot of emergency bedding aboard, mostly blankets, and at Naples many more bales were to be taken on, plus a thousand folding beds, five hundred tents and other camp equipment made available from American bases that were closing down. Even the poor old Jeep was going to be replaced by a Land-Rover, Father Leo said. English supporters of the Order had offered one. But what could crates so enormous and anonymous as these contain?

I stealthily paced out the biggest one. It was nearly fifteen feet long and six feet tall, clad in brown hessian. Where labels had once been affixed were only the torn corners. Some stencil markings were simply of code numbers, meaningless to me. It could have been a mobile operating theatre or something … I got Lisa to take some photographs, with me standing stiffly against the crates as a scale.

CHAPTER EIGHTEEN

I'd been counting the hours until I could be liberated from the iron hulk that had encased me for nearly a month. Typically, the day dragged ever more slowly. The last afternoon, thick with intimations of landfall, was slowed down to the treacle pace at which, in dreams, you strive to escape the pursuing thing. At the same time I knew that the end of the voyage would mean doing something — taking decisions — about the nagging worries which aboard ship I'd been able to suspend. Most of me wanted only to fly to home and Irby by the first available plane; one small stump of conscience needed first to be placated, at least as to the probity of the whole ramshackle expedition. There was also one of those less creditable considerations which usually seem to complicate the purest matter of conscience. In this case it was Lisa.

She had been an assiduous bedside visitor as I recovered, feeling — as usual after illness — washed-out, randy and emotionally raw. With the departure of Malcolm and the rest of the unit we were inevitably thrown together when I left the sick bay. Though at first Leo often joined us, in a curious way this only tightened the sexual tension that was building up. She was obviously drawn to his saturnine good looks. For his part he would — not exactly flirt with her, but make it clear he appreciated her femininity. He was an inveterate toucher, laying a hand on the arm of anyone he buttonholed, patting Lisa's bottom or throwing his arm round her shoulders. When chatting of medical matters he liked to show he understood, and sympathised, with ordinary human vanity. Once, talking about breastfeeding, and how it need not impair any woman's figure, he reached out and weighed one of her breasts in his hand — she was in her bikini — to demonstrate his argument. I felt all the time I was competing against him, although he was by definition out of the contest. It was like a game of three-handed whist in which the most favoured player forever called misère.

After the strafe by the two jet-fighters he was busy again in the sick bay, but his presence seemed to remain with us. I felt almost as if he were Trusting Us to continue the game, with me playing his hand for him.

I was not a toucher, not with Lisa anyway. She wasn't cuddly enough or soft enough or fragile enough for tentative endearments. She was tough and statuesque. If it was going to be anything it was going to be an all-night Decathlon. But for a physiological hindrance this would have come to pass the night after the attack. We'd attended the kids' debate, walked around the decks a bit. I said, 'Come and have a drink.'

'All right.'

In my clanking white cabin I poured out what was left of a last bottle of Scotch. She looked at me carefully over the rim of her glass. When she put it down, for once she looked — in the shadowless gloom — appealing and vulnerable. The image of her cowering against the blast of sound was still vivid in my mind. I bent to kiss her.

That damned mangled lip blurred before my eyes, finally wrecking any chance of any affectionate peck. An affectionate peck would just be a nice liberal gesture — look at me not noticing your lip. It had to be a great wet movie clinch.

She responded avidly. I held her tightly. She pressed herself against me. Now I wanted her. But even as I kissed her I thought I recognised a certain sourness on her breath.

She said, 'I guess I had to have it now.'

'Not really…'

'You don't think a girl would pretend at a moment like this.'

'There are other things one can do.'

'Not at first. Only after you've done the main thing.'

'When will you be okay?'

'Thursday.' Evidently her mechanism was consistent.

It was Thursday now. Indeed it was dusk on Thursday as the *Columba* finally dropped anchor in the Bay of Naples and the immigration and health and customs officials came aboard, plus a posse of journalists. While we waited for them to complete their various formalities we leaned on the gun deck rail and watched the lights and the reflections of lights come on to encircle us in a great tiara of lights. I thought, the last plane will have gone, anyway. Unless there were night tourist flights …

I said, 'The last time I saw these same lights was from a troopship twenty-five years ago.'

'I was just about born.'

It was after nine before we finally got ashore on one of the motorboats that gathered speculatively. Lisa had changed into a dress, and with a summer coat over her shoulders, and a touch of pale, pale lipstick and her thick yellow hair tied back with a bow, she really looked rather delicious. I had all my stuff, suitcase, Bolex, odds and ends. I could still find out about those night-tourist flights. But when at the quayside a tout with a uniform cap politely accosted us I didn't resist. He took the luggage and led the way to the hotel, which was a tall, anonymous block in the middle of a line of waterfront hotels. The receptionist completed the chain of events.

'Signor,' he said, 'Signora.'

I filled in the form for the two of us. In the lift Lisa said, 'This *is* what you had in mind? The clerk didn't add two and two and make five or something?'

'His addition was impeccable,' I said gallantly.

We ate at a little seafood place down by the Bastion — a pizza, mullet cooked in the paper bag, cheese, fruit and plenty of cool white Capri. I began to feel contented.

Then walking back to the hotel we had run into a bunch of the kids enjoying the release of being ashore again at last. They were laughing and singing and whooping, for once openly happy. In the centre of the group, being tugged along by a couple of girls, was Father Leo. For an instant I thought guiltily, irrationally, that's torn it, he must know what we're up to … especially as, after many weeks of his Dr Kildare outfit, he was in clerical black. But he only waved rather embarrassedly and shouted something cheerful and rueful as he was swept on his way.

Lisa, I could sense, had been thrown by the encounter as well. She was silent. At the hotel entrance she hovered and said, 'Do you think I should maybe get back to the ship after all?'

'No.'

'It seems kind of lousy suddenly.'

'Because of Leo?'

'Uh-huh. And you being married and everything.'

I said, 'It's too late. The sins have all been set up. What remains is only a technicality.'

'Yeah?'

'It would be like pulling out at the last minute — you know, coitus interruptus. And as frustrating.'

'I'm being silly, aren't I?' She leaned her head against me in a little-girl gesture that should have been absurd coming from a big girl, but was somehow touching.

The room was tiled throughout, cool and quiet and a long way up, with a picture window and little balcony overlooking the bay. After the cramped cabins of the *Columba* the ceiling was fifty feet high and the bed like a playing field.

From the bathroom came the sound of the toilet flushing. I waited until it was replaced by the sound of the shower running, and then another couple of minutes.

She was monumental, marvellous, all the honey colours from Canadian Clover gold to waxy white, with the needles of water bouncing off as she screwed her eyes tight and put her face right into the spray. The water streamed round her breasts, drenched her flanks, ran off in a little stream from the point of her little beard of body hair.

Sometime in the early morning I was floating voluptuously in and out of sleep, closing my eyes and drifting off into bits of dream, opening them again to re-locate the pale oblong of the window, the remote ceiling above, the moist, springy she by my side.

Later, she was out of bed, magnificently nude as she stretched and trod with buttock-swaying steps to the curtains, swished them aside and opened the little door on to the balcony. On impulse I slithered out after her, picked up the Bolex and without bothering to check the lens or trouble about the light, aimed at her and squeezed. She must have heard the sound of the motor. She turned her head, smiled and then, slowly, unselfconsciously, certainly uncoquettishly, the rest of her until she faced the camera in a gesture of utter contentment and candour. I let it run until the film was finished.

Behind me the phone gave a low buzz. I picked it up. A voice said, 'Is that — er — Colin Panton?'

'Speaking.'

'Oh, I've been looking everywhere for you. It's Ivor Rait, B.B.C. Rome. I came down to do a story on the *Columba*.'

'You don't want to talk to me, the kids are much better —'

'Oh, I have. I have. The stuff should be going out on *Today* this very minute. No, it's a message I was asked to pass on. It's your wife — apparently she's a bit worried. Something about the rest of the crew getting back and saying you'd been ill.'

'Oh Christ. I'll ring her.'

'Hope you didn't mind me disturbing you.'

'Glad you did.'

'Well, good-bye then —'

'Just a minute!'

'Yes?'

'Are you driving back to Rome by any chance?'

'Very soon.'

'Give me a lift, would you?'

CHAPTER NINETEEN

Rait was a gentlemanly young chap wearing a Guards tie with his navy silk suit. He said for the third time, 'I'm sorry if I gave you a turn this morning.'

'No, no. I'm glad you did. I rang her straightaway and put everything all right.'

We were speeding up the Autostrada del Sole in his nippy little Innocenti 1100. I wanted only to loll back and be sedated by the unrolling concrete ribbon, but no doubt he was worrying away at how it was I hadn't phoned Irby sooner, or who the girl might be I'd pecked good-bye in the foyer when he called for me after a hurried breakfast, or why I hadn't caught a plane direct from Naples…

Rait said, 'It turned out a good story.'

'What did?'

'The *Columba*, of course. And that chap landing on the deck and so on. Made all the papers. The Order is cock-a-hoop.'

'I expect so. Look, there's someone I must try and see in Rome. It's important.'

'Er, perhaps I can be of some help.'

I was hoping he'd say that. It was the idea that had occurred to me during the last days on the *Columba*, had grown and by now had become an obsession, something that would magically settle all doubts one way or the other, which would even justify the night in Naples. But I hadn't thought much about how to effect it. I tried the name on Rait.

He made dubious noises. 'They're difficult to see even with an appointment. Without … well, we can only try.' He thought of something. 'Wouldn't it be easier to go through the Nova Candia office?'

'I'd rather leave them out of it, if possible.'

'Well, as I said, we can only try.'

It was getting on for midday as we reached the B.B.C. office in the Via Propaganda, an address which didn't comfort me. Rait set a demure little Italian girl dialling whatever mysterious codes were needed to get through to the Vatican. In an upsurge of confidence I had a brief vision of an ancient switchboard staffed by nuns, the Little Sisters of our Lady of the Telegraphs, perhaps. Stuffing plug into socket, whirring little handles with dead white hands, they would cause to ring in dark offices stately instruments of ebony or chrysolite or — in the ultimate sanctum sanctorum — of purest ivory.

Sobering again, I tried to follow what was actually being said. It was operatic. Rait himself took over, to add a strain of Nordic tenacity. I heard the name and dignity of Cardinal Stefani being flourished, my own name spelled out and doggedly spelt out again.

Then all at once the soft Glasgow voice was on the line. 'How can I help you, Mr Panton?'

'If you can possibly spare a few minutes I'd be very grateful.'

'I'm sorry, but it's not at all convenient. With more notice, perhaps...'

I produced my little trump card, for what it was worth. 'I've still got that introduction I never used, if you remember.'

'I do. I do. A moment, please.' I could hear him asking something in Italian and the mumble of someone replying. Then: 'I am not sure if this would answer your needs. You have to go to the airport, I gather. I have to be at the Scots College at three o'clock. If that would be any good to you we might travel there in the car together. It could then take you on to Fiumincino.'

'That's marvellous. Most kind of you.'

'Not at all. Shall we say the Santa Anna Gate at two o'clock? I will look out for you.'

After an early lunch with Rait I strolled along the wide Via Conciliazone that leads to St Peter's — if you can talk of strolling when lumbered with suitcase, camera and raincoat. Hot and cross I fell a prey to familiar antipathies: the boutiques crammed with pious junk, the throngs of tourists, and in the great Piazza itself the banner-carrying parties being marshalled into line by photographers on immense stepladders — it was all so acceptant and cheerful and assuming, like one of those big families that forever try to make you feel one of them. Only Lourdes was worse, with dank wafts of superstition funnelling from the Grotto.

The St Anna Gate was farther on than I'd thought, a half-mile trudge under the beetling walls of the Vatican. It was evidently the workaday entrance to the little City State, with a single gendarme keeping an eye on arrivals and departures. I rested the gear near his sentry box and, with ten minutes still in hand, wandered inside and tried to cool off. I saw a truck laden with dustbins and a military picket marching along, not the exotic chocolate soldiery of the Swiss Guard but people in blue, perhaps the Palatine Guard. I found a little chapel dedicated to San Pellegrino and nodded grateful thanks for blessings received, i.e. hangovers warded off by the fizzy mineral water named after him. I could have used a bottle now but didn't know where to find the bars said to lurk in the Vatican, one in St Peter's itself. All around were great honey-coloured palace walls, castellated towers, yet also someone's little private yard fenced with corrugated iron, a row of new lock-up garages and a familiar green and yellow BP pump. It was like the kitchen end of an Oxbridge college, magnified a thousand times.

The cardinal's Mercedes announced itself with a seemly toot. The cardinal welcomed me into the back while the chauffeur stowed my luggage in the boot.

'It's very kind of you,' I said again.

'I'm glad the idea occurred to me. Now it's not really a very long drive to the college, so if you aren't too pressed I thought we might spin the journey out with a little detour.'

'By all means.'

'You have the time?'

'Plenty. The plane doesn't leave till five.'

The gendarme at the gate saluted the yellow and white pennant fluttering from the radiator. I wondered how to broach the subject on my mind. A frontal attack seemed best.

I said, 'You will know about the little comedy we enacted?'

'I'm not sure I understand you.'

'The great airlift from the *Columba*.'

He smiled. 'I gather it was more symbolic than real.'

'Some would say just a fraud.'

He said equably, 'The remainder of the supplies was landed conventionally, was it not?'

'On the island, sure. Where there are already hundreds of tons waiting to be flown in, much of it shipped there by your own agency — Caritas — and administered by one of your own priests.'

'That is true. But as I am sure you understand only too well, these days the mobilisation of public opinion is a necessary part of any such undertaking. Nothing which reminds the world of the plight of these poor people can be called entirely fraudulent, can it?'

I shrugged.

'Besides,' he continued, 'There is the future of the *Columba*. The operation of a former warship, in however pacific a role, has prompted misgivings in several quarters, some to be expected, some less so. You will have heard the many jokes about the Papal battleship, or the Holy Father's Navy.' He smiled again. 'Incredible as it may seem, some governments have chosen to take the matter seriously. The Italian government was obliged to give certain assurances whilst I have myself had to deal with representations made to the Curia.'

'Somebody made representations of another sort. They came down and had a look at us at slightly more than the speed of sound.'

I saw the eyes in the old slab face flick briefly towards me. 'So I heard,' he said quietly. 'We are making inquiries.'

'Through your air attachés?'

He nodded his head in acknowledgement of the pleasantry. He was wearing a simple black cassock without the scarlet piping of his rank, and a red skull cap. His black shoes, I noticed, were enormous — at least size elevens. The interior of the car was full of a faint, musty fragrance.

He said, 'The shape of an aircraft carrier, Mr Panton, declares the use for which it was intended as bluntly as — the shape of a tank or gun, or perhaps I should say, the spire of a church. I suppose we should not blame governments for being wary when they see a ship with a landing deck upon it. There were suggestions that in the case of the *Columba* it should be obstructed or foreshortened in some way so that aeroplanes might not make use of it' — he subtly stressed the final syllable in 'aeroplanes' to give it the exact definition he sought. 'We replied that this was one of the reasons why Candia had chosen an old aircraft carrier in the first place, and instanced just such a situation as that tragic one in Africa now. I remember pointing out also that since helicopters would be able to use the ship freely the objection was rather a theological one.'

It was my turn to acknowledge the joke.

The cardinal said, 'Should the little demonstration last week persuade these doubters both of the good intentions and the feasibility of the scheme, then it will again have justified itself.'

'You're saying that I should go along with the pretence?'

'That is not so harsh a word as "fraud," which you used before. It is still a troubling one.'

'I'm sorry. I meant, should I take the Order at its own valuation of itself, or at mine? I suppose what's really bothering me is whether it's as innocent and selfless as it claims to be. I can see that the kids are splendid. There's no doubt about that. But people like Durand — they're authoritarian, domineering, all the things that make people like me suspect Churches like yours.'

I hadn't meant to be so ill-mannered. It was perhaps a reaction to the impulse which had made me seek him out. Or it may have been the infection of Malcolm. But if the cardinal was angered he did not show it. He said, 'No one would pretend that the Order is above reproach. That is why the Church, in her wisdom, withholds her absolute recognition. Indeed, in common with other lay orders Nova Candia is the subject of occasional complaints of heresy laid before the Holy Office. There is, as you say, an unwelcome element of militancy among a certain faction. You must take cognisance of such matters. But at the end of the day you must always ask yourself, is there something being done in the world that would not be done without the efforts of these people?'

I would like to have asked him his exact connection with the Order but had already been impolite enough. He seemed to read my thoughts. He said, 'As I believe I told you when we last met, my work makes me forcibly aware of the needs of so many. Perhaps that is why the Order, sensing my interest, have assumed me to be their advocate at court. Or perhaps it is — ah! But here we are. I want to show you something.'

The car had pulled up outside a church in what seemed to be a prosperous working-class suburb, apartment blocks set back from a wide avenue, one or two villas, a cinema, hoardings, television aerials glinting in the sun. The church was large and clean and perhaps sixty years old.

'Every cardinal is also given the titular care of a parish church in Rome. You knew that, I suppose? The custom is said to commemorate the early days of the Church when the Pope was elected by the parish priests of Rome. It is also said that the most dilapidated churches are allotted to the richest cardinals, so that they will restore them. You can see that no one was under any illusion as to the wealth of a poor functionary dependent on his salary.'

Inside, the church was rather pleasant as well as immaculate. The floor was tiled prettily, the walls were washed a pale biscuit, bright reds and greens and lemon yellows streamed from a profusion of simple but not unattractive glass. Like all churches in Italy it seemed to be populated even on a week-day afternoon. People trotting purposefully here and there, or bobbing down in prayer. Many of them recognised the cardinal and bobbed again to him, and a priest glided up as if on wheels hidden beneath his cassock. As Stefani spoke to him, relapsing into Italian, I had another vision of his life in the tight little world of the Curia: the rustling of papers and squeak of nibs in dim brown offices behind yellow palace walls; the rustle of

129

starched linen and the chiming of bells; the endless cadences of Italian and the occasional honk of Latin; the peacock courtiers, the back-biting, the scheming and the gossip in which he would now be a leading character, an Eminence indeed, while outside those enclosing walls hardly known and beyond the frontiers of Italy, not at all. And I was curious to know what had brought him to this, from Glasgow!

The cardinal freed himself from the priest, executed a curiously clumsy, rather touching genuflection to the Cross and led me out again. As if again he guessed what I'd been wondering, he said, 'You know, the first day I knew I wanted to enter the priesthood I also knew I wanted only to be a pastoral priest. I wanted nothing more than a parish of my own. I had to become a member of the Sacred College even to pretend to one! But I try to celebrate one mass here each Sunday.' He reflected a moment. 'Perhaps this is the remaining reason, Mr Panton, why I take an interest in the order, particularly its *Auxilia*. Because these young people, whom you have rightly admired, are for me an unofficial flock.'

He didn't have the flabby hands I associated with Romans. They were very big and knuckley. He was an ungainly man. Before leaving the car at the college he said, 'I haven't been able to help you with your problem, have I?'

'Oh, I don't know —'

'I hope you'll make the film, Mr Panton. I believe you will make a good film. As to how you show the exploit, I am sure you have your own standard of professionalism and of accuracy — and of truthfulness. I shall be content if you abide by them.'

CHAPTER TWENTY

Irby was waiting as I emerged from the Customs. She was peering in the wrong direction and for a moment I saw her without her seeing me. She bit her lip and her eyes were narrowed in a little frown. She looked insecure and incomplete and a terrible fantasy pulsed once through my mind, that if I slipped by now I needn't see her, needn't ever be responsible for her again — and then she turned and smiled tentatively, and by the time I'd dumped the stuff she was up to me.

'I'm sorry about not letting you know.'

'It's all right now.'

'Oh, my love.' I'd forgotten how the top of her head just fitted under my cheek, how her hair smelled. Suddenly it was marvellous to be met, to belong. How many trips in my life had ended in a lone taxi ride, home to a flat full of uninteresting letters and fortnight-old washing-up? I was filled with sorrow for all those not being met.

She sniffed and pushed back to look up at me. A flattering tear glistened in each eye. 'You look thin.'

'I'm all right. You needn't have come out all this way.'

'I wanted to.'

'But how. Taxi?'

She looked insecure again. 'No, the car.'

Hell, the driving test. I'd forgotten it completely. 'You mean you —'

'Mmm. He said I needed more confidence but he was going to pass me.'

I hugged her again.

'I was a bit frightened on the motorway. You'll drive back, won't you?'

On the way I became loquacious. That was another thing about being met: being able to share all the things that demanded to be shared, starting with the most recent and the most vivid. I said, 'I've chummed up with a Cardinal. How about that?' And the beat-up by the unmarked fighters, and the old Jeep and the mad Englishman with the Twin Pioneer...

She listened quietly, perhaps not listening very hard at all, just content to have the sound of me again. She rested one hand on my thigh and looked at me and looked at all the stuff thrown on the rear seat and smiled to herself.

'What's in that canvas case?'

'Camera,' I said. 'They left it with me.' It was a line of inquiry that it seemed better not to pursue for the moment. I'd been reminded more than once, passing through Customs, of the incriminating film in the magazine. Locked in the tiny granules, needing only simple chemistry to make it plain, was — if it came out — my rather tactless study of Lisa. I changed the subject. I said 'What's new down our street?'

'Mrs Mooney had her baby.'

'Bully for her. What is it?'

'A boy.'

'Ah, they've only four boys, haven't they? They will be pleased.'

'Three. And they are.'

One thing hadn't changed about homecoming. The wad of letters looked no more interesting than in the old days: bills, bank statement, circulars, subscription renewal notices and the usual five pages of close handwriting from a man in Batley who sent me terrible comedy routines, I'd never discovered why.

Irby called from the kitchen, 'Oh, there was one from Canada — Fulton Goodman, I think. I took it to the airport in case it was important and forgot about it.'

'Tonight nothing is important except us,' I said loyally.

'It's in my bag.'

I poured another glass of plonk and rummaged among the keys and old snapshots and folded bits of Kleenex. It was from Fulton all right, in his own hand or anyway on his own portable. His spelling had always been erratic.

…the job is quite stimulating in a way I hadn't anticapated. It looks as if I will be able to exercise some creative function and not mearly an ass-polishing role. I listen when the kids come running to me with their problems and then I say, well why don't we try it this way instead? And they goggle, because no one in this office has ever talked that way to them before.

Laura and I both miss London, and Ottawa isn't exactly sin city. At the same time this is our country and its satisfying to be working for it/ in it/ what the hell despite it, again.

Now, as to your little querie about the late Mr Kuchinski I might have known that this would spell trouble in Canada like it did anywhere else. Even the mild persistance brought to the inquiry by the effeat colledge kids who pass as researchers here has landed us in dead schnuk with just about everyone from the Governor-General downwards. We've had the RCAF on to us, two government departments and probably the Mounties. However, by one lucky and I may say uncharacteristic stroke of entarprise someone thought of combing the book of rememberance in the RCAF chapel here, and sure enough your freind was there: Jerry Kuchinski, late Sergeant Pilot, lost presumed dead on Atlantic ferry flight, June 1959…

Fifty-nine! That was a slip, they meant sixty-nine, of course. But the whole episode seemed a million years ago, a million miles away. I couldn't summon up interest any more.

'What does he say?' Irby was calling.

'Nothing much.'

The smell of cooking drifted from the same direction. The bedroom door had been left half open. Within, the light was pink and dim and intimate. It was good to be home. Only later did the pent-up recrimination of five weeks break out. Couldn't I have written or phoned or something?

'I didn't want to worry you.'

'Colin. I'm your wife. I want to know what's happening to you. But you never tell me.'

'I told you lots —'

'Oh, you talked and talked tonight. That's something — I wish it could be like that more often. But you didn't really tell me anything. You never do.'

The awful thing was, she was right.

CHAPTER TWENTY-ONE

Malcolm hadn't neglected his researches either. Indeed he had neglected nothing. The film was back from the labs, the shot list neatly typed up, the editing facilities booked. It occurred to me that if I'd been back any later he'd have embarked upon the job as his own. Casting around in vain for some fault to find. I said grudgingly, 'You've done well.'

As usual he was besieged by imaginary conspiracies. Hayho had been very offhand, Programme Services had questioned his authority. And on a rather more momentous level the Middle East trouble was threatening to flare up again. He brought me copies of a journal ostensibly devoted to contemporary history, in fact almost exclusively concerned with Fascism and anti-Semitism and Zionism and Arab nationalism. 'You see,' he would say reproachfully, 'the Vatican is definitely on the side of the others. They even have nuncios in their countries but none in mine.'

'That's human nature. It's easier to talk to a stranger with whom you've nothing in common than to a distant cousin with whom there's an old family feud.'

'What do you know of this Professor Levegh?' He would persist.

'You're the researcher, amongst other things. What do you know about him?'

'Somebody of that name is writing on the Middle East situation in *Tribune des Nations*.'

'Well, even if it is the same Levegh, which I doubt, I don't see it has any bearing on the Order as far as we're concerned with it.'

When I casually described the buzzing by the two fighters he bristled with suspicions.

'What were they trying to do?'

'God knows, except scare everyone.'

'Scare people from sailing on the *Columba*?'

'I shouldn't think so.'

'Why not?'

'Because life isn't like that. The explanation always turns out to be something stupid and irrelevant like two foreign pilots getting the wrong target on an exercise. No doubt they're up before the Brass even now.'

'Were they Americans, do you think?'

'Why should they have been?'

One by one Malcolm proposed his other available bêtes noires: Franco then; or Arabs — the Algerians, perhaps; the French. I turned them down with mounting impatience.

'I tell you, I've no idea.'

'You didn't identify the type of aeroplane.'

'No.' I hadn't really intended to add anything else. I probably blurted it out from some suppressed need to justify myself a bit more heroically in the eyes of this prickly youth. I said, 'But I may have snapped one of them with the Bolex.'

'Really? Did you?' He was all eagerness.

'Probably it'll be only a dot on the corner of the frame.'

He ignored such self-disparagement. 'Where is the film? I'll get it to the labs.'

I hadn't yet decided how to process what was on two or even three counts a rather hot little property. I said, 'It's, er, in hand.'

'I'll chase it up.'

'It's all right.' But I knew he'd be checking with the labs the moment he was alone.

After lunch he produced a large blue volume from the reference library, which I recognised as *Jane's All the World's Aircraft*. I'd been intending to riffle through it anyway, but for appearance's sake I said, 'You're not still on about those planes?'

'A last small check, that's all.'

I stared at photographs and silhouettes of many MiGs and Mirages, not to mention Buccaneers, Phantoms, Thunderchiefs, Skyraiders and Attackers, even the curious canard shape of the Swedish Dracken. Several of them could have been the culprit, none decisively identified itself as such. Finally he held up a brutish, slabby thing with his hand masking the accompanying text.

'We're not playing games,' I said irritably.

'Was that it?'

'It could be. But so could several of the others. What is it, anyway?'

He moved his hand. The plane was the F-89 Firestorm. I might have guessed.

He said, 'I thought you might have looked it up when we were trying to get that other programme together. You know, the one about —'

'Yes, I know. It was your job to look things up.'

'I did, actually.'

I peered at the text. It was a brute, no wonder it had torn such a furrow in the Faeroese landscape. It was one of the types, along with the Northrop F.5., specifically made available by the Americans to 'allied and friendly' nations, which suggested its performance would be marginally below that of the equipment reserved for the Big Boys alone. But it certainly would be able to nose up to Mach 1 with a bit of dive, which was all the *Columba's* assailants had done.

I said, 'Who has it round those parts?'

He reversed the book to read the small print. 'Spain ... Morocco...' He looked up at me expressionlessly. 'Or did you mean in the North Atlantic? There it's Canada, the Netherlands —'

'I didn't mean in the North Atlantic. We're talking about this show, not the last one.'

'But it's an interesting coincidence, isn't it?'

'What is?' The only link between the two episodes was the fleeting glimpse of Hank Jansen in Venice, and I carefully hadn't told Malcolm of that.

He said patiently, 'That the villain of the piece should be the same both times.'

I said, 'Look — we don't even know it was the same yet. Besides, there can't be more than about twenty basic sorts of fighter still flying. Even if it were a Firestorm each time it would hardly be a miracle.'

'It is from accidents of this nature that one pieces the pattern together.'

'You've been reading too many spy stories.' But it was disconcerting that his reasoning should have short-circuited in this way. What was it called? Lateral thinking, the illogical, non-sequential, mental side-jump that could sometimes solve the insoluble.

He said, 'When we have your film, that, will perhaps settle the matter.'

'I doubt it.' I added casually, 'While we're on the subject I had a letter from Fulton Goodman in Canada. I badgered him to look into the Kuchinski business.' I threw it to him. 'The date must be a mistake. It would be sixty-nine of course.'

Malcolm looked up from the letters with an expression, rare for him, of indecision. It was as if his innate secrecy battled with his innate desire to be right at all times. He blurted out finally, 'That's not what I got.' He opened the big schoolboy wallet that he always carried in his inside pocket, and took out a long blue airmail envelope and from that a folded square of paper. I held out my hand for it.

'What is it?'

'Look at it first.'

It was clipped from something printed in bluish ink on thin shiny paper, the sort that's used for cheap gravure weeklies in Europe. The text, full of z's and c's, was obviously Polish. But what Malcolm wanted me to see was a photograph. It was of a group of aircrew posed in front of a jet fighter. They were very stiff and self-conscious.

'That one,' said Malcolm, pointing with the tip of a ballpoint. It was an ordinary, nice, Slav face with a shock of bristly fair hair above.

I said, 'There must be hundreds of Kuchinskis around the world. It's probably like Brown or Wilson.'

'But that happens to be our one.'

'In the Polish Air Force?'

'Exactly.'

'When did he defect?'

Malcolm smiled. 'He didn't, as far as anyone knows.'

I said, 'What are you driving at?'

'That nickname you gave the planes that buzzed you — the Worldly Air Force, was it?'

139

'Earthly.'

'The same thing. Perhaps you were nearer the truth than you guessed.'

'But I keep telling you, Kuchinski and the Faeroes business is one thing, those bastards that buzzed us are something else.'

'If the equipment were to prove to be the same, it would be interesting, wouldn't it?'

'A straw in the wind,' I said. 'But no more.'

CHAPTER TWENTY-TWO

What I did with the film was to take it privately to a lab in St Ann's Court, Soho, that I'd sometimes used on rush jobs. It was received by a knowing character in a grey overall.

'It's, er, slightly confidential,' I said.

'That's all right, squire.'

'That is, it's classified material. Plus one small sequence that might be described as Artistic.'

'Don't worry, we've seen it all. Some of it in focus yet.'

When I collected it he said, 'Nothing there you couldn't show the vicar, squire.'

Well, maybe he was acclimatised to full frontal nudity; others weren't. I still needed to be cautious about viewing the stuff. I wandered along to the News wing and ran it through on a Steenbeck machine which presents the result on a private, television-sized screen, rather like one of those old end-of-the-pier machines into which as an adolescent I'd hopefully peered, usually in vain.

My little sequence turned out to be about as revealing. Against the light flooding in through the window Lisa was no more than silhouette. When she turned the modelling of breast and buttock was briefly apparent, then she was just a black shape again. In my innocence I'd shot the tasteful undress scene which filmmakers had been obliged to contrive around, say, the early 1950s. The air-attack scenes were just plain inept; some empty, wheeling sky followed by bitty glimpses of the aftermath on deck, over-exposed, out of focus and — the amateur moviemaker's commonest fault — held for much too brief a period. The one usable sequence was the abrupt demise of the old Jeep, which did look rather good.

I could see nothing against running the film in the projection theatre the next time we were there. There were derisive cheers for the opening sequence.

'All right, all right,' I said. 'You wait.'

The Jeep bit looked well, as I'd hoped. They gave it a not altogether ironic clap. 'Very moving,' someone said.

I said, 'The last bit is just using up the film, nothing to do with the *Columba*, really.'

'Who's that then?'

'Your new P.A., Colin?'

'Buy him a light-meter, someone.'

And when she turned, more polite applause. On the big screen it was slightly less discreet.

I glanced at Malcolm. He sat expressionlessly. He was always rather a prig. He said, 'Can we have the beginning again, please?'

'Why not the end again?'

I signalled to the projectionist. Winding back a hundred feet didn't take long. In the very first few frames after the leader strip there was a smudge just vanishing from the corner of the emptiness.

'There!' said Malcolm. 'Can you get that again and hold it.'

The projectionist went back again and froze on one or two of the better frames. But even at the magnification of the theatre there was nothing that looked recognisable.

'What's it supposed to be?' said the film editor.

'The Earthly Air Force.'

'*What?*'

'A plane that beat up the ship. There were two.'

'It's hopeless.'

'We know that.'

'That one might just blow up,' said Malcolm.

'What for?' said the editor.

'For something else. Not the film.'

'I should hope so.'

I said. 'It's just a blur. Forget it. What about the old Jeep?'

'Pretty,' said the editor. 'A nice shot. Unfortunately, you've nothing of it being prepared, no close-up of it ready to go, no reaction shots when it does go. By itself it means nothing.'

The same thought had already struck me. I said, 'That disposes of that. We'll keep the spool for staff training as an object lesson in how not to do it.' But on the way out I took care to recover it from the projection box.

Back in the office Malcolm said, 'Oughtn't we at least try a blow-up of the plane?'

I didn't want him nosing after the film on his own. I snipped off maybe twenty frames from the beginning and tossed it to him. He put it in his great wallet and said, 'A pity about the catapult sequence.' He was nothing if not persistent.

'Yes, it is.'

'After all, it would quite stir things up in some quarters if they had proof that the *Columba* had such equipment in working order.'

'Malcolm, are you trying to own up to something, or is this just a line to impress me?'

He looked at me, not going to give anything away until he was quite ready. I knew that showing off was quite foreign to Malcolm's nature. From some tortuous motive or another he was manoeuvring me into being suspicious. I obliged.

I said, 'All these dark speculations, all that stuff about Kuchinski the other day — what's it all about?'

Still nothing.

I said, 'I'm not blind. I saw the stamp on the envelope, the one with the cutting in. Who do you know in that hard little country of yours?'

'I have friends there, of course.' This was what he wanted — or needed — me to know.

'But one special friend. Someone who helps you if you help him?'

'One exchanges small items of interest occasionally.'

'Who is he?'

'He is retired from active service now. He sits on committees, undertakes small errands, that sort of thing.'

I said, 'Well he's not having the film of the catapult launch. You've got those frames of the buzz plane. Send him one of those.'

He said nothing.

'Stuck under the stamp,' I said. 'That's how they do it in books.'

When we'd finished that evening and Malcolm had gone, I sealed the little tin of film with yellow Sellotape and took it home and put it in my sock drawer. Even if Irby came across it she wasn't likely to start looking at it. Next morning at the Centre I couldn't be sure, but I had the feeling that someone had been carefully through my desk.

Meanwhile there was the mass of Hayho's footage to be seen and evaluated. Most of it was superb. He was a remarkable cameraman. The ceremony of commissioning and the sailing from Venice were wonderfully pictorial. Shipboard routine was captured in dozens of sharp little vignettes. As for the operation off the African coast, it turned out disgracefully well, even to the feigning of dusk for the take-off.

We began to reject and select and assemble and shape it into a film. Malcolm was efficient and — preoccupied by Middle

Eastern affairs — for the moment content to do what I asked without discovering any fresh conspiracies. I was able to divert a good deal of attention to the script. On its tone of voice would depend much of the burden of what I wanted to communicate. But what did I want to communicate?

Some days it seemed easy. From civilised scepticism I would gradually allow myself to be won over to cautious respect. Snatches of the appropriate rhetoric whirled into reach — 'Whatever else we may say about the *Columba* and her crew, they represent one small good deed in a selfish world.' To Father Freeloader, who was taking an amiable interest in the course of the show, I proposed the title that increasingly appealed to me, *The Holy Father's Navy*.

'It's the Italians' joke,' I explained.

'Of course, of course. I'm not sure if His Holiness would be altogether flattered but it is explicit and it conveys a certain pleasant irony.'

'Stefani would certainly appreciate it.'

Father Freeloader was pleased that I had made the acquaintance of the cardinal but did not press me for details of what he had discussed. Perhaps I should have taken the opportunity of bringing my doubts into the open again, for on the bad days, when nothing went right, when Malcolm was surly, when from the draft script my fine phrases stared back at me in their dishonesty and mawkishness, the whole thing went sour on me again.

Then something happened to change the picture, literally. The evening paper bills said HUNDREDS FLEE QUAKE HORROR. Making allowances for bill-writers' hyperbole it was still an item to attract my now professional interest in disasters. It was in Yugoslavia, the part had been badly stricken once before; this time there appeared to be fewer casualties but a lot of houses had been destroyed and services disrupted. There was the usual need for food, blankets, medical supplies, emergency housing, and the usual helpful people like Oxfam and the American armed forces were rushing to help. The report petered out in speculation about British tourists in the area.

There was no mention of the *Columba*, but if she were anywhere within range this was surely the very kind of emergency for which she was equipped. In which case she might finally justify herself beyond doubt, and — I'm afraid this is the way television producer's minds work — justify my film into the bargain. I phoned Rome.

It couldn't have been better. After an Atlantic training cruise the carrier had been on her way back to Mestre for attention to a turbine that had been giving trouble. She was not only going to be on the scene, she was going to be first on the scene. By a stroke of luck, or divine intervention, nearer home, Hayho and his crew were within reach and could be dragged off a documentary about racing at the cost of a few grumbles from the man who was making it. We got them on to the late-afternoon plane to Zagreb while Malcolm tried to organise a helicopter at the other end. For obvious reasons helicopters were at a premium. We located one at Trieste in the end. It was another thirty-six hours before I was able to catch up with the action myself, via Zagreb again, a ten-hour bump in a hired Fiat and a dawn boat ride out to the *Columba*.

CHAPTER TWENTY-THREE

She looked serene and reassuring, anchored off the stricken little town. It must have been a nice little town. To tell the truth it still was, if you counted how many of the pink and white and saffron houses were still standing, how many of the cracked façades were repairable. It was some barrack-like tenements beyond the old harbour which had suffered the worst. But there were enough piles of rubble and battered motor cars and trailing telephone cables, plus the thick layer of dust over everything and a sort of quiet, corporate sense of shock, to give the authentic post-disaster atmosphere.

Aboard it really was impressive. Apart from being able to get a lot of stuff ashore they'd turned the ship into a floating hospital, refuge and general home from home. The sick bay was full and neighbouring cabins had been annexed for the overflow. The hangar had been converted into a dormitory with long rows of sleeping bags and at the head of many of them, forlorn little piles of personal possessions. The galleys were serving meals round the clock and even the chapel was working overtime on prayers of intercession, thankfulness at being spared and masses for the dead.

The kids were marvellous, needless to say. Most I remembered from the previous time, a few were new to me. They prepared and served the meals, organised the replacement of clothing, nursed the sick and held a children's school and playgroup on the flight deck. When they weren't hard at work aboard they went ashore and helped in the town. The great white ship had proved herself completely.

Unfortunately, from our point of view, she had also attracted the attention of the world. Journalists and television crews who'd come to cover the earthquake inevitably found the *Columba* their best story. Lisa Thompson was besieged by them, in half a dozen languages. Accommodation on an already grossly-overcrowded vessel was a constant problem. I ruled that our policy should be to remain as undemanding and unobtrusive as possible.

Father Leo was clearly under pressure, and we left him alone. Captain Belli looked better and was obviously bucked by the *Columba's* achievement. Even Durand was affable, either because he too enjoyed playing a useful role or because in the presence of so many journalists we lost our unique distastefulness. He said that as a result of his training programme the seaman crew had already been reduced in numbers; volunteers had taken over their duties. I noticed that some were now wearing the lanyard of office previously confined to his élite of ex-cadets. In general they seemed more disciplined and confident, almost as if they'd been seasoned in battle.

'We were buzzed again,' said Lisa.

'When? Where?'

'In the Mediterranean. Maybe six hours after we passed by Gibraltar. It wasn't so tough as the first time. They made only one pass each but there were three of them.'

'Did Durand do anything about it this time?'

'Complain like hell, I guess. Maybe not, though. He called everyone together and said we weren't to talk about it when we got ashore, or put it in letters home.' She added, with modest pride. 'I got a picture of one of them.'

'Let's see.'

'Not here. It's too public.' She was doing the P.R. job from the little cubby-hole in the bridge superstructure we'd used before as an equipment store. As if to confirm what she said, a noisy Italian photographer came in search of picture-wire facilities.

I had plenty of work of my own. It was nightfall before we could meet again. By now a small fleet of ships had anchored around the *Columba*, including a British frigate and a Russian helicopter carrier. Their lights were reflected in the happily calm waters of the Adriatic. Ashore, the town was still without electricity, but there were patches of light where digging was continuing under floods powered by generators landed from the *Columba* during the day. In one quarter the smudgy red glow lingered of a fire which had broken out during the earthquake.

Lisa had a cabin on the flat below the gun deck, well forward and comparatively quiet — she said — except when the anchor chain was running out. It was bigger than most, with a washbasin of its own, but had to double as a darkroom for rush jobs.

'Just a minute,' she called when I hammered on the iron door.

Inside, it smelled of a mixture of feminine things like soap and talc and chemical things like developer. Tights and pants and a cotton nightie were hanging to dry, amid them strips of 35 mm. Pan weighted with clothes pegs. She'd been loading another cassette into a daylight tank, and now she funnelled in the developer and set a timer ticking.

I said, 'You're cosy here.'

'Yeah.'

She hunted under the mattress of her bunk and pulled out a folder. 'It's not a good print. I haven't the facilities. But you can see the plane all right.'

Well, yes. It was climbing away from the camera. The three-quarter rear viewpoint wasn't the ideal one, and within the slightly fuzzy silhouette there wasn't much detail. It was still a great deal better than anything that might be blown up from my own poor effort.

'Can I have it?'

'If you don't let it get back to me.' She opened the folder again. 'Here's the one of you.'

'I'd forgotten about that.'

I was standing stiffly in front of the pile of crates in the hangar. 'Not exactly a Pulitzer prize winning shot,' said Lisa.

'It wasn't meant to be. I'm there as a yardstick. Is the stuff still there?'

'I guess so. Why?'

'Nothing.' I changed the subject. 'The film I made of you turned out to be so artistic that it might have been anyone.'

'That's just as well. When I was at college my room-mate took some pictures of me in the shower, for a gag. There were about fifty sets of prints around the campus within three days.'

She smiled and the smile turned into a yawn, which made me yawn too. I remembered I'd been up about thirty-six hours. I said, 'You haven't got a drink, have you?'

'Sorry, I should have asked you — Scotch all right?'

'Couldn't be better.'

She ran the drinking water tap for a minute and filled a plastic beaker. She said, 'They've got a kind of PX now, the kids. In that big place on the chapel deck that was being painted out when you were on before. Leo organised it. You can buy a lot of stuff, even this' — she was unscrewing an export bottle of Teachers. 'No drugs, though.'

The drink was warmish but welcome. I sat on the bunk. The timer rang its bell and Lisa tipped out the developer and ran water into the tank. I felt waves of tiredness invade me.

'I'm sorry. What was that?' Lisa had been saying something.

'Your sharp little friend Malcolm — you didn't bring him?'

'Not this time.'

If the crates contained emergency hospital equipment how come it wasn't being used? Surely this was the very occasion … I was yawning. I couldn't help it.

'Where are you sleeping?'

I said, 'I haven't worked it out yet. The others dossed down on the flight deck last night. Apparently it was all right until about four a.m. when they woke up freezing.'

Lisa finished rinsing out the film and tipped in fixer. She said casually, 'You can come in here if you like.'

I hadn't meant to, I really hadn't.

CHAPTER TWENTY-FOUR

The new material transformed *The Holy Father's Navy*. Without serious strain on the conscience it was now possible to advance from a conclusion of vague approval to one of positive applause.

The idea had been triumphantly vindicated. No other vessel could have brought to the scene such a combination of stores, supplies., electrical power, offshore accommodation, medical and spiritual aid and youthful enthusiasm. Of course, there was a strong element of luck in that the *Columba* happened to be close at hand, but if the Pope couldn't count on a little luck now and then, Jesus, who could?

Even Malcolm, after sulking for a day or two because he hadn't been taken along this time, permitted himself to warm slightly towards the subject of our labours. One morning at coffee time he slid the latest edition of his prickly journal across to me and said, 'It seems we can't divorce the Order of Nova Candia entirely from world politics.'

'How do you mean?'

'Page eighteen. Your Professor Levegh again. Far from upholding the Vatican view he seems to be advocating a holy war, to defend the Jewish State.'

The article was headed *France and the Arab-Israel Conflict: Some Dissident Attitudes*. The text, resting on a thick sub-structure of footnotes and attributions, analysed criticism within France of the official policy of withholding further arms for Israel and wooing the Arabs. A Professor Levegh was mentioned as the proponent of extreme views. Extracts followed from a speech to a reunion of Resistance *anciens* in Lyons. It seemed familiar, romantic right-wing stuff to me, dictated as much by hostility to Arab nationalism, Soviet communism and American imperialism as any burning love for the Jews. The Mediterranean was a European sea and should remain so. Israel was an outpost of European culture.

I returned the paper to him. 'You should be pleased.'

'I'm not in the least.'

'Why not?'

'Because such talk is as irrelevant and foolish and dangerous as the arguments of our enemies themselves.'

Malcolm! I couldn't keep up with him. I gave him the photograph Lisa had taken of the Earthly Air Force fighter.

He stared at it. 'Where did you get this?'

'It was taken from the *Columba*.'

'I'll get a positive identification.' He slipped the picture into his drawer and said, 'Thank you.' I think it was the first time I ever heard him use the expression. I didn't show him the other photograph, the one of me and the stack of crates in the *Columba's* hangar. That was another story, I still hoped.

Meanwhile there were plenty of other distractions, of which by far the pleasantest was Irby's discovery that she was pregnant again. Not that there was any great surprise about this: the interval prescribed by the specialist was up, we were trying again. As soon as she was a few days overdue she trotted along to Westminster with her little bottle and they told us the following week. This time it would be all right.

I allowed myself to think again how nice it would be to become a dad, to have a tiny unprotected creature in one's care, to watch it grow. The latest Mooney baby was in its pram. I crossed the street to have a look. He was sleeping, his head pressed into a grubby pillow. The veins showed faintly beneath his fuzz of hair.

'Dear little chap,' I said, bending low but bobbing back again rather quickly. There was a sour smell.

'Doan't wake him,' said a voice evilly. It was one of the intermediate Mooney girls, perhaps the fourth or fifth, it was hard to tell. 'Me mammy'll be mad if you wake him.'

'I wasn't going to,' I said. 'Dear little chap.'

The baby's face suddenly turned bright red and wrinkled. A single wail rent the air.

'Yer have.' the girl said accusingly.

'Well shut him up. You must know how. Here!' I gave her a ten pence piece and hurried away. *Our* baby would be quite different.

We finished the film in a rush because I was wanted for another project whose original producer had fallen sick, a heavyweight documentary about air traffic control, near misses, area navigation, all that. It had got badly behind schedule and I took Malcolm along with me to help out. The next few weeks were hectic. There were still a few loose ends left over from *The Holy Father's Navy*, which was to go out in the last week of December, presumably as one of the few hopeful emergences of the year. Moreover, one of the Sunday paper colour supplements had bought a portfolio of pictures from Lisa Thompson and wanted me to write the accompanying article. I hadn't done any real writing for a long time; it might be useful to accept, but they had to have the copy six weeks ahead, which meant like tomorrow, and it cost me a ruined weekend plus finally staying up most of Sunday night.

On top of everything came a message from C. Exec. Tel. to see him. I had to drive in especially from Ruislip, where we were filming. It could have been done just as easily on the phone.

He said, 'How's *His Holiness's Navy?*'

And how could he, occupying the job he did, have such a terrible ear for euphony? I said, 'I've only seen a grading print so far but as far as I know it's okay.'

'Has anyone in the — er — Order seen it yet?'

'Why should they have? H.R.O. saw the rough-cut and seemed quite pleased. So did his Catholic adviser.'

'Of course, of course. I heard they were *very* pleased. No, I just wondered if it wouldn't be a courtesy to let Geoffrey Moodleigh and perhaps *il Conte* from the embassy have an advance peep.'

'There'll be a couple of viewings just before it goes out. I'll see that they're invited.'

He sighed. For a young man he was already looking rather puffy round the eyes. 'I was thinking of something a little sooner.'

'As clients?'

'No, no, no. As — friends or benefactors, if you like, who first offered us the facility.'

I didn't need Malcolm's conspiracy-radar to alert my suspicions. A preview four or five weeks in advance of transmission allowed plenty of time for re-editing, even postponement. I said, 'It isn't necessary. It was made clear at the outset that we had a completely free hand. It would be our film and they'd have no yea or nay over it.'

'But Colin, who said anything about yea or nay? It's simply a courtesy.'

'It sounds like a word from the sponsor to me.'

C. Exec. Tel. smiled his most boyish smile. He said, 'Eleven thirty Tuesday, Crown Theatre, Wardour Street.'

They all turned up: Moodleigh with a carnation in his buttonhole even in November; the Count, elegant and powerful in a beautiful dark blue overcoat; the Rev. Gerald in his winter gear of roll-neck sweater and black Harris tweed jacket; Father Freeloader: Nick, the permanently harassed head of my department; and C. Exec. Tel. himself. Malcolm and I arrived late and last, having tried to spend the first half of the morning productively along at the airline pilots' guild.

'Perhaps we should run the film now,' said C. Exec. Tel., after they'd said polite things to each other.

It wasn't too bad. It asked the questions and raised the doubts without being sceptical in the world-weary, scepticism for scepticism's sake way. The episode with the nut-case pilot and the Twin Pioneer came over as something faintly ludicrous but brave and decent and a reflection on a world that wouldn't allow it to happen properly, and you got the feeling that the film — me, really — passionately wanted the thing to work. The actor who read my script did so without too many actorial flourishes. The last scene was of kids aboard the *Columba* after they'd been on the go for twenty hours or more during the Yugoslav operation. They just lay down on deck with a few blankets, boys and girls together, and slept. It was rather touching.

Afterwards there were drinks served by an aloof girl booted and skirted as if for the Russian winter. The compliments began to flow, gathering strength as everyone saw it was safe to enthuse. I nodded graceful acknowledgement and waited for the tentative 'Just one small point' that would gradually, implacably, lead to objections and from objections to suggestions: if the wording of the commentary could just be altered at one point, so as not to mislead ... was such-and-such a scene absolutely necessary, it didn't seem entirely relevant...

None came. The drinks were finished in an atmosphere of continuing cordiality. Geoffrey Moodleigh's smooth pink features were set in the contented smile of one who had brought a difficult exercise to an unexpectedly easy conclusion. C. Exec. Tel. made a few technical observations about colour matching, just to show he knew his stuff. H.R.O. beamed. Father Freeloader sipped a second dry sherry and wondered if anyone had organised lunch. Only when he had donned his beautiful overcoat and was about to leave did the Count rest a hairy hand on my arm and draw me aside as if to convey a last private commendation.

What he actually said was, 'This is the film exactly as it will be broadcast?'

'Except for a better print, I hope.'

'And the same will be offered for sale to other countries?'

'Yes.'

'There will be no fuller version, as I gather is sometimes the practice?'

He was either very knowledgeable or very well briefed. I said, 'Not in this case. There might have to be a shorter one for America, but nothing longer. Why do you ask?'

He hesitated. 'There were rumours of certain incidents whose inclusion in the film would have been … undiplomatic.'

It had come after all. But in the past speculative rather than the veiled imperative it was harmless. I said, 'If you mean the jets that beat us up, we didn't get them. It was after the cameraman had gone home.'

'Ah, yes.'

'By the way, there's been another case of it.'

He nodded.

I said, 'Whose planes were they?'

The Count hesitated. He saw Moodleigh approaching to escort him away. He said, 'Perhaps you would come to lunch one day? You can be reached at the B.B.C.? Good.' And with a whiff of expensive cologne he was gone. Two hours later I was wedged in the flight deck of a BAC 1-11 as we filmed a pilot's-eye view of Amber Three into London Airport on a murky late afternoon. Between spells of concentration I reported the morning's comments on our last job, ending with the Count's cryptic remarks.

Malcolm listened carefully. As we finally taxi'd along the perimeter track to the Maintenance Area he said, 'By the way, I got a positive identification of the plane in that photograph. It was a Firestorm all right.'

The pilot, overhearing, said, 'Firestorm? Overweight, under gunned, unforgiving. I'd as soon fly a London bus.'

CHAPTER TWENTY-FIVE

Christmas came. The air safety stuff was taking shape nicely, and the script was someone else's worry this time. It should have been a chance to relax, if only I'd been able to relax. I fussed around Irby, insisted on carrying the shopping for her, made her rest in the afternoons and secretly studied the medical dictionary and her Motherhood books on the subject of miscarriages. Actually everything was going well. Irby looked particularly beautiful and we were already at the three months mark, which according to the books was one of the critical stages.

We entertained Father Freeloader and, thinking he might be lonely, Malcolm Freundlich. He said he was taking six weeks leave in the New Year to go and work in a kibbutz, and brought me a Christmas present wrapped in a non-sectarian gift paper with a motif of stars and fir trees. It was very light and rattled and proved to be a Revell kit of the F-89 Firestorm. I made it up on Boxing Day, getting polystyrene cement on the carpet in the process. Decals, i.e. transfers, for six different air forces were supplied but I painted it black, with no markings. Set up on its little stand, its thuggish, snouty shape threatened the room like a short-barrelled revolver.

Among the cards were one from Fulton and another from Lisa featuring one of her own photographs of the *Columba*. She'd scrawled inside, *Am quitting to return to freelance work. May have some weird news for you soon!!!*

My own début as a journalist came in the *Observer* colour supplement the Sunday after Christmas.

The programme itself went out two nights later and drew good notices from the critics. I watched it again, of course, and people rang up afterwards and said nice things, but it seemed to me, re-reading the article for the eighth time, that it was there that I'd communicated more of the peculiar insubstantiality of the whole Nova Candia venture. I was suddenly nostalgic for the subtlety of prose; pictures were no substitute for ideas.

Curiously, a letter came from my old agent, complimenting me on the piece and asking if I had thought of doing a book on the subject. As usual, he'd just happened to be lunching with a publisher and had idly mentioned the idea. The publisher had expressed interest. My agent might be able to arrange for something to be commissioned... Well, it wasn't a bad suggestion. Indeed it was about the only cheering circumstance in an otherwise bad patch which I was entering.

From some anti-social citizen I had picked up a particularly foul refinement of influenza which made my glands bulge, the interior of my head try to beat its way out of its confining skull and my throat close up. Worse, I passed it to Irby, whose ensuing high temperature brought on the first scare of the pregnancy.

A gloom took hold of me and refused to be shaken off. It was partly the aftermath of the flu, of course. It was the time of year. It was being run down and anxious about Irby and powerless to do anything about it except keep up a false, bright surface optimism. There was perhaps some suppressed guilt — or anyway, dissatisfaction — at having neglected to do anything about the growing backlog of such assorted little mysteries as the identity of Kuchinski, the truth about the Earthly Air Force, the contents of those crates aboard the

Columba or what the hell Malcolm was up to. There was, lastly, the renewed threat of war in the Middle East.

This time it was different. It wasn't the usual midsummer shouting match. It was a cold, off-season crisis. For the first time one side had issued a formal ultimatum from which it would be hard to retreat. Moreover the super-powers had contrived to get themselves so involved, on opposite sides, that it seemed inevitable that they would be dragged into the showdown.

I said to Malcolm, 'You won't go to your kibbutz now?'

'Why not?' He looked at me in genuine puzzlement.

'And get overrun by foreigners?'

'I doubt it.'

'Look, this is a serious possibility of war, with the big boys joining in and a lot of people getting killed. You said you were against all that.'

'You don't understand, do you? I don't think you ever could. I am no longer a Zionist. Perhaps I never was. I do not say to myself, my people right or wrong. I disapprove of many of their policies. But if they are threatened then I am threatened. That is to be a Jew.'

'You are many other things, though.'

He looked as if he might be weighing up something. He said, 'This friend I have in Israel, this older friend —'

'Ah! The spy?'

It was meant to be a tease, with perhaps just a very small barb to it. Malcolm took it, as ever, unpredictably. He said, 'Not really. Not any more.'

'He was once, then?'

'He moved about on state business. But what I wanted to say was that in 1945 he was an officer in the British Army, decorated for bravery. Less than one year later he was fighting against the British Army. He tells me he was equally proud both times. That also is to be a Jew.'

'You saw him in Paris that time, on the way to Venice?'

He nodded.

'You'll see him again when you get to Israel?'

He changed the subject. 'Did you make up the model plane?'

'Of course. It's a great conversation piece.'

'How did you finish it? Whose colours?'

'Black and no markings. The Earthly Air Force.'

He said, 'I thought you would.'

The Count's invitation came suddenly, delivered on the telephone in a rather attractive, husky female voice: for the coming Thursday if that wasn't too short notice; at an address in Pont Street.

The other guests were pretty high-powered; a junior minister, another M.P., the editor of the *New Statesman*, a couple of Fleet Street specialists, two members of the embassy staff, the head of a department at Bush House and from Independent Television, where he had lately insinuated himself, my old adversary Mr William Wainwright. He seemed to bear no ill will.

He said, 'I enjoyed your film about the aircraft carrier.'

'What was that?' said one of the Fleet Street lot, ears pricking up by habit.

I explained.

Several others had seen it. For a while the activities of Nova Candia occupied the table talk. The *Statesman* editor was cheerfully scathing. The Count listened but did not join in, just as — I noticed — he drank none of the delicious Cinque Terre and Barolo with which his guests were plied; instead he had a bottle of Bass which a flunkey served, wrapped in a white napkin, as if it were champagne. It occurred to me that his connection with the Order was not generally known.

But inevitably the Middle East situation displaced all other topics. The privileged information that started to emerge was, if anything, more alarming than what was generally known. Again the Count preferred to listen rather than speak. He sat very still in his chair at the head of the table, his dark eyes resting unblinkingly on whoever held forth.

There wasn't much I could contribute, either. I remember bursting out, 'But you're not seriously suggesting, all of you, that grown, responsible men are going to — to hold *Armageddon* just because they're too stupid or too obstinate or too vain to back down?'

They stared at me, coffee cups and brandies and *sambuccas* half raised to lips. The junior minister spoke. 'Certainly not,' he said. 'I give common sense at least a, should we say, hundred-to-eight chance.'

As people were going the Count murmured, 'May I ask you to remain for a little moment.'

Only the two of us, plus the senior of the two embassy officials, walked through to a booklined study. I wished I'd paid closer attention when we were introduced. Inured to English inattention, perhaps, he re-declared his identity. He was on the staff of the naval attaché.

The Count closed the door carefully and sank into a deep leather armchair. He said, 'You will remember, Mr Panton, that I reassured myself that your film would not contain any reference to certain incidents involving the *Columba*?'

'Yes. It didn't.'

'That is true. There was an allusion in the admirable article you contributed to the *Observer* —'

'Not to the jet planes —'

He held up a hand. The palm was as pink and soft as the back was masculinely hairy. 'It is another incident I have in mind, at first sight of no great importance but which, if noted by certain careful readers of newspapers' — he glanced at the attaché — 'might lead them to draw erroneous conclusions.' He paused. 'You referred to a picturesque ceremony in which an old motor car or military truck was catapulted into the sea.'

'It could have been merely a figure of speech.'

'But was it?'

'No. They used the old aircraft catapult.'

He looked at me reflectively. He said, 'I think I must now take you into my confidence. May I rely on you to respect that confidence?'

'Of course.'

'You will understand that as a diplomat in the service of my country and accredited to yours, I have to keep my associations with the Order of Nova Candia strictly apart from my work. On its part, the Order sometimes spares me embarrassment by withholding from me its secrets.' He permitted himself a small rueful smile. 'I did not know about this catapult. The lieutenant would like to ask you one or two simple facts.'

The lieutenant asked how far, in my opinion, the vehicle had been hurled forward. Was it in fact a Jeep, as manufactured by the Willys or Ford companies? Could I estimate its speed on leaving the carrier?

I answered to the best of my ability.

The Count said, 'There is already enough suspicion of the *Columba* in the world. If it were to be learned — even worse, if it were to be demonstrated — that she had this capability, even in jest, her very existence might be put in jeopardy.'

'But surely,' I protested, 'an old tub that's had all her real teeth drawn long ago, manned by a crowd of young idealists, trying only to ship a little kindness around the scene.'

'That is precisely why we invited you to make your film, and why we are so pleased with the result. But it will be many months before it can spread its message widely.'

'There's a suggestion to enter it at some festivals.'

'That will help.' He had risen from his chair and stood by the window, looking at the Pont Street Dutch architecture across the street. 'In the meantime, a proposal has been made to use the ship for a somewhat different purpose. It does not have the support of all of us in the Order, by any means. It is not certain anything will come of the idea. If it does...' He turned and faced me again. 'This is extremely confidential.'

At last I saw how the bits might fit together.

He said, 'In the Middle East the Vatican has long been attempting to bring the two sides to the conference table. She is not alone in that, of course. Your own country has been active. But in a curious way Rome is at an advantage. She is old, she is patient, she has nothing materially to lose or to gain, she alone is not subject to economic or strategic pressures. Cardinal Stefani, whom I believe you have met, has established an unusual degree of confidence from the Syrians and Lebanese, in particular. If only one small agreement, in some relatively minor area of the dispute, could be gained — well, it would be a crack in the wall of hatred and distrust that divides Jew and Arab. And from one crack much can follow.

'But until that crack can be made, such is the obstinacy on both sides that even a physical meeting ground is impossible to find. There is not city or island or country in the Mediterranean acceptable to both parties. You can guess what I am coming to?'

I nodded.

He said, 'The proposal is that the *Columba* should act as the meeting point. She can position herself at some convenient point in international waters. She can guarantee complete secrecy, personal safety. Delegates would be able to arrive and depart freely by helicopter. It is not a wildly unrealistic scheme. I am opposed to it because I believe it to be a mistake for the Order to risk identification — however well-intentioned — with the politics of the world. It is not in the business of power. It is in the business of help and charity and...'

'Love,' I suggested. That word again.

'Indeed. The business of love. Unfortunately I am overruled in this matter. The proposal is already being communicated to the various parties. It may not be accepted. We must assume that it is. I do not need to tell you how hazardous it would be, both to the success of the negotiations and the safety of all aboard, were there any reason to suspect the *Columba* of being less innocent than she pretends.'

'But a decrepit old catapult launching an equally decrepit old Jeep — that's hardly very sinister.'

The Count looked at the lieutenant.

The lieutenant said, 'It is by such means that a catapult is tested for its real work. One uses a kind of tank on wheels which floats and can afterwards be recovered.'

'Okay, given it does work, what are you supposed to be using it for? An aeroplane's a big thing, it's not something you can hide away out of sight,' though even as I protested, I remembered those mysterious crates in the *Columba's* hangar.

The lieutenant said, 'One was not necessarily thinking of a conventional aircraft —'

'What then?'

The Count came in before he could answer. He said, '*We* may know the ship is no more than she professes to be. It is the interpretation of others that concerns me. Imagine what might be made from, let us say, a film record of that catapult launch.'

I stared at him.

'Did you make such a film, Mr Panton?'

'I'm a lousy cameraman. It wasn't usable.'

'So what became of the film?'

'It will have been scrapped by now.'

'Are you sure?' The dark eyes held mine.

I said irritably, 'Look, all this is hypothetical. If I were you I'd be more concerned about those rotten planes that have already beaten up the *Columba* twice. They are real, they are frightening and you never answered the question I put to you last time, whose are they?'

The Count said quietly, 'I do not know.'

I said, 'The first time we met — at that lunch at the B.B.C. remember? — we talked about a programme I'd wanted to make up in the Faeroes. It was to have been called *Act of God.*'

He inclined his head to show he did remember.

'The plane that crashed up there was a Firestorm, and there was a lot of hanky-panky as to whom exactly it belonged. They fixed the blame on Canada, but at least one Canadian wasn't too happy about that. Then the pilot — the pilot was supposed to be called Kuchinski, only that particular Kuchinski had been killed ten years earlier. There's some evidence that this Kuchinski was in fact an officer of the Polish Air Force.'

It was sounding wilder and wilder but I had to battle on.

I said, 'Those planes that attacked us were Firestorms, too. If they had any markings, no one saw them. Again, whose are they?'

The Count lifted his shoulders in a slow, resigned shrug as if to convey that there were things in the world beyond the ken even of diplomacy. He said, 'I'd be very grateful if you would make quite sure that piece of film has been destroyed.' When I got home that evening I checked that the tin was still in my sock drawer. I think I probably would have burned it. But in a 1955-built block in smokeless Pimlico, where can you burn anything?

PART THREE: *A GUIDED MISSAL*

CHAPTER TWENTY-SIX

It was Father Freeloader's idea to enter the film at Monte Carlo. There was an annual television festival there which I'd heard of before — an episode of *It Happened Here* had been shown in the Historical section and I had stood by to whiz out in case it won a prize, which it didn't; not even a mention. Apparently there was also a religious, indeed specifically Roman Catholic, television festival which followed and to some extent overlapped the ordinary one.

'We should stand an excellent chance,' said Father Freeloader, 'especially as it appears I am to be a member of the jury.'

'Will the Order mind? In a way it's their film.'

'They'll be expecting it. It will be useful publicity.' In six months Father Freeloader had been much tainted by the world. But he was right — had not the Count himself said that the more widely the film was shown, the better?

'You must come out yourself,' Father Freeloader was saying. 'They'll want to ask you all about it, and you can meet the Press, that sort of thing. It will be good for sales. I gather the hospitality is quite lavish. One is put up at the Paris, though I believe the cuisine at the Hermitage is better. Shall I set wheels in motion?'

'It's out of the question.'

'Why is that?'

'I can't leave Irby. Especially if there's going to be a war.'

'We have lived with the possibility of war for a quarter of a century now. There is much to be said for going about one's business until the actual knell.'

'Ah, but there isn't any knell these days. The fashionable thing is the pre-emptive strike.'

'In this case there does appear to be a named date, which is two or three days after the termination of the festival. As for the dear girl — why not bring her, too?'

That, of course, was even less to be contemplated. She had to stay near the hospital. It would be madness to venture abroad. And yet ... she was still looking peaky after the rotten flu. In London it was the crotch of the year. The iron wind bored between the office blocks. Snow came one night, speedily turned by the traffic into a khaki mush which it then sprayed at pedestrians. A spell in the sun might do her good. If the political situation did relax we could perhaps stay on — I had friends who lived near Grasse. Furthermore, and strictly from a selfish point of view, if I were to do the book this might be the opportunity to meet some of the French members of the Order, notably the outspoken Professor Levegh.

Irby said, 'It would be madness.'

'John doesn't think so.' John was our doctor.

She shook her head.

'You could lie in bed, swim in the pool, feed up. Those are all useful things.'

'No.'

'It's only an hour and a bit by plane.'

'I'm not going to fly, that's definite.'

'All right. We'll go by train.' It was a classic case of giving way on the minor argument to gain the major. And even this concession I could turn to my own advantage. We could break the journey at Lyons, where the professor lived. I wrote to him and received a reply in brown ink on a small sheet of university notepaper. As far as it was decipherable he seemed to raise no objection to being visited.

Packing for the journey, I contemplated the fateful tin of film. I could leave it. I could put it down the refuse chute. What I did do, mainly from indecision, was to slip it into one of the pockets in the lining of my case.

Though I'd lived in Pimlico for ten years now I'd never travelled abroad by train. It was really very civilised to eat at home and then take a cab the half mile to Victoria for the night boat train. On the ferry it struck me that heavy weather in the Channel wouldn't be the best thing for an insecure foetus. Luckily it was a still, cold night. We breakfasted in Paris and peered into a few shop windows before catching the Lyonnais. This was a T.E.E. train, very sumptuous and costly and warm within, which made the shock of being deposited in an icy Lyons all the more acute.

The sky was thick and grey. You couldn't see the Alps but you could feel the alpine air spilling over the plain. Snowflakes eddied across the great square in front of and below the Gare de Perrache. We booked into the Hotel Terminus, as recommended somewhere by James Bond — in France the station hotels were always comfortable, the station buffet could be relied upon and in bed at night one could hear the heartbeat of the town.

Irby settled for a couple of hours of afternoon heartbeat, which seemed to consist mainly of stealthy train noises and the muffled boom of traffic in the railway underpass. I telephoned the professor and took a taxi. It whirled me briefly along a broad avenue which had shops one side, the Rhône the other, before crossing the river at the Pont Guillotière. After that we plunged into a maze of one-way streets and I lost my bearings. But it only took about ten minutes in all. The entrance was one of those iron-bound portals that look as if they're designed to keep out the revolutionaries. I found the right bell and pressed it and presently some remote-controlled medieval machinery clanked it open.

CHAPTER TWENTY-SEVEN

Levegh was waiting at the front door of his apartment two flights up the echoing staircase. Though I didn't notice it consciously at the time I remembered afterwards that he had it open only a crack, and there was the rattle of a chain before he could usher me in.

He greeted me loudly and anxiously, the rubbery face creased into a mask of concern.

'You have had something to eat?'

'On the train, thank you. Not very good, but filling.'

'Ah, I know.' Concern became comic distaste.

I registered a large hallway with several doors opening off it and a passage stretching away. It was a big apartment, old-fashioned and dark, smelling of soup and linoleum and tobacco and somehow absolutely indicative of a celibate rather than a family establishment. Inside the study, piled with books and papers, warm from a tiled stove, he came quickly to the point.

'A book, eh, Mr Panton? I have not been told of any book.'

He was filling an enormous pipe with tobacco from a Limoges jar. He said, 'A book is not the same as a film.'

'Exactly. It would be less about the obvious manifestations of the Order, which by then will be familiar from television, and more about its origins, its aims, its philosophy … its relations with the Church, how its decisions are reached, how its members are selected…'

He struck a smoky French match and lit the pipe. He was wearing a droopy knitted cardigan over ordinary suit trousers. His feet were stuffed into carpet slippers.

I added, 'One hears of some conflict within the Order, between the more militant and the more conservative wings.'

He gave a short grunt of laughter. 'Mr Panton, you must also have heard that Nova Candia thinks of itself as a secret society. It would not have many secrets left if all those questions were answered. But I will try to help you.' He lowered himself into a deep armchair upholstered in what looked like an old Turkey carpet.

My first move as a prospective author of serious non-fiction had been to buy a neat little battery tape-recorder, by Philips. I set it down openly between us, so that if he had any misgivings about it we'd meet them straightaway. In the event it made no difference, unless it was to remind him to shape his replies into precise, professorial prose.

'Let us begin at the beginning. No! Let us begin at the end, at your last question — Is there a disagreement within the ranks of the Order? The answer is: of course there is! Tell me of any society or political party or trade union which is without such disagreement. But with us it is neither deep nor incapable of being resolved. We are all good Catholics first.' He waved his pipe at the heavy crucifix on the brown wallpaper, the framed photograph of the Pope.

'Perhaps I should say we all *try* to be good Catholics. We believe passionately in our Church and the values it teaches. We are jealous for it. We wish to see it an ever greater influence for good in the world. We believe that it is by the example of Catholics rather than their persuasion that this may be achieved. If young people see our young people of the *Columba* carrying food to the starving, or tending the homeless as they did in Yugoslavia, they will perhaps find that more inspiring than the antics of students who tear up paving stones and shout slogans. If the Church can be seen to be active in the world then the world may more readily heed the charity and tolerance which the Church urges. Now! Where do we differ? We differ only in the degree of assertion we bring to this common ambition. There are those, and they have been dominant in the Order until recently, who value discretion and adaptability above all other qualities. They believe the Order should conduct its affairs as the Church herself conducts her dealings with the temporal powers, by diplomacy, by infinite patience, by always leaving the door open and never closing it. There is much to be said for this approach. There are others — as there must always be others — who believe in a more militant attitude.'

He paused. I became aware of the ticking of an old gilt clock.

He said, 'You will know that Order was founded — or rather re-founded — only in 1932. So within a very few years the war came and we in France were separated from the members in Italy and Germany. We had to develop our own way. And our way as members of the Resistance was to be more daring and more determined than all others who opposed the invader. To this day we retain that more — more vigorous outlook. Again, it is here in France, logically perhaps, that we have chosen most strenuously to trace our true beginnings back to the old Knights Protector. They were a martial Order, Mr Panton. We inherit their martial character, you might say.' He laughed shortly again, as if to suggest this more picturesque atavism should not be treated as seriously as the Resistance theme.

The spools of the tape recorder silently turned.

'Look, Mr Panton, you have a saying in your country, "Why should the Devil have all the best tunes?" We might say in the world today, "Why should the Devil have all the best slogans?" For all their protestations of pacifism — let us make love, not war — the young people today are still excited by action, by violence. Who are their heroes? Guevara, Ho Chi Minh, Stokely Carmichael. Not a man of peace among them.'

'But *you* cannot advocate violence, as a Christian Order.'

'Of course not. Nor would we want to. All we want is to fire people with the idea that the service of God is not only contemplation and prayer. There is work to be done, there are battles to be waged.'

'And you would like to see the Church more militant too?'

'We would like to see it assert its authority in the world more forcefully, perhaps. You know, the Church has a long experience of the ways of kings and emperors. The ways of presidents and prime ministers are not so different. She already does much to reduce tensions and bring antagonists together. But it is all, as you say, behind the scenes. She is not often credited with what she accomplishes. Yet when she is rebuffed — insulted — that is remarked, without fail.'

Anger suddenly filled him. 'In Africa there, why should our work of mercy have been hindered at the whim of some intransigent…?' He didn't say 'black man' but it was implicit.

I said, 'What would you have done?'

'Ah, it is always easy to say what could have been done. It is less easy to do it at the time.' The mood of anger had subsided as quickly as it arose. 'But a great ship painted white, floodlit, emblazoned with the cross of our Lord, the eyes of the world upon her — surely it would need a very resolute tyrant to impede her by force.'

'You mean you would sail the *Columba* in against the wishes of a government?'

'Under certain circumstances it might be justifiable.'

'As now? In the Middle East?'

'Ah! You know about the plan?'

I told him the source of my information, lest he might become suspicious.

He said, 'Well, of course the Count is a "dove", as the Americans say. He has doubts about the safety of our crew. I myself' — he gestured broadly with his hands — 'I myself have doubts of another kind. I ask myself whether soft words can ever achieve peace between two sides so stubborn.' Impatience boiled up in him again. 'This whole situation in the Middle East is stupid and dangerous. It is disgraceful that we in Europe should have such a little voice in the matter. The Americans and the Russians are in command and they are equally stupid enough to let something start. But who will be the first to suffer? We in Europe, and our voice is not heard. Ah, but I must not talk politics. It causes me enough trouble already.'

'I heard of a speech you made.'

He shrugged. 'Perhaps something may come of our great intervention. It is very much Stefani's idea — Cardinal Stefani.'

He must have seen the interest flicker in my eyes. 'You didn't know that?'

'No.'

'Stefani is no fool. There is a proposal for accommodating the refugee problem. I do not know the details but one hears that it is an ingenious plan. That is Stefani's work. He has been advancing it slowly, a centimetre here, a centimetre there, for twenty years. You know that he was once nuncio in Syria? That is when it began. But he is not of the calibre of greatness. He is too — too soft. By that I do not mean what perhaps you think. I mean that in the service of the Church a man should be unbending in his principles. However subtle he may be in the conduct of affairs he must in the end be as adamant for Christ as a Communist is for Marx. Stefani has compromised. You know what he is called? — the Ice-cream Cardinal. It is unkind but not without justice. Once he was thought certain to become Secretary of State. Now everyone knows he will be passed over. The Red Hat was a consolation prize.'

An invisible telephone rang. The professor excavated it from beneath papers and journals.

'*Oui. J'écoute.*'

I peered ostentatiously at the pictures on the wall, studied my shoes, wiped my nose and did all the things you do to show you're not paying attention to someone else's phone conversation. As well as the crucifix and the picture of Pope Paul there were some old maps, a battle panorama, a photograph of a calm, rather handsome young woman with the hairstyle and clothes of when? — the late twenties, perhaps the thirties — and another of a studious young man in uniform.

But of course I couldn't help listening, or trying to listen. Much of the professor's contribution consisted of grunted affirmatives, neutral at first but becoming more enthusiastic. It was obviously something to do with the Middle East plan. He asked once, 'And the Jews. What of them?' At the answer he nodded his head vigorously. Then I pricked up my ears for the next name was the Count's and the one after that, Cardinal Stefani's — '*Stefani sera intransigéant,*' with tremendous emphasis on the adjective, giving it a declamatory ring as if at the end of a formal peroration.

The other voice reached me only as a faint, unintelligible quacking. But the intonation and the spacing of the words, especially, seemed familiar.

Just as it looked as if Levegh were going to ring off the other man must have raised another matter. The professor's eyes flicked up and at me and as if to be scrupulously polite, to ensure that I would not think I was being discussed behind my back he said very clearly, 'Yes, he is with me now. Of course, of course…' A moment later he did put the phone down.

For a moment he brooded in silence. Then he tugged an old-fashioned bell-pull which produced a distant jangle.

He said, 'That was Durand.'

Of course: I should have recognised the quacks.

'He was speaking from Toulon.'

'*Toulon*?' I wasn't expecting that.

'Ah, something else you did not know?' He seemed pleased that the Order still had some secrets from me. 'The *Columba* has been in for some minor modifications. From there she was to have shown herself off Monte Carlo when your film had been shown at the festival — you see we have learned from you, Mr Panton. We are now expert in publicity!'

As a compliment I wasn't quite sure about it.

'But naturally she must now sail earlier to keep her rendezvous.'

'When?'

'Tomorrow.'

The door opened and a comfy middle-aged woman entered, with a polite 'M'sieur' in my direction.

'Ah, Claudine,' said the professor, 'what do you propose for supper this evening?'

She busied herself switching on lamps and drawing the curtains against the sky, now quite dark, as she answered. There was a fine cockerel, or if the professor preferred, plenty of sausage and, always, cheese or eggs…

The professor thanked her and said, 'You stay in Lyons tonight.'

'Yes, but please don't —'

'You will join me. After all we have some small occasion to celebrate.' Suddenly he looked very pleased with himself.

'You see, my wife is with me —'

'Then bring her too! How charming.'

'Well, if you're quite sure…'

'It will be a great pleasure. And perhaps there will be time to talk more about what you wish to know, eh?'

As I prepared to leave he asked, 'How do you continue your journey tomorrow?'

'On the train.'

'Not by air?'

I explained about Irby. He beamed. 'Then that is something else we must celebrate.'

CHAPTER TWENTY-EIGHT

Irby said, 'Someone was trying to telephone you.'

'*Me*? No one knows we're here. Anyway, what do you mean by "Someone?" Who was it?'

She looked uncomfortable. 'I don't know.'

'Didn't you ask his name?'

'I think it was the operator. Something about a personal call.'

'But who was making the call?'

'I don't know.'

'Oh, for God's sake.'

'It's no use getting cross. I couldn't understand him.'

'That's marvellous.'

'They'll try again, won't they?'

I said, 'It doesn't matter.' But I hate puzzles like that.

Unexpectedly it was an enjoyable evening. The cockerel duly appeared smothered with truffles and fragrant with herbs, preceded by a little creamy quiche and followed by cheese and fruit and an almond cake. There was a white wine from the Dordogne, a Brouilly and a musky dessert wine which the professor served in a decanter. Irby flowered, looking strikingly beautiful in the light of the heavily shaded lamps which Levegh seemed to favour in every room. The professor, who'd donned an old smoking jacket of dark red velvet, flattered and fussed about her as if too long deprived of female company.

Except for the table covered with a thick ecru cloth and laid with heavy silver the dining room wasn't much distinguishable from the study: same dark walls, pictures, trophies, profusion of books and papers; same dedication to the comfort and convenience of one man. I accorded the wine and food priority and let Irby chatter. Her French was schoolgirlish in construction but she had a good accent. The professor gallantly tried out a little English. We heard in time that his wife had died during the Occupation and that his son, having survived the war, had been lost at Dien Bien Phu. He confirmed that his politics were of an impatient Rightest variety at once nostalgic for, and critical of, de Gaulle.

I remember arguing with him, especially about his Middle East views, but the most vivid image I carried away came later. It was when dinner was finished and we were in the drawing-room, which proved to be yet another version of the study, littered if possible with even more books and papers. I was relaxed warmly over coffee and an Armagnac. Irby was asking him about the pictures. The professor took down one of them from the wall. It was a woodcut from the fourteenth or fifteenth century, uncomplicated black outlines on yellow paper. It showed a luckless individual having his feet *flambéed* by a masked executioner. A small audience looked on, including a bishop type figure in a mitre.

'My predecessor,' said Levegh. 'His name was Jehan de l'Arbois, Grand Master of the Order of Knights Protector of St Mark of Candia when it was accused of heresy and its knights ordered to subject themselves to the Inquisition. Jehan refused to confess. They coated his feet in oil, as you see here, and set fire to the oil. They drove wooden splinters under his finger nails. They hung iron weights from his genitals' — he used the word without embarrassment in Irby's presence.

'But he died without recanting, which is perhaps why only in France do we still profess a link between that old order and ours today.'

In the echoing entrance hall he said again. 'You go on by train? Have a pleasant voyage.'

At the hotel two telephone message slips were waiting and a telegram that had come in on the hotel telex. Both messages were to the effect that a Mlle Thompson had called. The telegram said,

ESSENTIAL SEE YOU IMMEDIATELY SUGGEST QUITTING TRAIN LES ARCS CONFIRM LISA

'What is it?' said Irby.

'It must be something to do with the book. She's going to do the pictures.'

'Do we have to?'

'What?'

'Stop off at wherever it is?'

'*You* don't, whatever I do. You go straight on to that nice hotel at Monte Carlo.'

'But —'

'I haven't decided anything yet.'

'Not alone, I couldn't. Supposing anything … started.' She'd been hanging her dress in the wardrobe. In tights the rotundity of her belly was just noticeable.

'It would only be an hour or two. I'd come straight on.'

'Why couldn't I stop off with you?'

'Because.'

Because of what, though? Lying awake, I tried to sort out the fears that pressed in on me. It was something to do with the *Columba*, obviously. What had she been doing in Toulon? That was a naval base. And since the train passed through Toulon why couldn't Lisa and I have met there? Les Arcs was in the hills behind St Tropez, farther on.

There was another possibility, one nothing to do directly with the ship or the Order or the threatened war, one that

184

occurred to me the moment I read the telegram, which I'd then pushed firmly away, which now — in the middle of a sleepless night — came bulging back, nourished by all the similar fears I'd had in my bachelor years.

Lisa was pregnant.

That time on the earthquake mission, it must have been then. She'd muttered something about chancing it. I hadn't really wanted to sleep with her — or to be accurate, I'd been quite ready to sleep with her; there was nowhere else. I hadn't intended to screw her. Suddenly everything that was to have been — Monte Carlo, the child that Irby and I were expecting, the country cottage we would find, our whole future — seemed infinitely golden and precious — and imperilled. Why did I have to be such a bloody fool...?

I must have actually groaned for Irby whispered from the next bed, 'What is it?'

'Nothing. Just the bloody heartbeat.'

'What?'

'The heartbeat of the town. It's what you can listen to in station hotels according to James Bond.' I reached out across the gulf between us and found her hand.

Of course it wasn't the end of the world it had been when I was younger. The new generation tumbled in and out of bed as a matter of course. If anyone did slip up, abortions were easily arranged. Was not London the abortion capital? But even as I indulged the thought I knew that an abortion was far from nothing. An abortion was what the doctors called any termination of the pregnancy, sought or unsought. An abortion was what Irby had suffered. It was bloody and defeating and it had left her a different person at the end. Besides, I wasn't of the new generation. I had grown up and had my first awkward fumbles and my subsequent modest successes all under the

185

dread shadow of fecund Mother Nature. She'd cast her spell too well. And anyway Lisa was a Catholic and would almost certainly have scruples.

Later, I'd perhaps half dozed off and woken again, I remember calculating that Lisa would be about a month later than Irby and thinking, shamefully, that perhaps it would be a kind of insurance. If anything happened to Irby's again, maybe we shouldn't try again, perhaps we could adopt Lisa's. After all, it would be half ours…

Later again I dreamed a lurid, chaotic dream involving Irby and Lisa and the professor and a dungeon where the old Knights of Candia were being tortured. The executioner I saw with great vividness: muscled torso streaked with sweat, beneath the mask the kind of face you might find on a woodcut of a medieval cobbler, an attentiveness — a pride — in his skill. 'He's an old pro,' I was saying to the others, 'he'll hurt us as little as he can,' but at the same time I was filled with the injustice of what he was going to do to us. Why should he, why should he, why *should* he?

Blessed relief suffused me as I surfaced again and gradually, luxuriously established that it had been all a dream. I could feel the warmth of the bed, hear Irby whiffling and the cry of a distant train. Then the remembrance of Lisa barged greyly in again. I'd have to know, I'd have to organise something.

CHAPTER TWENTY-NINE

Les Arcs was a long platform and not much else. The train moved off again immediately as if resentful of having to stop at such a dump. I watched it go with the doomed resignation of a character in Greek tragedy. The ticket collector leafed through my coupons uncomprehendingly before making a tiny perforation with a large punch. Beyond him was a little hall with ticket office one side, luggage office the other. Beyond that a narrow street with a few parked cars and a notice drawing attention to someone's *caves*. Of Lisa, no sign.

This seemed entirely in accord with the day. The train was slower than the 'Mistral' which we might otherwise have caught. The journey from Lyons had taken five hours. At first, along the Rhône valley, there had been the modest distraction of identifying the vinous establishments of MM Chapoutier, Burton Père et Fils, Père Anselme and other benefactors of the race. Then even that was lost in a generalised wintry landscape. We clanked into Marseille and clanked out again. The sea beyond the airport looked a chilly grey. We paused in Toulon, where somewhere out of sight the *Columba* was preparing to put to sea on this latest crazy venture. I thought, I never care if I see her again. I've had enough of the whole thing. The book would be different, if I could make it work. That would be about ideas, dreams, delusions, ideals, all the things that television couldn't begin to convey. Television was that brave looney landing his Twin Pioneer on to the flight deck.

When the train moved away from the coast into the hinterland behind the Maures, I began to assemble my things.

Irby sat back in her corner seat, her head resting against the linen antimacassar. She looked pale and calm and resigned.

I said, 'Take a taxi to the hotel. Don't carry anything. Wait for porters.'

'I'll be all right.'

I resolved that it should be the last time: no more leave-takings. My marriage was like a piece of nice new luggage getting bruised and battered and the corners knocked off in airports and taxis and trains. Furthermore, an end to situations which could lead to partings; I would be fair but firm with Lisa and offer all I could offer, that was all. There was nothing like a slowing train on a dark day to prompt good resolutions.

Meanwhile, where *was* bloody Lisa? I walked back along the empty platform, past shuttered windows, padlocked doors, a sighing urinal, to a dim sign saying BUFFET. Inside it looked as if it had been built not so much of matchwood as matchbox wood, thin and splintered and painted the dingy green of the wartime NAAFI which it resembled. There was a juke box and table football; evidently the fun focus of Les Arcs. I asked for a Pastis and had just ascertained the gloomy news that there wasn't another train till evening when she burst in.

I looked straightaway for any tell-tale thickening but of course she was wearing a loose coat made from a blanket or something and, rather mysteriously in mid-winter, sunglasses. She was also a bit breathless.

She said, 'He wasn't on the train with you, then?'

'Who wasn't?'

'The Professor. When we heard he was coming we tried to warn you but the hotel said you'd already checked out.'

'What is all —'

'Was anyone else on the train?'

'Lots of people.'

'I mean, anyone else get off here?'

'I didn't notice.'

'Anyone waiting here, anything like that?'

'Look, what is all this cloak-and-dagger stuff? And would you mind telling me —'

'Never mind that now. No one saw you, then?'

'Not as far as I know.'

She looked around the bar. 'Okay, this way.'

There was another door, leading to the street. Outside stood a little Panhard 24GT coupé.

I said, 'I don't go anywhere else until you answer one of my questions.'

'Okay: one.'

The only thing was to start at the beginning and take it step by step. I said, 'How did you know I was in Lyons?'

'Easy. Kept calling the Press bureau in Monaco. They finally put me on to this network priest of yours, Monsignor whatever-his-name-is. He said how you were coming. Can we go now?'

'It'd better be important.'

'It is.'

She drove dashingly, with much brake and accelerator. After ten minutes we came to a busy *autoroute*, joined it, left it again and began to climb into a range of hills. The road was narrow and winding with, fortunately, not much traffic. Coming down the other side I saw segments of sea between headlands. Once or twice we passed snow that still lay on exposed slopes. From the signposts we seemed to be making for St Tropez, but outside the town Lisa took a fork which took us away again.

I tried again. 'Couldn't it have waited until I got to Monte Carlo?'

'No.' She frowned into the rearview mirror. 'Is there anything following?'

'Listen, if this is about what I think it's about, you're being unnecessarily melodramatic.' But I really didn't think that any more. It was a non-starter. 'Where are we anyway?'

'It's this little apartment I get loaned.'

'Where?'

'Port Grimaud.'

'I don't see anything.'

'It doesn't work much in winter yet.'

Now I saw buildings against the darkening sky, the glint of water. Then there was a little harbour, as neat and picturesque as a studio set for *Escape to Happiness*. The houses around it made an exquisite jumble of façades, each one a little higher or chunkier or deeper or paler than its neighbour, the pot tile roofs climbing and dipping in careful harmony. It was a Mediterranean fishing port magically preserved as it must have been a century and a half earlier.

'It's all a gorgeous fake.' said Lisa. 'It was a sort of swamp until a couple of years ago. Then they drained it and filled it and made the harbour and started building these little houses. In the summer it's getting très snob.'

But now only one or two windows showed lights within. Lisa stopped the car outside a bar that was shuttered and padlocked.

As she climbed out of the car I said, 'Just to clear up one small point —'

'Yeah?'

'You're not in trouble?'

'We're all in trouble.'

'I mean pregnant.'

'*Wha-?*' She was totally astonished. Her eyes flicked apprehensively up to an upper window.

'All right, all right. It was just a thought.'

'You must be confusing me with another of your friends.'

'I don't have any.'

She led me into the building next to the bar. There were raw cement stairs, at the top of them a raw cement passage half open to the sky, doors along it. Lisa fished keys from her handbag and opened the third one. Inside I saw a tiny kitchen, a bathroom, then we were through into a long low studio room with a tiled floor, a divan covered with a crumpled orange and white rug and crossing from the big far window with outstretched hand, his eyes meeting mine at once, Father Leo. He wore a chunky sweater over his usual black trousers, and when two people are living together there's no need for the evidence of shared disarray. There's a scent of cohabitation that is conclusive, something to do with curtains drawn in the afternoon; a mixture of bed and unwashed coffee cups and tobacco smoke and perfume and aftershave. I recognised it and they conceded it without the need for words. We could move straight on to more urgent matters.

Lisa said, 'He was alone on the train.'

'I wasn't,' I said irritably. 'I was with my nice little wife who even now is all alone and desperate —'

'She was referring to Professor Levegh,' said Leo. 'You saw him in Lyons, I believe. Did he tell you he was joining the *Columba*?'

I had to say he hadn't.

'No doubt he travelled by Air Inter. Did he say that Captain Belli is no longer in command?'

I had to shake my head to that, too.

'Captain Durand has taken over. Captain Belli has left for his home in Ancona.'

'You didn't get me off the train just to tell me that, did you?'

He looked at his watch. 'I am sorry about it but time is short and I hoped you might still be interested in the welfare of the children who have entrusted their young lives, and all they may one day make of them, to the ideal of —'

'All right. What about them?'

'Colin, I believe they are in great danger.'

I sat down on the divan.

He went on, 'You know of the mission on which the *Columba* sails in a few hours' time?'

'Yes.'

'Have you asked yourself why she should have prepared for it in Toulon?'

'There was going to be an appearance off Monte Carlo, wasn't there?'

'Oh, that was only a pretext. Look, we all know that Toulon is a military port and there must always be security arrangements in a military port, but for us they have been quite stupidly strict. Since yesterday no one has been allowed off the ship — I had myself to pretend I had drugs to obtain. And there have been technicians working in the vessel: not ordinary shipyard workers but specialists.'

'You're sure?'

'There is some new kind of radar. I am not expert in such matters, so I cannot say exactly what it does. Durand will only say it is for navigation. Then there is the aircraft catapult.'

'What about it?'

'Before, Durand was only playing. You saw the game with the old yellow car. Now I believe there has been some real work done on the mechanism.'

I must have looked incredulous. Leo consulted his watch again. He said, 'I must get back on board. We sail at midnight.'

Lisa said, 'I'll take you.'

'Just a minute. Exactly what do you think they intend?'

It all came spilling out, much as it had occurred to me in more fevered moments over the past weeks. If Leo had only just started to put two and two together, he was rather slow. Studying the big film star eyes as he strove to make sense of the jumble of surmise it struck me that in fact he wasn't very bright. He had been quite unsuspecting. Now he was jumping to the most lurid conclusions. It couldn't be as simple as that, I felt sure; not as crude, not as obvious, unless...

I said, 'That mobile hospital you're supposed to have packed away in crates on the hangar deck — have you set it up yet?'

'There has been no cause to.'

'What about the earthquakes?'

'The victims were brought aboard the ship itself.'

'Have you ever looked at it?'

'No.'

'That is the only possibility: that inside those crates is something that might be assembled.'

'An aeroplane?'

'They're not big enough for it to be a full-sized one. But perhaps some sort of missile.'

Leo said, 'I will try to see inside the crates. But I do not know if I will be able to get a message from the ship.'

Lisa said, 'Be careful. Don't take any chances.'

He was pulling the chunky sweater over his head. I found myself by the window. Outside it was quite dark now. There was a little balcony overlooking a beach of what looked like fine soft sand, beyond that the modest waves of the Mediterranean, and in the distance the lights of St Tropez.

I said over my shoulder, 'What do you want me to do?'

'You must go to Rome.'

'And there?'

'Seek help?'

'From whom?'

'From the one man the others will heed. Lisa tells me you have gained his confidence.'

'He saw me once. There's no guarantee he would again.'

'Will you try?'

It was the least I could offer.

'Tell him what we suspect, what we fear.' He was once more in his clerical uniform. He buttoned a black overcoat. Lisa jangled the car keys impatiently. 'I would go myself,' he added. 'But my place is with the young people. I'm still their doctor if it is difficult now to be their priest.' That was the only allusion he made to the ménage.

CHAPTER THIRTY

Supposing it was as he'd said, was that so wrong? If it worked, and the world gained a new force for stability, it could be the beginning of a new age. Even if it didn't work, it would be an insane, romantic gesture that might still change the course of history. But of course it wouldn't be allowed either to succeed or fail, not in any glorious way. The big bullies would see to that. Either outcome would be quietly, ruthlessly forestalled.

I went into the tiny kitchen, carved myself a sandwich and ripped a hole in a plastic litre of red plonk — what were the French coming to? But it was good rough Vin de Pays from Herault. With its help I screwed things into more worldly focus. Leo was imagining too much; probably his conscience was in a state.

Meanwhile, the important thing was to catch up with Irby. I realised I had no idea when Lisa would be back. There was a map pinned to the wall, given away by an oil company. God, it was sixty kilometres to Toulon. She'd be gone at least two hours. Then it was another couple of hours to Monaco.

I'd already located the telephone. Irby's train would be reaching Monte Carlo about now. I decided to give her another ten minutes. After five I noticed a snag. I'd been counting on the usual rustic curio with its little crank handle for summoning the friendly neighbourhood operator. In keeping with the rest of the studio this was a smart modern toy with a dial, and I couldn't see a directory or even a list of codes. It was an absurd predicament, like starving to death in the middle of Harrods Food Hall.

I scribbled a note to Lisa, pulled on my coat and was half-way down the cement stairs, two at a time, before another little factor hit me: from a ghost town on a winter's eve, there was no way out. The little square was empty. The few boats in the harbour were dark and shrouded. There wasn't a vehicle to be seen.

I went back and was just going to attack the telephone when it gave a little shiver and rang.

'Miss Thompson?' It was a heavily accented, rather musical voice.

'She's not here.'

'Ah.'

'Can I take a message?' I was trying to decide how best to exploit this fortuitous contact with the outside world.

'That wouldn't be Mr Panton by any chance?'

'Speaking.'

'Ah, how fortunate. My name is Sierdsma' — he spelled it. 'You have perhaps heard of me. I have an agency in Nice. Films, Television, Photo.'

I hadn't heard of him but I grunted affirmatively.

He said, 'Miss Thompson has lately honoured us by adding her name to our books. A charming young lady and a talented photographer —'

'Yes.'

He caught my impatience. 'I was wondering, Mr Panton, if you could spare a few moments —'

'Not just now, really. I must get to Monte Carlo.'

'Ah.' There was the briefest pause. 'You are leaving this moment.'

'As soon as I can find a taxi. You wouldn't know how —'

'But Mr Panton, let us be of service to each other. I will send my car for you, then it can take you on to your destination.'

'Oh, it's too far. If you could —'

'Not at all. It will be my pleasure. Better still, I will come with the car, then we can talk without wasting any of your time. I am already in Cannes so it is not so far. Wait for us, Mr Panton.'

It turned out to be an hour's wait, which gave me plenty of time for second thoughts. In the lurid context which Leo had been postulating, to jump into the arms of a stranger was obviously a little foolhardy. On the other hand it was a chance of rejoining Irby in the rapidest way.

After half an hour and another glug of wine or two I'd convinced myself that I had balanced the probabilities sensibly and was impatient to be on my way. When there was the sound of a car outside, though, I couldn't help hoping it was Lisa in the Panhard. It wasn't. It was a big black Citroën slowly sinking as the hydraulic suspension detumesced. A bulky figure in a peaked cap slithered smoothly from the driving seat. A rear window was wound down and the mellifluous voice called my name.

I saw a man of perhaps fifty-five years, bulkily huddled in one of those rather old-fashioned camel coats with a tie belt. In the front seat was a girl. I had an impression of lank dark hair, dark complexion.

I said, 'It's my wife, you see. She's all alone and expecting this baby, and it makes her nervous.'

'Naturally.'

The chauffeur had the door open for me. I ducked in beside Sierdsma. 'It's terribly kind of you.'

'Not at all.'

Suddenly I wasn't sure. The way he slumped in his seat like a successful gangster, the way the girl didn't speak, didn't even turn to look at me … in the darkness, once the courtesy light went out, my face burned not exactly with fear but with a curious acute embarrassment, as if I'd just committed a grave social gaffe.

'We are very interested in your film,' Sierdsma was saying.

'But it hasn't been shown yet, has it?' My voice sounded unnaturally high and casual.

'Indeed not. That is why I was so anxious to see you. Once the film is shown everyone will be out to secure the rights, yes?'

'Oh, I don't know about that.'

In the front the girl lit a cigarette. In the flame of the match I saw only straight dark hair and a cheekbone. Then it was dark again save for the faint radiance of the instrument panel.

Sierdsma said, 'For a small organisation such as ours, the only hope is to be able to make the first offer.' He added, 'When I speak of a small organisation, I should make it clear we are not without resources. I believe our terms compare with anyone's.'

I made a polite noise.

'We deal, in particular, with a large number of the so-called emergent nations. Individually, none of them might seem to have much money to spare for culture and entertainment and information, Mr Panton.' The stress on the last word was like a nudge in the ribs. 'But when they are all added together, it is surprising how the total can mount up.'

I said, 'You really need to deal with the B.B.C. you know. There's a special department called —'

'Shall we not waste time, Mr Panton?' The musical voice wasn't quite so musical. 'You have broken your journey to Monte Carlo first at Lyons now at Port Grimaud. Neither time was your business on behalf of the British Broadcasting Corporation.'

In the distance ahead were the cheerful lights of Ste-Maxime. From there it would be well lit and nicely built-up most of the way. I said, 'What rights did you have in mind?'

'Should we say the North African? Or perhaps, the North African and Arab World — does that sound of interest?'

'It could be. What would the rights entail?'

'Ah, Mr Panton, as you've no doubt guessed, it is not so much the film itself my clients are interested in as — shall we say — the background material? What a strange venture, this warship that is not a warship! There must be much you found out about the *Columba* which could not be expressed in a mere television film. You hinted as much in a magazine article.'

At last we were in lighted streets. Comforting things like cafés, other cars, people, gendarmes, were all about us.

'Furthermore, Mr Panton, one hears of a certain fragment which was not included in your finished film.'

I said, 'An innocent and charming little ceremony.'

'But one which does rather alter the light in which the activities of the *Columba* are viewed. Possession of that piece of film would be valued. Exclusive possession would be even more highly prized.'

'I'm not sure if it exists any more.'

'Come, come, Mr Panton.'

'I can telephone London. If it's still in the film store it might be possible to have it flown out.'

It was beginning to sound like the dialogue in any second-rate television thriller series, but I had a feeling that within this absurd idiom I had somehow done rather cleverly.

'Ah, we understand each other, Mr Panton.' He actually said it. 'The only thing is that time is against us.'

I said, 'I'll telephone you as soon as I know anything.'

'I'm sure you will.' Then he did rather an odd thing. He closed his eyes and went to sleep.

He slept through St Raphael, Cannes and Antibes. There was no sound except for the Citroën's Michelins hissing on the Corniche. Of the chauffeur I could see only the back of his neck bulging above his collar and — sometimes — his watchful eyes in the mirror. The girl sat with her head quarter-turned towards me, as if she were about to speak. But she only smoked. Her skin was tight on her face, giving it skull-like shadows. It was also very dark skin. She was an Arab.

On the outskirts of Nice the car turned off the main road and stopped outside a villa. Sierdsma woke up and said. 'Your luggage. Have we forgotten your luggage?'

'No, it went on ahead.' And with it, did he but know, the rotten scrap of celluloid he so coveted.

He eased himself out. 'We shall be in touch, Mr Panton.'

'I hope so.'

He waddled up the path without looking back. I heard myself breathe out rather noisily. The Citroën drove back to the Corniche. Ahead, the lights of the headland jutted in to the sea in echelon — Ferrat, Ail and in the distance Monte Carlo. Only a few minutes later, it seemed, the old terraces and steep cuttings and vulgar new towers of the town were closing in around us.

CHAPTER THIRTY-ONE

The air was faintly stale, wrong-smelling. Irby was in bed. She turned her head towards me but didn't raise it. Her hair spread over the pillow.

'Oh, Irby.' I bonked down beside her.

'*Don't*.' It was a scream.

'What's the matter?' But I knew.

'It started on the train. Like little — contractions.'

'Are you losing?'

'Not blood. Sort of pinkish stuff.'

'It's probably nothing … the journey, perhaps.'

She bit her lip, which I knew was the prelude to tears. 'Where were you?'

'I told you. I had to —'

'It's not *fair*,' All at once the tears streamed. She moved her head from side to side on the pillow as if trying to shake them from her eyes. They were warm to my lips. Her head was hot. Her hair was damp. She clung to me. She said, 'Don't let it happen.'

'I won't, I won't. I promise you. We'll get a doctor.'

'Make it come all right.' That had been a catchphrase the last time, a sort of comforter.

'I'll make it come all right.'

But in the corridor, hurrying towards one of the great rococo mirrors with which the hotel abounded, I looked at the reflection — familiar and yet suspect, this worried grey impostor — and felt with dull certainty that I would no more be able to make it come all right than I had then.

Even the doctor I finally managed to summon, after staging a small scene with the night reception staff, failed to be the pillar of quiet confidence I'd hoped for. He was my age, abstracted, almost nervous. He said, 'It is not necessarily serious but certainly she should stay in bed a day or two.'

'Of course.'

'If you prefer' — with elaborate unconcern, to make it clear he wasn't trying to sell the idea — 'I have a little clinic up the hill. It is very small but there is always a nurse, and we could keep your wife under sedation.'

I looked at Irby. She'd heard and wasn't protesting. I said, 'Yes, let's do that.'

The clinic: I remember it vividly and I don't remember it at all. That is, the particular rhomboid outline as it first loomed into view from the escalier, the narrow iron gate, the little room where Irby lay in a prescriptive doze, the fearful examination room, of course — these are etched on my mind's eye; but of the waiting room nothing remains. There must have been a waiting room.

By car it was a devious zig-zag between beetling cliffs, both manmade and natural. By the escalier, or old marble stairway of the kind with which Monte Carlo is laced, it was a breathless climb but it didn't take much longer and it gave me a vague feeling I was doing some kind of overdue penance. It climbed and twisted steeply, past decaying villas and cracked urns and little dusty gardens, crossed an abandoned romantic railway line and served as a lavatory for innumerable cats.

I suppose I actually made the journey only about five or six times. It just seems more. During the day the little place was quite busy, with patients waiting to see the doctor. Evening was my favourite time, when it was quiet and deserted but for the night nurse. At first there was one other girl, who'd just had a baby. Her delight in her achievement and her child were in trying contrast to Irby's plight, but then Irby was largely insulated from reality, and the second day mother and child went home. I would chat away. Irby would lie there, dreamy and creamy. Sometimes she'd ask a question, sometimes her eyes would close and she'd drift off.

Between visits life resumed fitfully, like a television set left on in an empty room. Even on the night of arrival some foxy corner of my mind remained open long enough for ordinary business to remind me to extract the incriminating film from my suitcase and deposit it in the hotel safe. It began to seem an anti-talisman that had brought nothing but bad luck, but having hung on to it this far I might as well keep it a bit longer.

Lisa telephoned the next morning and I was brusque with her ringing off impatiently, regretting it afterwards. Father Freeloader fared little better. I was cashing a traveller's cheque when I felt a touch on my elbow and heard my name softly spoken.

'Just in time, young Colin,' he said. 'We were beginning to wonder if you'd forgotten about us.'

I said, 'I'm busy now, can we talk later?'

'But it's on at eleven.'

I stared at him blankly.

'The film. *Your* film. It's to be shown at el —'

'To hell with the film.' Again I was sorry as soon as I'd spoken. I said, 'It's Irby, she's not very well.'

His expression changed instantly to one of comical woe. I explained briefly. Actually, it didn't sound so grim when I put it into words. We walked through the gardens, past the swelling white breasts of the hotel, under the balcony of the suite Churchill had occupied all those times, out on to the esplanade that curved down and away to the harbour. Somewhere along the road the night before, Sierdsma's big Citroën had carried me across the invisible, shifting frontier between temperate and Mediterranean climes. The sea that had been grey off Marseilles and Toulon was now distinctly blue. The air was warmer and more fragrant. In the orange trees hung small, dusty, inedible oranges.

The Palais de Congrès had flags fluttering and a banner proclaiming the Festival. It was set into the cliff, an upside-down building. The entrance was in the top floor and you progressed downwards into the bowels. Father Freeloader led the way through a door marked DELEGUES. Inside many TV sets were arranged, some black and white, some colour. On every screen a procession wound slowly up a hillside, rather underlit. Abruptly they all changed, like a squad of well-drilled troops, to a close-up of a child carrying a candle, much better illuminated, so that the whole room seemed to brighten. A chorus of identical voices ground out a commentary in a language I didn't recognise.

'Not us yet,' said Father Freeloader. He ushered me back into the hall. 'We might take a little something.'

From yet deeper down in the building rose a sibilant murmur of voices, in all the intonations of Europe, together with whiffs of tobacco smoke, coffee and aniseed. At the foot of the stairs was an area fenced off with potted palms and set with small tables. A bar ran along one side. A motley collection of clerics and others peopled the scene.

'This is where much of the viewing seems to take place,' said Father Freeloader apologetically. 'But I'm sure there will be a very good turn-out for us.'

He led the way to the bar, nodding in reply to many greetings. Evidently everyone knew him. I had missed breakfast and had a coffee and brioche. Father Freeloader settled for a small brandy, to calm the nerves, he said.

'We stand an excellent chance for a Silver, if not the Gold,' he added.

'For what?'

'For a Silver Virgin, of course.'

'Oh yes,' I said vaguely. I remembered that the prizes in the Festival were in the form of gold and silver and bronze statuettes of the Virgin Mary. I surveyed the assembly carefully. I had this feeling there was someone I should expect but I had only a vague idea who it would be, and no inkling how to recognise him…

'Ah, not long now,' said Father Freeloader. There were more screens dotted around the bar. They showed an interval signal.

We went back to the delegates' viewing room. The squad of interval signals were just fading in unison, to be replaced by a squad of captions reading ROYAUME-UNI. Then at last my opening sequence was filling the line of screens, a pilot's-eye swoop down to the *Columba's* flight deck which Hayho had shot from the helicopter. As the titles came up, people were still crashing in from the bar. Others were whispering to each other or fidgeting with the controls of simultaneous translation gadgets — a blast of tinny German welled up beside me before the owner hastily turned it down again. How could any film look its best in such conditions? But perhaps it was the same for them all, and after a while there was reasonable attentiveness. At the end there was a buzz of exclamations and a few even clapped.

Afterwards there was the Press to meet. They formed a respectful group around Father Freeloader and myself in the bar. Was I a member of the Church myself? Ah, no. Of the Evangelical Church, then? So? Had the Order given one complete freedom to operate? How many metres of film had been turned? Was it a fact that the head of the B.B.C. was now a Catholic? But no longer the brother of Graham Greene the Catholic novelist…?

At the back of the group was a man who asked no questions himself, but in whose direction I found myself directing half my replies. He must have had that quality called magnetism. He had a powerful, rather military face and thin sandy hair through which his brown skull showed. He puffed at one of those pipes with a futuristic metal stem and kept, hard blue eyes on me the whole time.

When the others began to drift away I waited for him to make himself known.

'Eshri,' he said. 'Israel Television.'

'Ah.'

'You are surprised?'

'Not at all. Tell me, which was your entry?'

He grinned. 'Our service is still young and inexperienced. We have much to learn. You could say we came chiefly as — as observers.'

I nodded.

'I must compliment you on your film, Mr Panton. It would be interesting to talk some more about it.'

'It's surprising how many people have said the same.'

He was busy re-filling the technological pipe. He said casually, 'I imagine so.'

'What rank did you say you held in your country's television service?'

He struck a match and got the wood alight before replying. 'Colonel,' he said.

I watched him suck and puff. For a technological pipe it produced clouds of the usual old non-technological smoke. I said, 'And how is Malcolm?'

'Malcolm,' he said, 'sends you his warmest regards.'

'Look,' I said, 'I've told you all I know' — which give or take a bit of speculation was the truth. Malcolm would have long since told him what few solid facts we had. The rest was only guesswork, anyway.

Eshri said, 'And this little film of the ceremony with the catapult?'

We were lunching at the Hermitage, whose dining-room, as Father Freeloader had unerringly predicted, was superior to that of the Paris both in the cooking and the atmosphere. Father Freeloader himself was with a merry bunch of fellow-clerics who, he explained regretfully, had been counting on his company. A large centre table was given over to a crowd of French journalists covering the festival, for whom it was obviously one long cheerful reunion. We were tucked away in a nice discreet, secluded corner.

I said, 'Why is everyone so interested in that?'

'Everyone?'

'You have competition along the coast.' I described the meeting with Sierdsma.

'I have heard of him. He's of no great account, I think. But you should be careful. Behind him there will be Algerians. This part of the world swarms with them. And if they get pressed they're not always so sweet, you know.'

I fished in my pocket. Already there had been two message slips at the hotel to say Sierdsma had telephoned. I said, 'I'll give him a ring and say they couldn't find the film in the film store.'

'And where is it?'

I looked at him candidly. 'That's the truth. It was probably thrown away.'

'Of course,' he agreed. 'On the other hand you did deposit a tin of film in the hotel strongroom this morning.'

We were eating *crudités*, those delicious mounds of raw fennel, tomato, celery, radish and palm hearts that you douse with oil and vinegar. I stopped a forkful in mid-progress from plate to mouth. 'Who told you that?'

He shrugged. 'There are usually people in large hotels who will furnish such titbits for a consideration. There are receipt pads, daily inventories, that sort of thing.'

It was a little disquieting. If he could learn about the film so easily, presumably others could as well.

Eshri said, 'Now I will tell you why there is so much interest in that scrap of film. From the trajectory of the Jeep one can work out the capability of the catapult — whether it would be able to launch a jet aircraft, to which the answer is probably no; in that case, what kind of propeller-driven plane —'

'I know all about that. And I don't believe that for one instant you're in the least concerned by it. It's about as likely a contingency as if our Monsignor there' — I nodded to Father Freeloader — 'were to stand up, open his cassock and flash it.'

Curiously, Father Freeloader chose that moment to rise to his feet, though fortunately with no more sinister purpose than to greet another churchman who was just entering.

Eshri smiled. 'Privately I may agree with you. But look from the point of view of my country. We are surrounded by our enemies. A strange aircraft carrier proposes to anchor only a few minutes' flight from our coast. Our enemies will be invited aboard her. Are we unreasonable in wanting to find out exactly what she might have up her sleeve?'

'She will be equally near the coast of one of your enemies.'

'Not the one we have to worry about.'

I said, 'Sierdsma made it clear what really interests you all — the propaganda bit. If the talks were going too well for someone's liking, if the hawks of either side were losing and the doves were winning, what a foolproof way of sinking the whole thing! Get that bit of film on to television everywhere and the *Columba* is discredited.'

'Sure, sure. As we who work in the medium know only too well.' But he could switch back to seriousness in the same breath. He said, 'If I promised you that the film would not be put to that use…?'

'I don't know. I'll think about it.' At least it would get rid of it, once and for all. I could unload the responsibility of it.

He said, 'Don't leave it too long, that's all.'

I looked across the room to where someone was just coming in.

He must have seen my expression. 'What is it?'

'Trouble.'

'Who?' He didn't look around, didn't show any awareness. I suppose that was his training.

'Not who you're thinking. Other type trouble.'

It was Lisa. She scanned the room and must have seen me, but didn't come over. One of the journalists from the big centre table hailed her and she joined them. Instead, she caught me as I was following Eshri out of the restaurant.

'What brings you here?' I said cordially.

'It so happens I have an accreditation.' She thumbed the Press badge, with her name inset in plastic, that was pinned to her dress.

'Good. I'll see you around.'

'I'm sorry about the other night — leaving you like that. I should have thought of something.'

'It's all right. Your friends got me here.'

'Listen, I don't know that guy from Adam. What's his name? Sierdsma. He's just someone I met at a party. He runs a picture agency.'

'It doesn't matter.'

She held my arm and hissed, 'When do we go?'

'Go where?'

'Jesus! To Rome.'

'We don't — or anyway I don't.'

'You promised.'

I could have explained. I wanted to explain. I even started to point vaguely in the direction of the little clinic room that for the moment, for me, was the limit of the world. But suddenly I was too tired. No words came.

Lisa said quietly, 'You bastard.'

I signalled to Eshri not to wait.

'You inert, soft, spineless British bastard. You let Leo sail off in that ship with just a little espionage job to do, that's all. You let those kids sail off to Jesus Christ knows what, and you can't even be bothered to make a nice safe little trip to Rome.' She drew breath. 'Those kids — all that shit you talked about how marvellous they were. It was a lot of sentimental boloney. You don't understand them, you don't know them, in truth you don't care a fuck about them. Correction: that's the only thing you do care. You fancied some of the girls but were too inert even to do anything about that. So you made do with me.'

The French journalists had fallen silent, except for the low monotone of one man finishing off a simultaneous translation for the benefit of his non-English-speaking colleagues. After a moment they politely applauded. I could only slink away.

In the evening there was a reception at the Royal Palace. Father Freeloader and I shared a taxi up to the toy town edifice on its headland overlooking the sheet piling and bulldozers with whose aid the Prince was reclaiming a bit more Principality from the sea. Toy town soldiers toddled up and down in the courtyard. Toy town flunkeys took our coats.

We waited in an ante-chamber, took our turn to file past their Serene Highnesses, bowed, shook hands, received a nice smile from Grace and passed into another salon where more flunkeys circulated with trays of champagne.

'Charming couple,' said Father Freeloader.

'Radiant.'

The showing of the film seemed to have made us minor celebrities. People came up and felicitated us upon it. Others inquired further as to its provenance. After half an hour my voice began to get husky from talking continuously above the hubbub, and my head ached from the effort of listening to, and trying to talk in, foreign tongues.

Finally I got trapped by a tedious Russian whom everyone was treating with exaggerated respect. Apparently he was some big wheel in Soviet Television who had stayed on after the regular festival ended. He had one of those heavy Slav faces set in an expression of stupefying self-certainty.

'Was interesting film,' he honked. 'Quite interesting film. We have thought only that in some scenes the composition could have been better, for example the landing-on of the aeroplane.'

I thought of that brave, scared nut-case plonking down the Twin Pioneer with about five feet to spare, and all this gorilla could notice was the composition. I said, 'It was better on the final run-through.'

My eyes strayed again to Lisa, across the room. Her hair, tied back loosely with a wisp of chiffon, shone in the light of the chandeliers. Her arms were bare, and there's something about bare arms which is very bare indeed. But she saw me and looked stonily away.

'Please?' The Russian was saying. 'I do not understand you.'

I said, 'Who does?'

Eshri intercepted me as I was making for the door. 'Going already?'

'I hear they begin putting the champagne away soon.'

In the courtyard I looked vaguely for a taxi, but they hadn't started to return yet.

'Should we go on somewhere?' It was Eshri again.

'I have to see Irby.' He knew about Irby.

'Of course. Let me give you a lift.'

In the car, which was a Simca and rented, I guessed, I said, 'Oh Lord, what was she wearing?'

'Who?'

'The Princess. Irby's sure to want to know.'

'A green dress, I think.'

'You wouldn't do any better than I will.'

I wasn't sure how to approach the clinic from this direction but he seemed to go there without hesitation.

I said, 'Thanks, Colonel. I'll let you know in the morning about that other matter.'

I hurried into the clinic, the way that was already so familiar, through a door that led into a little passage, thence straight into Irby's room. A hand was rammed over my mouth and something thumped me hard in the base of the spine.

CHAPTER THIRTY-THREE

I was hustled into a room I hadn't seen before. It was tiled, brightly lit and dominated by a piece of apparatus whose purpose was appallingly specific, a gaunt skeletal chair that could be tipped and tilted to present its occupant's rump to the world, with legs hooked out of the way above him. It was an obstetrician's examination table. At this moment the occupant was the Algerian girl who had been in Sierdsma's car. She was wearing stretch pants stretched very tight indeed by the action of the chair and she squinted at me between her suspended knees. She also held a nasty squat little automatic pointed in my direction.

Sierdsma was standing against the wall in his tied camel coat. He looked pale and uneasy and he began talking at me at once. The pleasant voice had a peevish tone. He said, 'You have wasted forty-eight hours with your lies and evasions. Now only forty-eight remain. Where is the film?'

The hand loosened on my mouth. I said, 'Let me go. Just who the bloody hell do you think you —'

The hand clamped back. It tasted of petrol and garlic and something sour, like urine. It was the chauffeur's.

'Simply answer: where is the film?'

'I told you. It must have been thrown away —'

'Don't tell more lies, please.'

For the moment I kept quiet. The girl swung herself athletically off the apparatus. I thought with horror, are they going to put me on it? But they weren't.

Sierdsma called, 'Raôul.'

A man I hadn't seen before came in. He was Arab, too, or half-Arab. He had a rather kindly, pock-marked face and he was in his shirt-sleeves, with the sleeves rolled up. The night nurse followed, her eyes full of shock. She was wheeling a rubber-tyred trolley. Irby lay on it under a red blanket. When she caught sight of me I could hear her catch her breath. But her voice was still dazed.

'Oh, darling.'

I must have tried to reach her, for an iron clutch pulled me back.

'What's happening? What is it?' She was terrified.

I heard my voice mumbling the words of reassurance I'd mumbled so many times before.

'That's right,' said the man Raôul. His voice was kindly, too. 'Just a routine examination…' He'd been doing dextrous things with a hypodermic. He pushed back the sleeve of some white garment she was wearing, dabbed the soft white inside of her arm with cotton wool and flicked the needle into a blue vein. She looked at me all the time, as if it would be all right as long as she could see me.

'You will feel sleepy,' said Raôul. 'Even more sleepy.'

She moved her head in agreement. Her eyelids started to droop, then she pushed them open again.

'Now, please, can you come?' He had his arm under her narrow shoulders, helping her slither off the trolley. The garment was one of those shroud-like operation smocks that tie at the back. Two bumps of her spine showed through one gap, through another the curve and cleft of her bottom. Her skinny legs faltered as they took her weight, then Raôul was half guiding her, half lifting her on to the monstrous chair.

Suddenly it was unbearable, for her to be naked and prised open like an oyster in front of these people. I hacked back with

214

my foot at the chauffeur's shin. I heard him grunt and his grip loosened for an instant. I'd got my mouth open to shout, to scream, then he was jerking me back and round to face him. He hit me somewhere just over the diaphragm. There was this awful thump of pain and the next few seconds, or hours, were consumed in a desperate attempt to breathe again. I must have ended up on the floor, for the first sensation of which I was otherwise aware was of being hauled to my knees and having my head pushed between them.

Sierdsma was saying, 'That's exactly what we're trying to avoid, you ape.'

The chauffeur grumbled from somewhere just above me. 'He was going mad. What else could I do?'

For once in my life I wasn't bodily afraid. If I could, I'd have gone for anyone, everyone. In the event I was just beginning to take some agonised breaths. One of the chauffeur's iron hands held my wrists together behind my back while the other pumped my head up and down.

'That'll do now,' said the girl, in French. It was the first time I'd heard her speak. She was leaning against the wall with her arms folded. When she saw my eyes on her she waved the gun in a small, economic motion. She said, 'Don't do anything else silly.'

The man they'd addressed as Raoul had the anaesthetic mask over Irby's mouth. He looked a bit sick.

The girl said, 'Don't worry. He's a doctor. We won't damage her. She'll be able to have another baby, even. But not this one, unless you co-operate.'

I wheezed, 'You can't, you can't. It's not fair.' In an odd way it was the terrible unfairness of it that was uppermost. The outrage only came later. I started to rave at them, as best I could, blaspheming and screaming until I ran out of breath again.

The girl said, 'You should be glad she can't hear you.'

Sierdsma said, 'Now, please, tell us all you know about the *Columba.*'

'There's nothing to tell. You've got it all wrong.'

'Tell us anyway.'

I told them. I answered all their questions.

Finally: 'And the film?'

'It's in the hotel safe.'

Sierdsma looked at the girl. She said, 'You and Raôul wait here. I'll go with them.'

They put me in the back of the Citroën. The girl rode in the back, too, keeping the gun aimed at me. The tyres squealed as the chauffeur swung round the hairpin bends.

At the hotel she said, 'Don't try anything if you want to be a papa.' She put the gun in the pocket of the stretch pants and followed me in.

The hall porter looked at me curiously and handed me my key and a message slip. Still dazed, I took them. The message was from Sierdsma, the ninth or tenth in two days and timed a couple of hours earlier; a last attempt to avert extreme action, perhaps.

I caught an oblique reflection of myself in a mirror in the office beyond the reception counter: ashen, a bit wild, but nothing that would be noticed in a crowd. I signed for the wretched tin of film and the girl jerked her head towards the door again. It was a big lobby, with tables and leather seats around the central area and an overflow of people from the bar talking and drinking. I had time for just one agonised look in their direction. If only Colonel Eshri saw me he would guess something was amiss. But I couldn't spot him.

Outside the girl held out her hand. I gave her the tin and preceded her into the car. The square was alive with lights and more people, people doing nice normal things like hovering outside the Casino or sitting in the Café de Paris or browsing over the magazines in the bookshop. We squealed away from them and back on to the zig-zag climb to the clinic. I closed my eyes and lay back and thought dully, it probably won't make much difference. The only thing was that I had just been making up my mind to play along with Eshri. His side wasn't perfect, but it was the few against the many and anyway, no country could be all that bad that aroused the enmity of the lousy Russians. I should have taken the decision long before, back in London when Malcolm was dropping his hints. As usual, I'd been obstinate and inert and muddled. Lisa was right.

In my pocket I was still holding the hotel room key. It was a big old-fashioned key and it was attached to an onion-shaped lump of brass big and heavy enough to make it unlikely to be borne away by absent-minded guests. Was it big and heavy enough to be a weapon? If I held the key and let the onion swing free it might be. There was a rubber ring round the middle to stop it damaging the paintwork of the door. Carefully I wriggled it off. It was damage I had in mind. When I could be sure Irby was all right, when Sierdsma had got what he wanted and would be thinking only of sending it on its way — I might just be able to get one of them, the chauffeur or this hard, skull-headed girl, to make up in a small way for the humiliation and pain and terror they had given me.

The car pulled up outside the clinic. The girl motioned me out. I followed the chauffeur through the gate, she came last, jabbing me in the ribs with the pistol as a reminder — then it happened very quickly. The chauffeur had just entered the building. He was turning to hold the door open and see me in

217

when he gave a sort of grunt and started to buckle at the knees. The girl moved fast behind me. She had the gun held high and was shifting sideways and down into a crouch. I swung the key weight and hit her on the side of the head as she aimed. It didn't seem much of a blow but it made an ugly sound and down she went. Eshri, coming in a low rush from the door, snatched the gun from her as she fell.

He was puffing hard — well, he must have been in his fifties. He said, 'Were there any others?'

'Just the two who stayed.'

'Good.'

We stepped over the chauffeur. Inside the examination room Sierdsma scowled at me. His hands were tied behind his back with the camel-hair tie from his camel-hair coat. His feet were bound with the electric cable running from an instrument steriliser. The man Raôul was standing in a daze. His face was covered in blood and he was still mopping at his nose with a blood-soaked handkerchief. The monstrous chair was empty.

Eshri said, 'She's back in bed. She's all right.'

I sped into the little room. Irby was sleeping peacefully — the only good aspect of the whole business was that she was to remember nothing of it. The night nurse was there, looking distraught, and with her the doctor — the real doctor. He was babbling apologies and explanations.

I went back to the examination room. Eshri had pulled the chauffeur in from the passage and was working on him with a wet towel. The chauffeur started to come round and was sick on the floor.

I said, 'How did you know?'

'I watched you come in, read the name on the brass plate, outside, made a phone call, came back to check up.'

'What will happen?'

He glanced at Sierdsma. 'Don't worry: we should be able to fix something up. Come to some arrangement, even. There's only one complication.'

'What's that?'

'We're professionals. You aren't.'

'What do you mean?'

'I guess you killed that girl.'

It was my turn to heave up. I couldn't help it. It was the finality of it, on top of the strain, on top of the smell of blood and anaesthetic and someone else's vomit.

I hated them all. I hated them for dragging me into their squabble just as their countries threatened to drag the world into *their* squabble. I hated and feared the violence that had so easily made the violence ring in me.

Eshri said, 'You should go now.'

'Yes.'

'The film?'

'It's in her pocket — the girl's.'

'Okay.'

He threw me some keys — KEYS! 'Take my car.'

At the hotel, Father Freeloader was waiting. 'Let me be the first to congratulate you,' he bleated.

I stared at him.

'We won the Gold,' he said, 'the Golden Virgin.'

CHAPTER THIRTY-FOUR

Irby was sitting up, propped by pillows. With her hair brushed back and held by a ribbon she looked ethereal and calm. At some stage in her drugged meditations she had decided she was going to keep her baby, and that was that.

I said, 'It's all arranged. We're on the B.E.A. flight this afternoon.'

We had decided to fly home. The doctor agreed. He too was satisfied that there was no physical threat, it had been mostly psychological — 'When a girl is nervous, insecure at being far from home, she can … er…'

'Imagine?'

'Not exactly. She can — magnify. And now, after the terrible business last night, it is best she should be away from here.'

I sat on the bed. She said. 'What about the prizegiving?'

I was supposed to receive the Golden Virgin at some gala ceremony that evening. I said, 'That's the last thing I'm worrying about.'

'What are you worrying about then?'

'Nothing'

She took my hand. 'Will you never learn, love? Do you think I can't see you're all screwed up? Just for once try and tell me what it's all about.'

It was no good. I'd been a single man too long.

She closed her eyes. She said, 'Colin, if you can't, if you won't, I tell you we can't go on together. I'm not a child. I don't want to be treated like one. I just don't want to be excluded. Can you see that?'

'All right.' I plunged in somewhere, I can't remember where. And suddenly it all came spilling out: what Leo had said, what Lisa had shouted, what Eshri had done, what Malcolm had been up to, the whole morass of speculation and suspicion. Only the Arab girl I kept back, I had to keep that back, at least for now. But I came clean about Lisa.

'Is she the one on that piece of film?'

'How do you mean?'

'I unwound it when you were in Yugoslavia. I couldn't think why you had it there, with your socks.'

I couldn't be sure whether she was laughing or crying.

When I finished she said, 'You must stay. You must find out what you can do, and then do it.'

'It's out of the question.'

'It is not out of the question. What is out of the question is that you should let a whole lot of people down just to fuss round me. Look, if it happened five years earlier I could have been one of those volunteers — I was silly enough for anything like that. If anything happened to them that you might just have prevented I'd — I'd never sleep again. Father Freeloader can take me — he was going tomorrow anyway.'

'He hates missing a party.'

'He'll miss one for me. And ring Mummy to come and stay with me for a few days.'

'Are you sure?'

She said, 'It's settled. Don't argue. But Colin —'

'Yes?'

'Only what you've said you'll do.'

Eshri was settling his account at the hotel when I got back from seeing them off at Nice. He said, 'Everything has been fixed. You don't need to worry.'

I nodded stupidly at him. I still hadn't assimilated the events of the night.

He drew me aside and murmured, 'The Citroën went off the road above La Turbie last night and crashed into a ravine. The girl died from multiple injuries. The police are making only routine inquiries.'

'You're going back to your own country?'

He nodded. 'At a time like this it is where I should be.'

I said, 'Remember me to Malcolm.'

'Of course. You return to London now?'

'I suppose so.' In truth I didn't know what to do. Despite the undertaking I had given Irby, a lone expedition to Rome seemed doomed to failure and probably pointless anyway. If Lisa had encouraged me, I might have persevered. But Lisa banged down the phone when I rang her room. Did this let me off the hook? At least I should maybe collect my prize before doing anything else. After all, I was due a little enjoyment.

Until about half-way through the evening I even persuaded myself I was getting it. I'd telephoned home and talked to Irby and her mother. Everything was fine. I'd bathed and put on my dinner jacket and had a couple of drinks in the Paris bar and strolled round the corner to the Sporting Club. I had chewed my way through the banquet and, by dint of intercepting every passing bottle, had downed about three people's share of the Pouilly Fuisse and Château Lynch-Bages. I had lurched up to collect my prize from the Princess and say a few blurred words in French. But when the band began to play, deafeningly, and the floor of the big, plushy room was cleared for dancing, spectres began to rise. I saw the lean, sexless shape of the Algerian girl as she slithered down from the awful chair; heard her voice saying, 'If you want to be a papa' — saying it almost as a joke; thought of that narrow, bony head ruptured by my blow, imagined the dawn ceremony of arranging her behind the wheel of the Citroën and releasing the handbrake and letting it roll away down the steep road…

I would find another drink and talk animatedly to someone and for a while feel better. Then it would be the turn of the *Columba* and an onslaught of guilt about her. Had I really imperilled those kids? Rationally, the answer had to be no; irrationally, the possibility began to overwhelm me. Soon it would be midnight. Thirty hours remained.

Lisa was with the party of French journalists. They sat in a noisy huddle in one of the galleries overlooking the main floor. A chap with federale moustaches and a turtle-neck pullover was being very attentive. I had an idea, waited until they went down to dance and intercepted her.

'What do you want?'

'A word.'

Federale glowered but she turned on some North American charm and excused herself.

I said, 'If you still want to see him, I know where we ought to find him.'

'Where?'

'Rome.'

'When?'

'In the morning.'

She grabbed my hand to look at my watch. 'I'll get the car.'

I said, 'But I haven't danced with Grace yet.'

'You don't get to. Only people she knows.'

I was disappointed. I'd been planning to ask her if she came here often. But it couldn't be helped. For some reason I felt suddenly cheerful.

If the frontier people at Ventimiglia were surprised to clear a couple in evening dress, one clutching a statuette, they didn't show it. To the customs man I declared one Golden Virgin in a loud voice. He looked appreciatively at Lisa and said, 'Congratulations.'

Still full of obscure relief I dozed off contentedly in the passenger seat of the Panhard. There were fresh problems looming but for the moment they were four hundred miles and eight hours away.

When I woke again, with a stiff neck and gummy mouth, we were only just clearing Genoa and two hours had gone. Even in the middle of the night the big trucks and trailers swayed along, blocking off up to two thirds of the available road.

'We're not going to make it,' I said liverishly.

'It'll be okay when we hit the autostrada,' she answered.

This we did between Viareggio and Pisa, after filling up at an AGIP station, where Lisa also sucked a Coke from a machine and we changed places. Initially it meant a detour eastwards but once we were pointing the right way on the Autostrada del Sole the miles reeled by reassuringly. The Panhard was sweet to drive and for a twin-cylinder, 850 cc. motor surprisingly fleet. In the overdrive fourth it whirred along effortlessly at 130 k.p.h. on the clock.

We stopped for coffee and bread rolls in the company of truckers and drove into the city in the first grey light of day. I wasn't sure how to find the cardinal's church, so we started looking immediately. By some sort of luck we went straight to it.

We sat in the car for a while, listening to bits of the city gradually wake. An early bus rumbled by, a man on a scooter, another man carrying fishing gear. A bell began to ring a few streets away.

I said, 'Has it occurred to you that apart from our duty to those young swingers on the ship we have a duty to our professions?'

'Say again.'

'Me as film-maker, you as photographer — we ought to be recording it all for posterity.'

'I guess so.' But she didn't sound convinced. She rummaged round the junk in the Panhard. 'Nothing here — wait a minute, is this your tape machine?'

It was: the little Philips. I'd completely forgotten it.

She said, 'You left it in the apartment.'

'No camera?'

She shook her head. Her mouth was full of pins as she tried to fix her chiffon scarf as a covering. Posterity would have to be served on sound only.

We went into the church and sat at the back. There were one or two other people already there. More came in, including another angler who stood his rod near the door. Without any preliminaries a priest began to say the mass. People continued to drift in, and some to drift out. I looked anxiously around: was he not coming today?

Lisa whispered, 'Are you sure this is the right one?'

'Of course.' But there could have been other unlovely churches on other windy corners.

'Maybe he isn't coming today.'

'He said every Sunday.'

The mass finished. Those who'd partaken left. But more and more people were coming in. There was some air of expectancy.

Then without much ceremony — an acolyte swinging a censer, another carrying a cross — the cardinal entered. His bulk was cloaked in crimson silk, his great blotchy face set off by the incongruous, feminine lacy whiteness of his vestments. On his head he wore the biretta.

As he climbed into the pulpit I switched on the tape recorder. Maybe this would be some definitive statement. But he spoke only a short time, in Italian of which I understood very little. All I could say for sure was that there was no direct reference to the Order, to the *Columba*, or the belligerent countries.

Afterwards he stood at the door as people left, like the parish priest he'd claimed he always wanted to be. The men gave little bows, the women curtseyed. Many kissed the ring on his outstretched hand. To the children he bent himself with smiles and jokes and once an expression of comical dismay as if at some reported naughtiness.

We hung back until everyone else had passed and Stefani was turning to follow the priest back into the church. Lisa bobbed. He nodded at her, then saw me. For a moment I saw the uncertainty in his eye as he tried to place me, then he smiled with real, and flattering, warmth.

'Mr Panton. I didn't expect to see you here' — and still coming as a minor shock, the soft Scottish burr.

I said, 'We have to talk to you. It's urgent.'

'Would that be about the *Columba*?'

'Yes.'

'I see.' He murmured in Italian to the priest, who nodded his head in vigorous assent.

The vestry smelled of wax and old clothes and very faintly of tobacco. The priest stood aside and elaborately closed the door on us. The cardinal drew a chair up to a table of plain varnished wood and motioned for us to do the same.

We spoke in turn and sometimes together and even against each other. It was garbled and badly organised but every possibility emerged.

The cardinal asked no questions. When we finally dried up he said, 'Thank you for coming to see me. I understand your fears and they do you great credit. I believe I can set most of them at rest if I assure you that neither Captain Durand nor Professor Levegh will be in charge of the *Columba* when she fulfils her task.'

'Who will, then?'

He said simply, 'With God's help, I shall.'

CHAPTER THIRTY-FIVE

We watched the cardinal's Mercedes draw away. Everyone in the street seemed to recognise it and wave.

'What now?' said Lisa.

'Before anything else, find some other clothes.'

'You could be a waiter on your way to work.' It was all right for her. She'd found a cotton showerproof in the car and slipped it on over her party outfit.

The decision was taken out of our hands. I was looking down, fiddling with the tape-recorder. She said, 'Shit, did we park on a cab stand or something?'

'What do you mean?' But already I'd seen what she'd seen. There were two motor-cycle policemen, knee-breeched and helmeted. One still sat astride his machine. The other had propped his by the Panhard and was fussing round the car. I even saw him check the number against something written in his notebook.

I had one of those sensations of pure dismay, that interior cavity that suddenly yaws. It could only mean one thing: the truth had come out about the Arab girl; once Eshri had gone, the others must have changed their story — could we pretend we were nothing to do with the Panhard and just pass by? Or turn and make a dash for it? It was too late: the policeman on the bike had got us marked already.

They were quite polite, in the non-committal way of good city cops. They talked mostly to Lisa, realising that she had a better grasp of the language. They asked to see our papers. They requested us to follow them.

One rode ahead, one behind. They didn't turn on their flashing lights or sirens but even so it was noticeable how obliging other drivers became.

'Don't worry,' said Lisa. I must have been looking pretty grey, for she gave my hand a reassuring squeeze. I allowed myself a sliver of hope that it might be something else. When they led us not to a police station but into the courtyard of an old office block somewhere in the vicinity of the Quirinale, I began to tremble with the possibility.

It seemed to be some ministry building — a uniformed guard had waved our small convoy through the archway. We parked in the corner of the courtyard, empty on a Sunday morning, and were shepherded up a short flight of steps to where another attendant was waiting for us. It was a dark blue uniform, almost a naval uniform. He took us into a waiting room furnished like any waiting room in any ministry anywhere in the world. We were left alone just long enough for me to work out whom we were awaiting. In the event I was only half right. I had a greeting ready for the Count, swarthy and stocky in his beautiful overcoat. I wasn't ready for the tall figure that followed him.

Nor was Lisa, evidently. We exclaimed together.

'Mr Olsen!'

'Commander Jansen!'

'It's been a long old haul since last we met,' I must have said to Jansen. I can't remember everything that I heard and said and saw that day: from the meeting at the ministry the cumulative effect of too much happenstance and too little sleep began to confuse the hours into a blur of arguing and listening and travelling. Worse, the capacity to be surprised had dried up completely. But this, I know, was in the official car that at some stage was speeding us all to the NATO headquarters in Naples.

Anyway, he replied rather dismissively, 'Yeah, quite a coincidence.'

'What is that?' said the Count courteously.

'Mr Panton and I encountered each other last in the Faeroe Islands. You know, the SACLANT Base there.' Several noisy clusters of initials had entered the conversation by now.

The Count looked at me sharply. 'Would that have been the time you wanted to make the programme we spoke of?'

'It would.'

'I'm lost,' said Lisa.

'One of our aeroplanes came down, causing a civilian fatality,' said Jansen quietly. 'It was a sad, but minor incident. Now, if we may get on to —'

I said, 'It took me a long time to work out the connection.'

'What connection, Mr Panton?' It was the Count again.

'Between what happened there and what we're all trying to prevent happening now.'

But Jansen was signalling fiercely. In my dopey state I realised at last that he was trying to head me off from this topic. Even in the alliance which united us all they were playing at keeping secrets. The oddest part was that when I got Jansen alone he maintained the pretence that the two things were unrelated.

I said, 'Come off it. You know that wasn't a NATO plane. You just took the rap — or rather, Canada did.'

He said nothing.

'And Kuchinski — you still pretend he was a Canadian? The only Canadian Kuchinski died ten years earlier.'

He changed the subject. Yet on intelligence about the *Columba* he was perfectly forthcoming.

I said, 'When did you first start checking up on the *Columba*?' This must have been in the operations room where plotters moved tokens on a huge wall map and Jansen was handed a signal to the effect that Cardinal Stefani, accompanied by a flat wooden crate, had landed at Athens on the scheduled Alitalia flight.

Jansen crumpled the message form and said, 'Oh, from early on, as a matter of routine. Your pictures were very helpful, Miss Thompson. We were able to account for every cubic metre of deck space.'

The Count said, 'You would have been welcome to examine the vessel at any time, I'm sure.'

I said, 'That would have put them all out of a job. You can't do that.'

Jansen said, 'We were reasonably satisfied that the instinctive reaction to the activation of a former aircraft carrier was in fact unjustified. There was no realistic possibility of her carrying or launching offensive aircraft. A modern warplane is a lot of hardware. It is also a massively documented product. The whereabouts of every one made is known.'

'Until the exception crashes in the Faeroes —'

He scowled at me to leave that alone. He said, 'The opportunity of flying on an older type of aeroplane remained. There are plenty of old Avengers and Helldivers still flying, including some of which the manufacturers have lost track. But we felt a policy of mild surveillance would take care of that.'

'It wasn't always so mild,' said Lisa.

'What about in Toulon?'

'Though the French are not at present members of the Alliance, we can count on their co-operation in many matters. No aeroplane is aboard the *Columba*.'

I caught the Count's eye. 'Your attaché hinted that time in London, that it wasn't exactly an aeroplane he had in mind.'

The Count nodded.

Jansen said, 'We call them drones — small unmanned planes used for target practice. Some are launchable by ordinary catapult.'

'They break down and could be packed into crates?'

'They do.'

'And could be fitted with an improvised warhead?'

'Exactly.'

'Is that what you fear?'

'It is what we cannot discount.'

The Count said, 'There is one further possibility which I think we have all dismissed too readily.'

We waited.

He said, 'The possibility — indeed the very strong probability — that the *Columba* is no more and no less than she claims to be: a ship of peace.'

Jansen said, 'You may be right. But it's too late now. If enough people think she isn't, the damage is done.'

He was handed another message. The cardinal and his box had caught the Olympic Airways connection to Cyprus. On the great map the token representing the *Columba* was just to the south-west of that island. Jansen pointed to another symbol that had just been moved, north of Cyprus.

I said, 'What is it?'

'It's an American carrier, the *Oakland*. It's where we're going, Mr Panton.'

We left the Count and Lisa at Naples. I shook hands with the one and kissed the other. No one was in the mood for sentiment. She said simply, 'Give my love to Leo. All of it, tell him. And be safe.' She called after me, 'I'd go in your place if I could.'

But of course she couldn't. I was the only one who had guessed the truth. On the bumbling Navy Convair to Athens, too tired to sleep, I worked out the last equation. Jansen would never admit anything about the Firestorm that had crashed in the Faeroes, about its pilot Kuchinski, about the whole institution I had later nicknamed the Earthly Air Force. He couldn't. It was by definition not to be admitted. It was only because a million to one coincidence had already exposed me to the inadmissible that I was being allowed to help.

'They call this the Beach,' Jansen was saying.

'What?'

'The Beach — the airfield here.' The Convair was making its final approach. 'Ever since World War Two in the Pacific, I guess, any shore base has been the Beach to Navy flyers.'

This Beach turned out to be the military end of Hellenikon International Airport. Waiting for us was a little Grumman S-2 Tracker.

CHAPTER THIRTY-SIX

The Grumman was a throwback to childhood, the kind of little aeroplane whose pictures I'd pored over in *Flight*, which I'd modelled crudely in balsa wood, which one blissful day I'd actually looked over when an uncle turned out to know the local airport commandant. I remembered marvelling then at the compactness of a Lockheed Orion which I'd previously visualised as a giant airliner: the cabin in which even a thirteen-year-old — admittedly a gawky thirteen-year-old — could not stand upright; the littleness of the windows, the proximity of the engines, the nearness of the ground. Zipped into a Dacron overall, bundled through something that was half door, half hatch, into the still tinier fuselage of the Grumman, wedged in a narrow, rear-facing seat, I couldn't suppress a certain thirteen-year-old excitement.

But once we were airborne the nostalgic beat of old-fashioned petrol engines combined with lack of sleep to lull me into a doze. I woke to look down on wrinkled blue-green sea and occasional rocky islands. My foot developed a cramp and I began to wonder what you did about having a pee on a little plane like this. Thirteen-year-old excitement had evaporated.

It returned, mixed with a good deal of forty-three-year-old apprehension, as we prepared to land on the *Oakland*, I'd seen too many old newsreel shots of spectacular deck-landing mishaps. I caught one glimpse of the carrier, ridiculously small below, the deck a complex pattern of white lines, the long wake spreading astern. Then she disappeared from view as the pilot continued his circuit. The wings straightened, the gear came down a yard from my nose and the airscrew note took on the edge of fine pitch.

I braced myself. I just saw the lip of the deck — nets, lights, white markings — and forgetting the landing deck was the angled section, thought Christ, we're going to slide off over the side, then there was the scrape of the hook hitting the deck a fraction of a second before the thump of the wheels and the next instant the little cabin was full of bits of loose equipment flying about as the arrester cables grabbed us to a halt.

'Sorry,' said the navigator cheerfully. 'We really must remember to button down that stuff.'

'Yoh,' said Jansen.

The deck crew had already got the Grumman on to the overhang lift, and its wings folded. As we sank to the hangar level someone opened the hatch and we wriggled out. I waved a vague farewell to the crew and followed Jansen. An officer in tan uniform approached with a casual salute. He was young and clean-featured — then there was another, indistinguishable from the first. I worried briefly in case I was subsequently required to tell them apart. Both were lieutenants.

The first, or it may have been the second, led us through the hangar. I looked round interestedly. This was a real warlike carrier, so like the *Columba* yet so different.

'You are familiar with carrier vessels, sir?' asked the second officer, if it wasn't the first.

'Only the Pope's — which isn't quite the same thing.'

He laughed politely. 'The *Columba*, you mean. She's our problem right now.'

More S-2s were ranked on either side, some sprouting monstrous carbuncles from nose or belly or spine, all with wings primly folded.

'They're all tracker ships,' said the officer. 'Carrying various types of radar and airborne sonar.'

'You don't have any strike aircraft?'

'The S-2s can carry small bombs but no, primarily ours is a search and tracking capability. While we're with the Sixth Fleet we also carry one light fighter for interception. That's the Skyhawk over there.'

We came to a kind of focal point, a thronged hallway from which companionways radiated and doors opened in all directions. Colour portraits of the captain and some forty or fifty officers, in matching gilt frames, each neatly captioned with name and post occupied most of the remaining wall space. I noticed with renewed dismay that *they* all looked alike too, if older and leatherier and more often bespectacled.

One of our officers poked his head round one of the doors. Withdrawing again, he said, 'The Exec, is with the captain. He suggests you gentlemen might care for a cup of coffee. He'll be with you just as soon as he can.'

The wardroom was informal and clubby, with leather chairs set round small tables. We helped ourselves democratically at a buffet table where coffee simmered in Cona flasks and there was powdered cream in a dispenser. With a throat dried by tiredness I'd have preferred tea or a beer but neither was available. There were many small stares at my crumpled *tenue de soir*.

The executive officer bustled in. He was a bulky commander with a crew-cut. He seemed to know Jansen and they swapped some gossip and some guarded news of the war situation. For the moment I was content to loll back and leave it to them. Just to be aboard this big, efficient ship with its teeming crew, its laconic instructions and summonses broadcast over the public address system, its world-weary air of having been doing this job for a quarter of a century, was reassuring. The *Columba* would be sympathetically but firmly dissuaded from her adventure.

In a map-hung command room to which the Exec, presently led us, vague optimism waned. The captain was a pink-cheeked man in rimless spectacles who could have been a vice-president of General Motors. He jabbed a pointer at the largest map and said, 'Well gentlemen, this is the approximate position of the *Columba* as of now. Maintaining her present course and speed she will enter the war zone within four hours. If she then continues that course she will arrive at her stated offshore rendezvous in a further two hours.' He paused. 'Up till now she has ignored all requests to call off her mission or — as we have been urging — to make for Cyprus until the position clarifies itself.'

Jansen said, 'Are you able to intercept, sir?'

The pointer jabbed again. 'Effectively, we could have interception any time after midnight. The difficulty is that at present we have no legal cause to interfere with the vessel's movements in international waters. Naturally we are keeping her under discreet air surveillance.'

'What will happen if she does continue?' That was my question.

'Our assessment is that she will come under attack.'

Put that way, it sounded worse than any of the more lurid forebodings I'd heard. 'But all those kids aboard?'

'Sure,' said the commander.

'Who could do it?'

'One, any organisation opposed to the peace talks, beginning with some four or five different Palestine Liberation groups. Two, any Arab government likewise opposed to the talks, of which there are more than publicly admit the fact. Three, one or other of the parties which are agreeing to the talks in principle —'

'Or both,' said the captain harshly.

' —if for any reason they suspect that the invitation to the *Columba* is any kind of trap.'

The captain said, 'Of course, we are hopeful that reason may yet prevail with those in command of the ship, at least as far as permitting the evacuation of all personnel who wish to leave.' He picked up a message flimsy and added, 'For your information His Eminence Eugenio Cardinal Stefani left Nicosia airport by helicopter at eighteen forty-five Eastern Mediterranean time and was landed aboard the *Columba* one hour ago.'

I said, 'It could be done — the airlift?'

'Let's say it's no problem. Our own helicopter complement is limited but we can turn 'em round fast. Then there is *Bulwark* of the Royal Navy' — he tilted his vice-presidential head about one degree in my direction — 'which will be within range around dawn. As an amphibious warfare vessel she has plenty of helicopters. Finally the Soviets also have a helicopter carrier in the southern part of this sea. The problem is how to get the persuasion through in time.'

Jansen said, 'This is where Mr Panton may be able to help. He is — or was — accredited to the Order as its official film-maker.'

The captain said, 'I understood that one of the prime assurances given by the Order, when this operation was first proposed was that no observers, no Press, no outsiders of any kind would be aboard.'

'Nevertheless, I believe I might be received if the approach were made to the right quarter.'

'To his Eminence?'

'Yes.'

They thought about that.

I added, 'By the way, is there a movie-camera aboard I could borrow? Anything would do.'

The commander said, 'I guess the Public Affairs section could fix you up.'

'And a change of clothes?'

He almost smiled. 'Sure.'

The captain said, 'What message would you send?'

'Just tell them that I'm with you, and I want to see him. And ask them' — I closed my eyes to work it out — 'ask them to tell him that what must be done should also be seen to be done.'

'What's that again?'

I wrote it down. The commander took it away. I had a shower and put on a blue denim shirt and a pair of tan trousers they'd found for me. It was marvellous to be out of that damned dinner jacket at last. A cheerful boy who introduced himself as Seaman-Journalist Jackson entrusted me with a battered old Bell and Howell hand camera. We went to the wardroom again for a meal and it must have been between the steak and the ice-cream that I fell asleep where I sat.

When they woke me, I'd been laid on someone's bunk. I splashed my face with cold water and went up to the flight deck. In the moonlight the *Oakland's* great radar scanner endlessly revolved. The wind was steady and cold. I shivered and gratefully accepted the offer of a thick woollen jacket.

Out of the sky came a winking dot of colour to settle among the *Oakland's* bulky Sikorsky SH-3s like a dragonfly among maybugs. It was the *Columba's* little Agusta-Bell.

CHAPTER THIRTY-SEVEN

To land again on the *Columba* was to fly from the seat of Mars to the skirts of Jesus. It was after midnight and the great white ship was deserted, all but lifeless. Three improvised, unwinking floods made a little pool of light for the helicopter. Three volunteers silently ran from the shadows to seize and secure the little machine. But astern I saw, as I wriggled from the glass bubble of the cabin, the long wake creamed and gleamed. The fabric of the ship throbbed with a purposeful rhythm I did not remember from before.

Leo was waiting. His eyes were dark-shadowed, but the anxiety which had filled him at Port Grimaud was quite gone. He seemed filled with joy. 'Colin, Colin,' he said as I tried to give him Lisa's message, 'we were so wrong, we were so foolish and unjust in our suspicions —'

'Just a minute, where is the cardinal first?'

'You shall see him presently. He is at prayer. When he came aboard I could have beaten myself with remorse for ever doubting the goodness of the undertaking. But even as we sailed — let me show you. Come with me.'

He led me down to the hangar deck. I blinked. In the centre of the dimly-lit cavern something like a great tent — or tabernacle — glowed with an unearthly radiance. It *was* a tent, its guy ropes anchored to bolts in the deck, its pristine white nylon illuminated within.

Leo drew back an entrance screen and motioned me inside. I blinked again. It was the size of a small hall. A long table had been set up, covered with a green cloth, set with pads of paper, pens, ashtrays, glasses and carafes of water. A dozen chairs waited stiffly for their occupants. But what had astonished me was the bank of flowers massed against the far end of the tent. There was mimosa, clouds of it. There were lilies, freesias, roses and flowers I could not name. Their fragrance filled the tent.

'The children bought them,' said Leo. 'They managed to send out before we sailed. They emptied the flower shops of Toulon. I cannot think how much they will have spent. They emptied our refrigerators of fresh meat in order to keep the flowers cool and dark. They devoted the night, until a little while ago, arranging them. It is their way of trying to help the talks that will be held here. In the presence of the flowers all hatred will be forgotten.'

'If it were so simple,' said a voice.

I turned. Professor Levegh had entered behind us. He was now subdued, the rubbery face set in a neutral mask. It was as if he and Leo had exchanged the states of mind in which I had last seen them. He looked at his watch. 'Now we await only the delegates.' He said it without expression, not as an expectation, not as a wish, without irony, simply as six flat words laid down like counters in a game.

Leo was bubbling on. He touched the nylon wall of the tent. 'But Colin, this is where we were wrongest of all. Do you recognise it?'

'No.' Even as I said it I guessed the answer.

'It is one of the tents of the mobile hospital! We unpacked it from its crate over there' — he pointed into the shadowy recesses of the hangar. 'One of those crates you and I supposed might contain an aeroplane or missile.' He turned to the professor. 'You see: I am so happy to be wrong I do not mind if you laugh at me.'

But the professor didn't laugh. His eyes met mine. We looked at each other for a long time. Then he gave a small shrug.

We paced back through the hangar, down to the gun deck, down again. The iron corridors were lit only by dim blue lights. Once we passed through a mess deck where two figures slept under a thick red blanket. The girl had thrust an arm out. It shone in the gloom, pale and fragile.

Waiting outside the chapel we made a tableau of men each lost in his own thoughts. Levegh closed his eyes. Leo composed his faultless profile. I found myself referring every minute to my watch. As long as I stared at the hands they moved not at all; look away, and they leaped on. Beneath our feet the iron plates pulsed with the vibration of the machinery driving the *Columba* eastwards. In four hours now she would make her rendezvous with peace or war.

At last the door opened. The cardinal rustled out. His face was calm. For a moment he stood unspeaking, perhaps bringing his thoughts back to present realities from some empyrean plane. Then he smiled in greeting.

He said, 'Mr Panton, I was intrigued by your message but let us first deal with other appeals I have received, from such persons as the captain of the United States Ship *Oakland*. Mr Panton, these are not *ruses*, are they?' The word sounded very Glaswegian.

'I believe they are quite genuine. I have also brought you a letter from the captain.'

He read it. 'Very well, let the children be called together. Father Leo, would you see to that?'

When he'd gone, the cardinal said, 'You must think me a hard old man not to have complied earlier. But had there been any … deception, the lives of these young people would have been in danger just as great as the one you fear. They are impulsive and would have resisted any attempted seizure of this vessel.'

'Of course.'

We began to pace slowly back the way we had come, the cardinal between Levegh and me. I felt his hand on my arm. He said, 'Even now I do not know how many will heed a plea that they should leave.'

'I am sure you can persuade them.'

'I will try. And if I fail, then you shall have your opportunity.'

I couldn't be sure whether it was more than a pleasantry.

We ascended slowly to the hangar. The cardinal paused to admire the tent, like a great lantern. He said, 'You have been in our conference chamber?'

'Leo showed me.'

'The flowers are beautiful; such a simple thought but would it have occurred to any of us? It must surely soften the hearts of the delegates.'

I said, 'Unless any of them suffer from hay fever.'

The cardinal chuckled. 'And only you would have thought of that, Mr Panton.'

'But there won't be any delegates, will there? No one will come.' I might as well continue the role of the man who faced facts.

The cardinal's hand tightened perceptibly on my arm. 'They have not refused the invitation. It is true that nor have they positively accepted. But as long as the possibility remains we must fulfil our part of the bargain. We must be where we promised at the time we promised. Captain Durand assures me that we shall be.'

'Suppose the delegates arrive not in peace but with bombs and guns?'

'Why should they?'

'Because it isn't what you are that matters any more, it's what they suspect you might be. Neither side is quite sure' — and how much of that was my fault? I closed my eyes in pain. 'Either, or both, could reckon it's not worth taking a chance. An unarmed hulk lying at anchor — it wouldn't be a difficult target.'

Levegh said, 'He is right.'

The cardinal spread his hands. 'But we are transparently innocent.'

I said, 'Look, until I saw that tent, I still believed that this ship might be planning to launch a buzz-bomb or missile or something — and I'm on your side.'

The cardinal evinced no surprise. He said quietly, 'Our only weapon is prayer. It is perhaps a weapon the world fears more than steel or explosives.' He brightened. He added, 'If I may attempt the kind of word-play in which you excel, Mr Panton, we have no guided missile — only a guided missal.'

The volunteers were assembled by the aircraft lift, which had been raised a couple of feet to make a platform. The cardinal spoke first. He spoke very briefly, first in Italian, then in French. He said that the *Columba* was entering the war zone. Inevitably there was a danger of her being inadvertently involved. It was common sense that as many as could be spared should remain in safety until it was clear that the ship's presence was accepted by both sides. He appealed for everyone to co-operate.

Then without warning he introduced me, and stepping down from the platform, left the assembly, the ranks of volunteers parting and dipping to make way. Levegh followed him. I was alone.

I looked at the *Auxilia* and Lisa's scornful words in the Hermitage dining room came ringing back to me. She was right. I had been professing this sentimental admiration, but secretly I had feared and envied them all the time.

I said, 'How many of you will go?'

About half of them put up their hands, the more dutiful ones. Among those who didn't I remembered several from old hangar debates as being militants. They began to call out slogans, 'We stay, we stay!' Others jeered at the faint-hearts. One started to climb on the platform.

I trod on his hand, not too hard, and shouted for silence with a force they hadn't perhaps expected. There was a moment of silence. It was now or never.

I took a deep breath and plunged in. 'Look, it isn't just the two sides in the war. There are the Russians —'

'Or the Americans,' bayed at least a dozen voices. They didn't like the Americans.

I just managed to regain attention. 'Or the Americans, quite right. Or the NATO force or the French, they're all around, with their fingers on the trigger. But I think the greatest danger comes not from any of them but from someone else.'

I risked a brief oratorical pause.

'I think there's another force around, one that is neither Russian nor American, neither British nor French. One that's all of us but none of us — whose name is Legion!'

For the moment I had them.

'We used to call them the Earthly Air Force — remember? They beat up the ship a couple of times.'

They remembered that all right.

I said, 'I can't be sure. No one can be sure. But there's been a fragment of evidence here, a fragment there. I was in some remote northern islands last year when one crashed. They said it was a Canadian, but the pilot was a Pole — not a defector either, a real Polish Pole. They come from East and West alike, all volunteers. The planes carry no markings. Even the component numbers have been filed off. And what do you think their job is?'

They waited.

'Their job is to do the dirty work, to keep the balance as it is. The *Columba* is something new, something they can't be sure about. You might upset this balance they've been charged to maintain. So she'll have to go — and you with her, if you're unlucky.'

One last message: I shouted it. 'And what will that avail? Nothing! It'll all be hushed up. It will be un-happened. You won't even shame the system, because it's the system that's going to do it! Now choose: will you go?'

At first nothing happened. Then they began to murmur among themselves. I saw heads bowed, heads nodded in agreement. Diffidently, a few hands were raised. Some more followed. Others looked for a lead from friends or elders. Suddenly a whole thicket of arms was held aloft, then more and more until only a last hard core of militants stood defiant and isolated.

The throb of the *Columba's* engines had subsided. From the bows came the rumble of the anchor chain. On deck I watched the spreading phosphorescent wash gradually peter out. It was misty and somewhere above a foghorn began its monotonous call.

The helicopter lift began at first light and was completed within an hour. They hung in the sky, winking red and green and white against the paling sky, then clattered down in turn. Two or three would be loading on the deck at the same time. Some were from the *Oakland*, others bore the markings of the Royal Navy. At Stefani's request I made myself known to no one, nor allowed myself to be seen, but watched from my old vantage point in the aviation bridge.

The regular crew were taken off first. I'd left them out of my calculations. There were twenty or thirty in all, mostly engine room staff. They smoked and laughed nervously and shouted to the kids that everyone would be back on board by midday. But some, I noticed, carried bundles of possessions.

The *Auxilia* crowded together silently at the side of the flight deck. Against the chill morning air they wore thick sweaters or duffel coats or anoraks. Some of them carried parcels and one of them a guitar. Only a dozen or so were being allowed to stay, mostly drawn from Durand's élite, to maintain the ship's last essential workings. Without sufficient crew to sail her she could only wallow helplessly at her anchorage. If a storm blew up … but the morning was windless and misty. The sea blurred into the sky. Of the embattled land thirty miles to the east there was no hint.

When the last American Sikorsky and the last British Westland had dwindled and faded, and only the *Columba's* petite red Agusta-Bell was left, I climbed to the captain's bridge. Somehow I was not surprised to find Durand dressed in French naval uniform, not his best but one that must have seen some service, smooth at the elbows, the gold braid tarnished, the cap with its circling gold rings frayed at the rim. He gave me for the first time a look that was without rancour, a kind of rueful ships-that-pass-in-the-night nod of recognition.

The cardinal's situation should have been equally astonishing, and again wasn't. He filled the swivelled throne, gently swinging from left to right and right to left through about fifteen degrees. I can't swear to it, but his watered-silk skull cap seemed to be pushed back on his head. Levegh had changed into a dark suit. The rosette of his Legion d'Honneur nestled in the buttonhole of his lapel. Also present were one of the élite cadets, who stood stiffly on watch, and the helicopter pilot. Though he'd flown us for some aerial shots in the early days of the *Columba's* maiden voyage, and ferried me out to the ship twice now, I'd never got to know him well. He was a small man with a heavy moustache that made him look like some Socialist martyr of the twenties. Now he came and shook my hand vigorously as if he'd been waiting for me. There was a pot of coffee on the map table. The pilot poured me a cup. It was hot and strong and beautiful. I felt hungry and helped myself to a piece of bread.

An inter-com phone buzzed. Durand answered it. He said to the cardinal, 'Eminence, we have a message from the Americans. All the crew and volunteers are safely aboard the *Oakland*.'

'Good.'

For a while no one spoke. The sluggish motion of the *Columba* was magnified here in the bridge, half-way up a superstructure welded almost as an afterthought to the side of the hull. We swung slowly, stickily, from side to side like an inverted pendulum. The cardinal's creaking oscillation, I now saw, was in time with this larger motion and partly caused by it. Even the mournful blast of the foghorn seemed part of the same ponderous rhythm.

The professor was staring into the mist. I followed his gaze.

'Somewhere over there is Haifa,' he said in a low voice. 'Nearby, the old Crusaders' city of Acre. This is where we began, seven hundred years ago. It is rather symbolic, no?'

'For a while I thought it was also where you were going to pick up where you left off.'

'How do you mean?'

'Brandish the sword again for Christ. Or to be exact, brandish a buzz-bomb for him. Just to add weight to your mediation.'

His features bunched briefly in the old rubbery grin. He murmured, 'The idea did cross our minds. But regretfully we abandoned it. We are too old for such antics in Europe, Mr Panton. What we try to do instead is better.'

The cardinal fished beneath his cassock and produced a little gold pocket watch. He held it at arm's length as if he were longsighted and opened it with a tiny, precise click.

He said, 'Presently we are going to celebrate mass, those few of us left aboard this vessel. It can only be a brief version. Few could be spared to go down to that beautiful little chapel, so everyone must crowd in here as best they can. Mr Panton, although you are not a member of our Church you would of course be welcome to join in —'

'If you don't mind I'd —'

'— But I am asking you to do something else instead. I wish you now to leave us, to ascend in the helicopter with the pilot here, who has already accepted my wishes in this matter.' He held up a hand to still a protest I hadn't actually intended to make. 'Apart from the fact that we have undertaken not to have any outsiders aboard when the delegates arrive, as I pray they will yet do, I have not forgotten the message you sent from the American warship. Do you recall it? 'What must be done must also be seen to be done.' It is an adaptation of a legal maxim, is it not? I was intrigued by it and believe I know what you intended. If what you fear should come to pass, you will agree that you can only see what is done as an external observer. That is what I propose you now become: our impartial observer, our witness before the world. For the moment, Mr Panton, we bid you farewell.'

CHAPTER THIRTY-EIGHT

We stooged around for a quarter of an hour, occasionally glimpsing a wary Grumman. Suddenly I knew there was something else in the sky. It was nothing that could be heard above the enclosing sound of the helicopter, nothing that could be discerned in the enveloping haze, just a sensation of violent displacements in the atmosphere, a trembling of the spheres —

'*Look*!' The pilot spat out the word.

It was below us, moving immensely fast but hard and sharp in outline against the mist, the remembered brutal shape like a pistol barrel with wings. It was going in low for a pass at the *Columba* which lay to the corner of my field of vision as I twisted in my seat. Now the helicopter was turning. The *Columba* swung back into full view, white and unreal like a china ornament, the red cross baked into the glaze of her deck. The dark shape flicked towards her — and then, Christ, it was different. Something exploded whitely in the sea a length away from the ornament. A puff of brown smoke blossomed from the side of the ornament itself, in its centre a flash of fire that was unnaturally bright and orange as a stage effect.

The pilot was yelling, yelling away in Italian, whether to me or into his radio-telephone I didn't know or care. I remembered the Bell and Howell and grabbed for it under the seat and thumped the pilot and pointed at the *Columba* for him to get nearer and lower. He just carried on yelling like an opera singer.

There was another plane going in already. This time there were two ugly brown blossoms, two orange fires. And to one side, approaching from a fresh angle, a third dark, detailed shape — I could even see its wings making a small, stiff inclination as the pilot corrected his course — followed the second.

I squinted through the camera viewfinder and pressed the button to try and get something on to film. The pilot stopped shouting and we started to descend. Already the *Columba* was half hidden by the smoke which drifted away in a thick grey smudge. Somewhere in the middle a fire was burning. The pilot had clawed off his R/T earpiece and faintly but distinctly I heard an American voice saying, 'Keep out of thirty miles radius of location as long as the attack continues. Repeat, keep away from location. This applies to all crews.'

At last we were getting in closer. It was terrible. The smoke rolled away oilily, the flames were very high, the ship leaned over in a steep list. I had the sliding door open and had wedged myself half out with the camera. I glimpsed a float in the water and figures in it, then at that moment there was another attack, and the thump of the explosion was for the first time tangible and violent and frightening.

As we hovered, trying to see the float again it occurred to me that we might be a target for the fighters as well. I just hadn't thought of it before. It happened that very moment. The helicopter gave a lurch that all but slung me out. I grabbed wildly at the nearest thing, which turned out to be the door handle. The door slid to, hitting the leg with which I'd been bracing myself. I opened my mouth to scream blue murder, the pilot was already screaming, something hit the chopper with an almighty bang, and the sea was suddenly very close. The pilot had the nose right down so the rotor clawed us forward. The engine racketed at full throttle.

Ahead was the long pall of smoke from the *Columba*. 'In there,' I tried to shout above the din, but he was already making for it. Actually, he was a very good helicopter pilot.

A second plane took a long poke at us just before we gained the cover, but slow and tiny we can't have been an easy target for someone sealed into a thousand-mile-an-hour projectile. I watched the line of cannon-shells or whatever they were perforate the sea safely wide of us, then we rocked in his efflux as he whooshed overhead and climbed away. I even saw the fire of his afterburners.

Inside the smoke it wasn't as shielding as I'd briefly hoped. I could see out through great gaps and rents in the cloud; perhaps it worked better the other way, like one-way glass. The pilot had throttled back and now we hung unmoving.

I let go a breath I must have been holding without realising it. Beside me, the pilot made a different sort of noise. I looked at him. He turned to me with a curious expression, perplexed and hurt and waxy-white. I said, 'What's the matter?'

He had a hand over his ear. He took it away and it was covered with thick bright blood. He stared at it in dismay. Oh Christ, he was hit and going to die or faint or otherwise flake out and I could no more drive this precarious contraption than walk a tightrope. I said, 'Make for the carrier, make for the carrier.' I don't know if he understood, and if he did, *what* he understood. I'd meant the *Columba*, which even afire and sinking astern of us was better than the huge sea. But he headed away, in the opposite direction, out through the farthest tendrils of the smoke into clear — or relatively clear — air. I looked apprehensively around but there was no sign of the planes, and somehow their presence had gone, too. The world was empty again except for the long drag of smoke and at its far, far diminishing end the sacrificial fire of the stricken ship.

The pilot was trying to call up the *Oakland*. He put the earpiece to where his ear should have been, groaned theatrically and brought it away sticky with blood. The collar of his overall was now sodden and it was starting to dribble bizarrely over his yellow life-jacket. I twisted to lean behind him as best I could in the confines of the bubble. There was a lot of yuk which I didn't investigate too closely, and a bit of ear definitely in the wrong place. He pointed to a little first-aid box which had been staring me in the face and I wound on a dressing of sorts. There were some anxious minutes when he again seemed to be going to swoon and I willed him not to, then he rallied and fiddled with his navigation equipment. The sky had cleared; There was now a recognisable horizon. At last I saw with dull relief the distant, unmistakable profile of the American warship. We got down in more or less the right place, the pilot collapsed and was borne off, they pressed in on me, and at last I was possessed by the enormity of what I'd seen.

On the slopes of Mount Carmel, above Haifa, they heard the strike like distant thunder and waited for the war to come their way. Trackers from the *Oakland* located and circled over the *Columba's* float until a helicopter rescue crew could take off the survivors. These included Captain Durand, seriously wounded; Father Leo, shocked; two officers who had remained aboard and seven young volunteers. Levegh, another officer and four kids were known to have been killed. The cardinal had administered Last Rites.

The cardinal himself had apparently agreed to join the boat party, but when Levegh was hit and lay dying had stayed with him. The others had gone to find a boat still capable of being launched as the doomed ship listed ever more heavily. They'd succeeded only in getting a float into the water. Confused by a further attack, and with Durand hit, they'd drifted away without seeing the cardinal again. The pilot of an S-2 claimed to have seen a figure on the deck under what he described as an enormous red umbrella. Another, when the burning carrier slowly tilted and slid, thundering, beneath the waves, reported that amid the flotsam, in the centre of the great expanding slick of oil, bobbed the same great cartwheel. In later days, when the legend began to grow, they said it was the cardinal's red *galero*. But that is never worn, only hung over a cardinal's tomb after his death; and anyway, the Pope had abolished the *galero* a year before.

Who had done it? Israel came under automatic suspicion from the Communist world, and is not free of it yet. In America a few accused the Arab governments. But the world mostly accepted, with cries of outrage concealing a good deal of relief, the claim of one — or rather, the rival claims of two — of the Palestine Liberation movements that it was all their handiwork. The story was that the two planes had been hijacked, in the face of minimal resistance, from a base in Syria and flown to an abandoned R.A.F. airstrip in Jordan to be armed. They returned to the same field and were blown up by the pilots and ground crew before they vanished into the landscape. The photographic and other details of the 'heroes' that were put out seemed particularly unconvincing and I remained firmly of the belief that it was all a convenient fabrication.

'It was the Earthly Air Force, wasn't it?' I demanded of Malcolm, back from the Promised Land with a deep tan and the eyes of a man who'd stood sentry under a hot sun.

'It was the enemy.'

'But Malcolm, it was your idea as much as mine.'

'What was?'

'Come off it! Without actually spelling it out to each other, we agreed there might be some final, anonymous, fail-safe bloody arbiter of what is and what isn't allowed. The Earthly Air Force, we called it.'

He put on his stoniest stone face. 'That was just an image we kicked around.'

'And Kuchinski? What about Kuchinski?'

'A common enough name.'

'You didn't think so before.'

'Anyway, Kuchinski was killed.'

'Other Kuchinskis soldier on.'

He said, 'Look, as far as I'm concerned it was a couple of Palestinian Arabs. The man who crashed in the Faeroes was whoever they said it was. Because it doesn't matter who they are, or where they come from, or what is painted on the planes, or what you call them. It's what they do that matters. It's like the square root of minus one in mathematics. You can't comprehend it but you can use it.'

Father Freeloader put it a different way. He said, 'If one believes in a force for good in the world, or in God as I would put it, then it is necessary also to believe in a force for ill. The difficulty sometimes is to determine which party is which. The difficulty in this particular instance' — he tilted a glass of Cru Pauillac appreciatively beneath his nose — 'is to be sure which of them in fact was performing God's will.'

CHAPTER THIRTY-NINE

In the event, the sinking of the *Columba* somehow acted as a release. The tension diminished. The threat of war receded. A fresh attempt to hold talks followed a few weeks later, and as I write there is still hope.

Irby's pregnancy went to full term and, perversely, two weeks beyond. Our daughter is round and pink with ash-blonde hair. She is called Stephanie. Lisa Thompson sent congratulations and the news that Leo was relinquishing holy orders to marry her. She also enclosed the transcript of the cardinal's little address in his church that morning, as preserved on my Philips, which incidentally I've never recovered from her. They'd translated it between them, she said.

Dear friends, in the few months I have enjoyed the privilege of having titular care of this church I have come to enjoy these occasions more than a member of the Sacred College should perhaps admit. Some of you may know that in fact I was never lucky enough to be a parish priest. The Holy Church called me as a young man to service in another field, and if I have thus been able to fulfil God's will in the smallest degree I am humbly grateful. But in the few minutes remaining before I must leave you in pursuit of those duties, I would like to ask of you here today something that only a pastoral priest can ask: the support and prayers of his flock. It is not all a one-way traffic, you know. As the priest may guide and sustain his people — and in Father Tomasso you have a wise and good guide — so he receives back from the people their love and their prayers. I wish to borrow your love and your prayers.

When next we meet, it will be Lent. This church of ours will be hung with purple and black, the picture over there covered.

We shall be moving towards the solemn climax of the calendar, when we remember the Crucifixion and Resurrection of our blessed Lord.

Anthropologists sometimes argue that Easter, like Christmas, is but the Christian adaptation of ancient pagan myth, that in the deepest fabric of man there has always been — and always will be — a need for violence, for bloodshed, for the ritual purging of the tribe by the death of one victim. This is not the occasion, nor have I the time, to discuss the ultimate fitness of this theory. But none of us would deny that it was such cravings which drove the mob to clamour for the death of Jesus two thousand years ago. Today we hear the clamour for violence throughout the world: in the great cities, in the fields, in the rich countries and in the poor. We hear it raised as the only solution to the conflict between different races, and even as the last recourse in the differences between different branches of the Christian religion. And most urgently and most dangerously we hear it urged as the only release of the tragic hatred between Jew and Arab in the Middle East. But how much bloodshed, how many victims, before the clamour is stilled and the craving satisfied? Would it be less than the destruction of the whole world?

My friends, the Church is active with the many other governments and institutions to avert this catastrophe. But let no one suppose that this deep, dark need of violence is easily turned aside. As I go to play my small part in the attempt, I ask you not simply to pray for peace, which is an abstraction, but to pray for every man or woman in whom any of the decision rests, that only love may guide them. And above all, I ask you to pray for me. In nomine Patris et Filii et spiritus sancti. Amen.

A NOTE TO THE READER

If you have enjoyed this novel enough to leave a review on **Amazon** and **Goodreads**, then we would be truly grateful.

Sapere Books

Sapere Books is an exciting new publisher of brilliant fiction and popular history.

To find out more about our latest releases and our monthly bargain books visit our website:
saperebooks.com

www.ingramcontent.com/pod-product-compliance
Lightning Source LLC
Chambersburg PA
CBHW060414180626
46817CB00007B/2579